© 2022 Robyn Singer

Robyn Singer
The Sunrisers

All rights reserved. No part of this publication may be reproduced, stored in a retrieval system or transmitted in any form or by any means, electronic, mechanical, photocopying, recording or otherwise without the prior permission of the copyright holder.

Published by: Cinnabar Moth Publishing LLC
Santa Fe, New Mexico

Cover Design by: Ira Geneve

ISBN-13: 978-1-953971-57-9
Library of Congress Control Number: 2022944269

The Sunrisers

ROBYN SINGER

Dedicated to my Goblin Gal

CHAPTER 1: YAEL

A peculiar amount of folks I'd been hired to steal from recently had been recreational joggers. It was possible the people of the universe found it as pointless and annoying a hobby as I did. Anyone with half a brain knew the only ones who did it were too lazy to run but wanted to feel like they were doing something more than walking.

Crouched on the roof of a skyscraper across the street from the Syler Hotel, I vigorously slurped a cup of ramen. Compared to all the other noodles I'd tasted, these wouldn't have even cracked my top 1,000, but comparing them to the ones I'd had on this planet, they'd come in 6th.

Glancing at my watch, I checked the time. Mr. Amatyn would be leaving the hotel to go for his nightly jog in approximately three minutes. I slurped up all of the noodles remaining in the cup and chugged back the remaining broth, some of it missing my mouth and dripping down my chin.

"Not bad, but it needed something else," I said, wiping the broth off my chin with my sleeve. "Not sure what, though."

I tossed the cup and fork aside, grabbed my mask, and leaped to my feet. Stretching out my arms, I tried going over my finalized plan in my head, but I couldn't get past how relatively lackluster the soup on this planet had been. On Benkin, like on all the worlds which made up The Cykebian Empire, save for Cykeb itself, there was a disgustingly gargantuan divide between the rich and the poor, which meant the former probably hogged all the good soup for themselves, and left the hardworking ramen-in-a-cup salespeople with crap.

"Focus, dummy."

I had a bad habit of concentrating on the wrong things at the wrong times. Especially times like right then, when I was freezing my ass off. Making things worse was my brain's tendency to go off on tangents that didn't even have much to do with the original thing I was distracted by. Like the time I was being dangled off a skyscraper by my ankle, I should have been focusing on how to save myself, but instead I was thinking about a recent game I'd played with Aarif, which led to me thinking about my board game rankings and—

"AHHHHHHHHH!" I screamed, muffling the sound by burying my face in my hands. "Your window's gonna open in less than two minutes! Get it together!"

I put my hands down, closed my eyes, and took a deep breath, in and out, like I'd practiced with Aarif. With each breath, I pushed a thought to the front of my mind.

Mr. Amatyn is a scumbag. Mrs. Amatyn needs her heirlooms back. You've already received half your payment. Don't fuck up.

By the time my head cleared and my brain refocused, my window would be opening in less than a minute. I kept my eyes glued to my watch until it turned to exactly 21:00. I was ready. I slipped on my mask, drew my grapple gun from its holster, and aimed it at my target. The model I had wasn't the most up-to-date, but it was still equipped with a computerized guidance system, a silent motor, and a maximum range of 20 yards. With the target already programmed in, I pulled the trigger, propelling the drill-tipped cable across the air and into the side of the hotel, right above the penthouse balcony on the 32nd floor. I sprinted forward and, clenching my gun tightly, leaped off the rooftop.

The cable was nearly invisible and my stealth suit against the backdrop of the night sky kept me from being seen by the naked eye, so I didn't have a worry in my mind about being spotted. I did however have a single passing thought about potentially losing my grip and falling to my untimely death, because doing crap like this wasn't something you ever got used to.

Having successfully swung 15 yards across the air, my boots made contact with the black marble wall. I breathed a sigh of relief as I hopped down onto the balcony and holstered my gun. The next step was getting inside, which was a far less life-endangering matter.

Syler hotels all used the same passcode system for all of their doors, including entrances to the balcony, and it was designed so the balcony doors couldn't be opened from the outside. The doors slid open when the passcode was entered and you could only input the passcode inside the room. If the door or the sliding mechanism were to be damaged, a silent alarm would be triggered.

For a hotel, it wasn't bad security. But it couldn't keep up with the toys the black market had to offer. I reached into my suit and picked out the micro-decoder Jellz had gotten me a few years ago. Like my grapple gun, it was outdated, but it still suited my needs. With the press of a few buttons, it wirelessly connected with the passcode system and entered every possible combination. It took 5 minutes and 43 seconds to work and open the door, leaving me with about 14 minutes to complete the job.

"If I was a stolen jewel being hidden by an abusive asshole, where would I be?" I whispered as I stepped inside and turned on my night-vision lenses. The suite was nothing too fancy, it was only a Syler hotel after all, but it was still nicer than anything I was used to. It was several times larger than my room, there were two king sized beds, a giant TV was implanted in the wall, and there were flowers all over the place scenting the air.

I sorted through the closet and the drawers underneath it, but didn't find anything except suits, socks, ties, underwear, hats, and dress shoes. Next, I turned over both of the beds to see if he'd hidden anything in the multiple soft covers on each bed, but again, I had no luck. Before continuing my search, I re-made both of the beds. It wasn't something I ever did with my own bed, but I still had Sunriser training in the back of my head.

When I found the old-fashioned safe Mr. Amatyn had hidden underneath one of the beds, I had ten minutes remaining before my window closed. It was a far weaker hiding spot than a clever arrangement in the closet could have pulled off, but I wasn't exactly dealing with a criminal mastermind.

I could have taken the safe and ran, but I couldn't be 100% sure Mrs. Amatyn's jewels were inside, and it'd be a stain on my reputation if I brought her back a safe full of normal rocks instead of her heirlooms.

Low-tech combination locks were outside my area of expertise, but I'd practiced cracking them a few times for fun. I'd always practiced with a stethoscope though and it always took me several hours. Even if I had that much time, I doubted my naked ears were up to the task, no matter how much tampering had been done with them. Thankfully, unlike the balcony door, there was no silent alarm to worry about with this thing. And more than enough tampering had been done with my muscles.

I wiggled my fingers and licked my lips before, with one forceful tug, I ripped the door of the safe off its hinges, revealing a gold, emerald-encrusted necklace and two gold rings, one with a ruby inside and the other with a sapphire.

"Very, very nice," I smiled down at the jewelry. Just because I didn't wear the stuff didn't mean I couldn't appreciate how pretty it was.

After stuffing the safe's door inside the safe so it kept the necklace and rings from falling out, I checked my watch and saw I'd finished the job with slightly under nine minutes to spare. All that was left now was for me to grapple away and hopefully not drop the safe as I did so.

This hadn't been my most exciting job, but I liked not having to avoid lasers, turrets, and armies of security guards every once in a while. Sometimes, a relaxing robbery was what a girl needed. Before I'd taken this job, I'd asked Lulu why she was hiring a thief and not reporting the theft of her jewels to the local authorities. After all, she was a well-respected woman around these parts. Her answer had made me like her enough to do this job for half my usual fee.

To amuse myself on the trip home, I went over my jewel robbery ranking while I grappled. My caper on Hudrup was still easily #1.

"Antella powder!" I shouted as I grappled away. "That's what those noodles needed!"

The parking lot I'd left my ship, Ricochet, in was next to a

Levi's Swamp Burgers. Aarif had thought this was a terrible idea, as I'd stolen their once-"secret" recipes when I was 20, but I'd figured it was safe. After all, no one knew I'd done it.

Sometimes I thought anonymity was overrated. That it'd be cool to have a wanted poster. Especially with how I'd improved my looks over the last few years, I wouldn't have minded the universe getting a look at my grown-out brown hair, my mostly cleared up skin, and my increasingly large muscles.

"Anybody home?" I called out as I walked up the ramp into the ship, closing the entryway behind me and tossing off my mask.

Ricochet wasn't a large ship, made up of only a common area, two bedrooms, a single bathroom, a tiny kitchen, an engine room, and a cockpit. I'd bought it when I was starting out and only had the money from my first heist to my name. A few times, I'd thought about getting a new ship, but I'd never had the heart to go through with it.

What Ricochet was was completely filthy, the sweet scent of age around every corner. Walking through the common area, the thick layers of dust covering the floor coated my boots, a cobweb got in my face, and I spotted the rat who'd been living in an empty can of beans. I'd named him Kidney.

The state of the ship disgusted the occasional passenger we had, but there was no point in cleaning up when it would just get dirty again.

"Aarif? You around?"

BARK. BARK.

Instead of a response from my full-time engineer and part-time maker of good life choices, I received one from, without hyperbole, the greatest dog in the universe. Juri came rushing into the common area from the kitchen and leaped across the room to tackle me onto my back, assaulting me with a barrage of kisses.

"Hey girl!" I laughed as the kisses continued.

Juri was slightly bigger and quite a bit heavier than me, but I'd become used to her affectionate assaults. I put one hand on her side to pet her curly brown fur, while my other hand scratched her head.

"You want a treat? I'm in the mood to give you a treat."

"Don't give her any more treats." Aarif appeared, climbing up from the engine room, his clothes covered in dirt and grease. "She already convinced me to give her two days' worth."

"You spoil her too much," I said, Juri getting off of me and rushing over to my partner.

Aarif excelled at both of the jobs I had for him, but what had gotten me looking in his direction in the first place were his tattoos. Aarif almost always wore a tank-top to show them off, recreations of fantastical things he'd dreamed up covered his arms. A dragon and a chicken eating a giant meatball together, precious jewels erupting from a volcano, and a trio of stuffed animals armed with medieval weaponry were just some of his mind's creations that had taken on ink form.

"She's a queen, she deserves to be spoiled," Aarif replied as he bent down to pet Juri.

Long before Aarif and I had met, he and Juri had been a duo, struggling to survive together and looking out for each other. I considered Aarif my best friend, and he felt the same way, but if he had to choose between saving me or Juri from falling off a cliff, he'd probably pick our dog. And I was cool with that.

"Got the jewels?" Aarif asked.

"Got the jewels."

Aarif pumped one of his scrawny arms into the air in

triumph. "Wooh! Not our biggest score ever, but I'm always up for a payday."

"With all the evil CEOs and aspiring warlords we usually work for, it feels nice to be helping out a robbed divorcee. Good for the conscience." I walked over to Aarif so we could pet Juri simultaneously, her favorite experience not involving food. "I'm thinking after we receive our payment, we take a little vacay. We could finally go lava rafting on Seko VII."

Aarif chuckled and shook his head. "We haven't taken a vacation in two years. If one's actually on the table, my vote's for any place where I can relax."

"'Relaxing'", I mocked. "There's nothing fun about relaxing."

"Trust me, you'll change your mind about that when you turn 30."

I laughed, pounding my chest. That day was a long three years away, and even if it was tomorrow, I had no intention of ever becoming boring.

"We all set to take off?"

"Should be. Just finished fixing the condor coil."

"Hell yeah!" I cheered. Finding out I didn't have to wait for something always perked me up. "Let's do this!"

I sprinted up the staircase, my boots clanging against the metal steps, and ran to the left, toward the cockpit. Said cockpit was a cramped compartment with barely enough room for two people. It was also the stickiest part of the ship, as I'd spilled several sodas inside since I'd first gotten the ship. The fact the controls still worked at all was a miracle.

As I was about to sit down, I realized I was still in my tight and uncomfortable stealth suit. "Should probably get changed first."

I kicked my boots off and ran back across the walkway, into my room. My quarters were only marginally bigger than the cockpit, but I'd done what I could to personalize them. My walls were neon blue and my sheets were neon yellow, I had a mini-fridge which I always kept stocked with beer, and, on my desk, surrounding my tablet, was my collection of fidgets from across the universe.

I picked up one of my fidgets, a crank made from high-quality bluequartz wood a rich client had tipped me, and spun it around a few times.

And another few times.

And another few times.

It was crazy to think that when I did turn 30, I'd have been doing this job for twelve years, nearly half my life. Sometimes I thought about whether I'd be happier if things had gone the way I'd planned as a kid, protecting people, saving worlds, and being beloved by everyone... but then I remembered the Sunrisers were a bunch of stuck-up shits, and those thoughts went away.

"Stop!" I shouted, putting the crank down after a few hundred rapid spins. "You have things to do."

I took off my stealth suit and, one look-through my closet later, changed into a yellow blouse, jeans, and a short-sleeved leather jacket that stopped half-way down my waist.

"Let's do this!" I shouted as I exited my room. "For real this time!"

"You wanna call ahead and let Lulu know we're coming?" Aarif asked, now being licked by Juri, as I passed back through the common area.

I aimed my pointer finger down at him. Aarif had taught me a lot of the reasons I'd been shot at came down to a lack of "social etiquette." I didn't get a lot of the things he'd told me, or why people would be annoyed by them, but I trusted him. So I'd give Lulu a call. To make sure she didn't shoot at me.

As I re-entered the cockpit, I took a seat in my chair and pressed down on my watch's screen. "Call Lulu," I said. The dial tone sounded for half a minute before a projection of Lulu popped out of my watch.

"Yael!" Lulu exclaimed, looking excited to hear from me. "Do you have some good news?"

"Your jewels have been retrieved and your ex is none the wiser," I told her, smiling back.

Lulu placed her hands over her heart and took a deep breath. "Thank you so much. You can't imagine how much this has been weighing on me."

Not that my life had been easy, but she was right that I didn't know what it was like having priceless family heirlooms stolen… or what it was like to have priceless family heirlooms.

"I just did what any genetically engineered thief would have."

"Maybe so, but I wouldn't have even been able to afford your fee had you not agreed to such a generous deal. Are you on your way over now?"

"I am," I answered, shifting around in my seat, already struggling to maintain eye contact. "And that's why I called. Because it's the polite thing to do."

"Splendid!" Lulu clasped her hands together. "I'll prepare a magnificent meal for us! Will the partner you told me about be dining with us as well?"

Unable to control myself any longer, I looked up, away from Lulu, and scratched my head. "Yeah, and, if you wouldn't mind, maybe put something out for my dog too?"

"Not a problem," she answered.

BEEP! BEEP!

"Uh, I have to go," I said, looking down at my watch to see who was calling and noticing the number was unknown. "I'm getting another call. See you in a few hours?"

"Sounds like a plan. Have a nice flight!" Lulu called out as I tapped my watch and switched over to the other line, the projection of her made-up, polished face replaced by one of a man far grimier, far more untrustworthy, and who I partially owed my successful career to.

"Jellz! How are ya? New tongue still giving you trouble?"

Jellz slowly circled the circumference of his mouth with his metal tongue. "I still can't taste anything sour, but other than that, I've got it worked out." He shifted his head, looking to either side of him. "Are we on a secure line?"

I nodded. "You got a job for me?"

Jellz shook his head as a smirk formed, showing off his rotten natural teeth and his numerous robotic replacements. "Nah, kid. I got something much bigger. But you're gonna have to come to me for the details."

"Can you at least give me a hint to what this is about? Because I was planning on taking a vacation."

"Vacation can wait." Jellz's eyes widened and he pointed a finger at me. "The Order of the Banshee are interested in you."

I jumped up from my chair and my jaw dropped. If I'd been slurping any noodles, they'd have been spit out all over the controls.

"The Order of the Banshee? Are interested in me?" my voice cracked.

"Meet me at my office on Trionga," Jellz said with a satisfied smile. "This is the break we've been waiting for." Jellz ended the call, his projection fading away, as Aarif entered the cockpit and bore witness to me standing in place, awestruck.

"Everything okay?" he asked, waving a hand in front of my face.

"The Order of the Banshee," I repeated without looking at him. "I think I'm getting invited to join The Order of the Banshee."

Aarif's jaw dropped as far down as mine had. "The Order of the Banshee…but they never bring in thieves under 40."

"I know."

"And they certainly couldn't be impressed by your maturity or professionalism."

"I know."

"So they must just think you're really good at stealing shit!"

"I know!"

Leaping up, I wrapped my legs around Aarif's waist, grabbed onto his shoulders and kissed him on the forehead, my hands in a flapping frenzy.

"We're gonna be rich!"

CHAPTER 2: MOLINA

Everyone thinks their home world is the best planet in the universe, but mine actually was. Technologically, culturally and socially, Cykeb, along with all the planets under its dominion, was centuries ahead of the rest of the universe. It was the birthplace of the Sunrisers and the head of the largest empire the universe had ever known. Poverty was non-existent and discrimination based off gender, race, religion, and sexual orientation were things of the past.

If I had any issue with Cykeb, it was the annoyances that came from having its crown princess as my closest friend.

"You *must* come with me to dinner tomorrow night," Kaybell said as we walked down the glistening, platinum halls of Zenith Command. "I can't stand being alone with my father's old, gross, boring friends."

"I'd really rather not, Kay."

"What? Why? Are you suddenly some kind of anti-social freak? If you ever become supreme general, dinners with the emperor will be commonplace for you."

I side-eyed her. "By the time I'm supreme general, *you'll* be the emperor."

"Which is why it's a good idea for you to do me this favor."

I shook my head as we continued toward my father's office. It had been almost a year since I'd last seen the supreme general in person, and, even then, my most recent visit hadn't been a long one. I'd been on the planet attending a conference about new potential rehabilitative programs for incarcerated citizens and had stopped by for dinner before I left. We'd mostly eaten in silence, but I had shared some of my recent exploits with him and he'd seemed happy to listen.

"If your hesitation is coming from nerves about potentially not making captain, you should put them at ease. There's no shame at all in losing to Princess Kaybell Kose Bythora, daughter of Stephen and descendant of Leon, first emperor of Cykeb and founder of the Sunrisers, future ruler of The Holy Cykebian Empire."

Somehow, she never got tired of using her full title.

"Listen, I'd just really prefer to not attend. I'm not as adept at dealing with your father's 'old, gross, boring friends' as you are."

"*That's* certainly true."

"But I have a plan. Before dinner, the three of us can have tea and go riding. Your father loves me, so maybe I can get you out of having to go either."

Kay tilted her head up and curled her lips up her face. "A potentially sound strategy. Provided you don't fall off your horse and embarrass yourself like you did during our shore leave on Eltista V."

"Gods, are you ever going to let me live that down?"

"I shall not. But I will consider bringing it up less if your plan works."

"Well then, I guess I can't fail." I smirked. "Like you will at making captain."

Kaybell laughed in her usual, haughty way as she wrapped her arms around me. Especially when she was smiling like this, Kay was possibly the most beautiful member of the Sunrisers. Her eyes were the same shade of vermilion as her hair, her skin was porcelain, she had a flawless figure, and her grin could light up a star system.

"Molina!"

My heart sank into my stomach. From behind a corner stepped my little sister, Morphea, flipping her long, bright-pink hair. She wore a venomous smile and had five gold earrings in her left ear, four indicating her rank of commander and the fifth, shaped like a star, signifying her as the supreme general's adjutant.

"I was so excited when I heard you were coming," she continued.

I gritted my teeth and forced myself to smile back as I shook her hand, which was as soft as a moon callie's feather. The scent of her mango lotion was far too strong.

"I assure you, the feeling wasn't mutual," Kaybell remarked as she let go of me, her smile as effectively deceptive as Morphea's.

"Kaybell, I've missed you most," Morphea said, pointing a finger at her before looking back at me. "If you were wondering how Father's been doing, he recently recovered from a bad case of Poxin plague. It was pretty touch and go for a moment there and he would have loved to hear from you." Her smile widened. "But he knew better than to expect a call."

My blood boiled. I'd graduated first in my class, I could list every Sunriser rule and regulation off the top of my head, and I'd even received special commendations for creative thinking during combat situations, but when faced with Morphea I couldn't think of witty retorts to save my life. Luckily for me, Kay hated my sister as much as I did, and was much better at delivering tongue lashings.

"Not everyone has the privilege of ample free time that a desk job permits," Kaybell said. "And when the time comes to choose a successor, I'm sure the supreme general will care more about who achieved greatness, and not who spent the most time as his side. So why don't you quit trying to guilt Molina and go get us all some tea while we wait for our interviews to begin?"

When I was a kid, I'd had someone else to protect me from my sister. And while Kay wasn't as passionate as she'd been, she still performed excellently.

Morphea didn't look perturbed in the slightest, but I could sense Kay had chipped her armor. "Such an optimistic view of the universe." Morphea tilted her head to the side. "You can ask Father's secretary to get you tea if you'd like. I have to go speak with General Hossington." She spun around and clasped her hands behind her back. "Good luck to you both."

As my sister walked down the hall, I whispered to Kaybell, "When we're running things, our first order of business has to be locking her away in the deepest, dankest cell we have."

Kay laughed. "I can't wait."

Reaching our destination, I put my thumb on the office's entrance scanner, signaling the supreme general that I was here. Moments later, the doors slid open, revealing Father seated at his desk.

"Commander Langstone, Commander Bythora," the Sunriser supreme general greeted us as we passed over the threshold. His face was cold and unreadable and his stocky body was stiff as a statue. While we were on the job, he was nothing but my superior officer. "I hope you had a pleasant journey home."

"Thank you, sir," I replied, Kay and I standing with perfect posture and blank faces. "No problems were encountered."

"Excellent," he nodded. "And I trust you're both prepared to set off on the Noriker as soon as its new captain has been determined?"

"Yes, sir," we said in unison.

The supreme general leaned forward. "Commander Bythora, please step back outside. I'll be speaking with Commander Langstone first and will send for you when we're finished. Understood?"

Kaybell nodded, turning around and walking out of the office, the doors sliding closed behind her.

"Please, sit down."

I did as I was told and crossed my legs. My father picked up a tablet from his desk and focused his eyes on it, rather than on me. I didn't know what kind of questions the supreme general would be asking, but I was prepared for anything and my record spoke for itself.

"Commander, would you have handled the recent situation on Rondow any differently than Captain Asparago?"

That wasn't the type of opening question I'd been expecting, but I had an idea of how to best answer it.

"For the most part, the situation on Rondow was handled through standard procedure. I did question the captain's order to terminate the terrorist leader instead of arresting him, but given the circumstances, I completely understand the reasoning behind her decision."

Not entirely true. I felt no pity for someone responsible for the deaths of so many people, but the fact he co7uld have so easily been taken in alive still nagged at me.

"I see," the supreme general said, writing on his tablet.

"And what do you think are the largest problems currently plaguing the universe?"

Again, this wasn't the type of question I'd anticipated. It was true he was already aware of everything I'd accomplished in my career, but I'd figured that was still what he'd be asking about.

"From how I see it, the biggest problems facing the universe are the prejudices held by more primitive cultures. Along with being toxic to themselves and their societies, when held by those with great influence, they can inspire a great deal of death and destruction. The people of the universe outside The Cykebian Empire need better education."

Father's eyes didn't move away from his tablet, his finger continuing to glide back and forth across it. "And do you think the Sunrisers should be responsible for delivering said education?"

I swallowed before answering. "It is not the place of the Sunrisers to get involved in civil affairs."

"Then do you think there's anything we could do if aiding their education programs is outside our purview?"

There had to be a reason he was asking questions like these. These matters were of relevance to generals, not captains. Either I was up for a bigger promotion than my father had stated, or he had a very specific mission in mind for me.

"We could institute more strict anti-discrimination laws on all the worlds where we have jurisdiction, but we'd have to introduce them slowly and take care to not cause the bigots on these plants to gather and riot."

The supreme general set his tablet down on the desk. He sat up straight and looked me dead in the eye. "And what of the planets outside our jurisdiction? Surely the toxicity on those worlds will only spread farther."

I looked back directly at my father. "Unless a planet has signed an agreement with the Sunrisers, we have no place getting involved in their affairs, as per regulation 1C-4A."

Father gazed down at his tablet before looking back up at me. There was now a small smile on his face. It was strange to see him show that expression outside the house, but I had a feeling I knew what it meant.

Following the supreme general's surprising smile, the interview went on for another 20 minutes. We moved on to questions more like the ones I'd been expecting, and by the end, I was feeling as confident as I could, although Kaybell would no doubt excel in her interview as well.

While I waited for Kay's interview to conclude, I was sent a video of an orchestra performance from my third year at the academy. I barely knew Dr. Kurama, but they'd sent it out to everyone from our graduating class. I enjoyed music as background noise while I was working out, but sitting down and listening to it had never been enjoyable to me. I'd attended all the concerts Kay had participated in during our school years out of support for her, but in my memory, they were all a blur.

Kay had tried getting me to join the orchestra many times, but I'd never been interested. She thought I needed more hobbies outside of my sword collecting and training, but the way I saw things, with the amount of time I'd put into my studies, pursuing any other leisurely activities would have led to me spreading my time thin and not enjoying myself at all.

A half hour later, the doors to Father's office slid open, the supreme general and Kaybell walking out together. Father wore the same blank expression he'd worn throughout our meeting, while Kaybell looked even more smug than usual.

As Kaybell walked up right next to me and turned around, Father clasped his hands in front of him. Kay's arrogance didn't dissuade me at all. The only thing I was nervous about was how irritating she'd be once the supreme general was no longer present.

"Commanders, thank you both very much for your time. I'll be taking the rest of the day to mull over my decision and discussing the matter with several of my advisors. You're free to spend the rest of the afternoon however you'd like, but I want you both on the bridge of the Noriker at 2000 hours for the promotion ceremony. As per tradition, every available general will be present. Understood?"

"Yes, sir!"

Father nodded. "Dismissed."

The rest of the day proved uneventful. We had lunch at Cyrus's and then went to the hotel we were staying at to rest and edit the thank you speeches we'd written over the past several days. They were meant to be short and to the point and so I'd kept mine under a minute long. Kaybell's, however, went on for over five minutes, and went over many of the legendary members of her family who'd served in the Sunrisers before her, as well as many of the reasons The Cykebian Empire was the greatest the universe had ever known. While I had nothing but respect for her family and I agreed with her points about the empire, she was definitely overdoing it.

At 1900 hours, it was time to change into our dress uniforms. Unlike our standard uniforms, which were designed primarily for practicality, these were meant to be more "stylish," primarily indicated by a lack of pockets. The black on our uniforms was swapped out for white, gold sun-shaped brooches were worn over our heart, and the com devices in our right ears were exchanged for a number of earrings to match the ones in our left ears, connected to them by gold chains.

We returned to Zenith Command and took a shuttle up to the shipyard outside the planet's atmosphere. Inside it were ships of all classes, each impressive in its own way. There were Parallax-class ships like the Mangalarga and the Noriker, which were massive and designed to be able to handle any and all situations, as well as White Thunder-class ships, Horizon-class ships, and Eclipse-class ships. White Thunder-class ships were the smallest in our fleet, with room for only a single pilot and designed for maneuverability and direct combat. Horizon-class ships were significantly larger and built primarily for short-distance travel, and finally Eclipse-class ships were the largest of all and designed for transporting cargo.

The Noriker was approximately the same size as the Mangalarga, and had a near-identical design, being a burnt-orange octagonal prism, with the Sunriser logo displayed prominently on one of its sides. From what I'd read, it was exactly 1800 meters in diameter and staffed by a crew of 12,000, including command officers, doctors, engineers, and security personnel, with 30,000 ground troops also living on board, always ready to be deployed at a moment's notice. Whoever became captain would be responsible for all 42,000 of these lives.

Stepping on board, there were some minor aesthetic interior differences, but it was mostly the same as the Mangalarga. The color black stretched as far as the eye could see and the burnt-orange symbol of the Sunrisers was plastered everywhere.

Upon reaching the bridge, we found that not only were the supreme general and several of the great people directly beneath him present, but other highly influential people within The Cykebian Empire were also there.

We took a few minutes to greet all the generals in attendance and enjoy the refreshments that were laid out, Morphea thankfully not being present to make me even more anxious. I would have to thank Father for not inviting her.

Eventually, everyone else was instructed to sit down, while Father, Kaybell and I stood in the middle of the bridge.

"Commander Langstone, Commander Bythora," he started. "it's always a pleasure to add a new captain to the Sunriser's ranks. And to be frank, I'm especially pleased to see two brave and brilliant young women I've known for so long become worthy of the position at such a young age." Despite speaking of the joy he was feeling, his tone was as flat as usual. "However, there is only room for one new captain today. And that honor goes to… Molina Langstone."

His words pierced my eardrums as they were met with the sounds of applause from many of the most powerful and influential people in the universe. Far more shocking than the promotion itself was that Kaybell was applauding, with what seemed to be a genuine smile on her face.

As confident as I'd been, I'd been equally prepared for the next words out of his mouth to be "Kaybell Bythora." While I would have been disappointed, and it would have been a new experience for me, I would have taken no issue with serving under my friend… so long as she could maintain a professional attitude about it.

Father brought his hands out from behind him, and inside them was a gold earring. Still in shock, I leaned forward almost automatically and allowed him to put it on my left ear.

"You deserve it," Kaybell whispered.

This wasn't the reaction I'd anticipated from her at all, but I was happy to see it. Maybe in spite of all the teasing, she'd actually done some growing up.

"Congratulations, *Captain* Langstone," the supreme general said as we shook hands. "I hope you don't mind me saying this somewhat publicly, but we already have a crucial mission in mind for your first outing."

I recomposed myself and looked my father straight in the eye. "With my team by my side, I'm prepared for anything. I'll uphold the legacy of all the captains who've preceded me and do everything in my power to spread peace and order across the stars, no matter what the mission."

"I'm glad to hear all of that. Because we've finally managed to track down a priority target we've been after for centuries." He paused, and I waited with baited breath to find out which long-time criminals I'd be bringing to justice. "Captain Langstone, your first assignment is to take down the thieves guild known as "The Order of the Banshee."

CHAPTER 3: YAEL

"Yael, welcome!"

Lulu approached me with her arms open for a hug, and I braced myself for impact. She wrapped her arms around my shoulders, her grip not too tight but not too gentle. By all rights, it was a perfect hug, but that didn't stop it from sending tingles through my body.

A sense of relief overcame me as Lulu let go and turned her attention away from me. "And you must be Aarif," she said, hugging him the same way she'd hugged me.

Aarif was more responsive to it, hugging her back with a single arm. "Nice to meet you."

Lulu was a small woman with neat black hair she kept short. She couldn't have been younger than 40, her skin was incredibly dark and flawless, and she smelled like fresh roses. In contrast to the casual clothes we were in, Lulu was wearing a Benkinian-style floor-length black dress with poofy silver sleeves, a star-shaped broach, black leather gloves, and an extravagantly designed hat covered in feathers and lace. Underneath her dress, on her feet, were no doubt high-heels that would make me vomit if I saw them.

BARK. BARK.

"And what's your name, girl?" Lulu put on a baby voice as she bent down to pet our doggo.

"It's Juri," Aarif told her. "She's a cross between a Spanish water dog and an American water spaniel, and she's the best."

Juri aggressively licked Lulu, most likely noticing her nice scent.

"I don't doubt it," Lulu chuckled. "I've got some tasty fish laid out for you, yes I do." Lulu stood up tall, her posture perfect. "And of course, I have food for all of us as well. Shall we adjourn to the dining room?"

"First things first," I said, pulling the safe out of my bag. "Your jewels."

Lulu's smile widened as she took the safe from me. "You're an angel, thank you."

Lulu turned around and walked, Aarif and I following behind as she led us through the massive entrance hall. The St. Shiala School for Girls was Lulu's entire life. For four generations, the women of her family had been responsible for educating the young girls of the Cykebian nobility in the ways of high society and teaching them to be the future leaders of society. This place had meant so much to Lulu's grandmother she'd made it her home, and the family had lived here ever since. The school was as large as a castle, a necessity given the various teaching facilities and hundreds of girls who lived here at any given time, so living space had never been an issue for them.

A dark, gloomy lavishness was present throughout every part of the building I'd seen. Black and silver were The Cykebian Empire's colors and the school was proud to show off its interplanetary pride, nearly all of the décor and furniture being of the same colors, with hints of purple mixed in, and a massive Cykebian flag hung up on a wall, a black base with twenty-four silver stars on top. Walking through the dimly lit, polished and pristine entrance hall, it felt like I was in the universe's fanciest dungeon.

The dining room was as spotless and the color palette was as bleak as the rest of the school, but the lighting was more upbeat, a row of chandeliers shining brightly above the long table.

Even if this room had turned out to be an actual dungeon though, I wouldn't have cared with the spread Lulu had put out. Matzah ball and kreplach soup, Thai papaya salad, bottles of blue wine, and baskets filled with the freshest rolls and pastries I'd seen in months lined the table. And I had a feeling these were just the appetizers.

"Mine!" I shouted, charging at the food.

"Yael, we're in someone's home!" Aarif called out to me as I stuffed a French baguette into my mouth.

"And she put the food out for us," I replied, only realizing half-way through my sentence they probably couldn't understand a word I was saying.

Lulu giggled as she put the safe down on the floor against the wall.

"It's quite all right. I got a pretty clear idea of Yael's personality when we first met and I fully understood what I was getting into when I offered her a meal."

"See?" I swallowed the baguette mostly whole.

Aarif rolled his eyes before taking a seat next to me, Juri already chowing down on the bowl of yellowtail that had been left waiting for her in the corner.

In the past, I'd had someone else to call me out when my behavior was "socially inappropriate," but she'd been pretty bad at her job because of her inability to not find my inappropriate behavior adorable. Wherever she was now, I hoped Moli was happy.

"You know, I received quite a bit of money from my ex-husband in the divorce," Lulu said as she sat down opposite Aarif. "I could take my first vacation in over a decade. It's not something I've ever felt an incentive to do before, but it could be a lovely way to start off my new life."

I was only half paying attention at this point. Most of my focus was on the delicious matzah ball I'd just tasted. Lulu wasn't a noble, but all her food was fit for them, and it seemed like I'd been right; they kept all the good soup to themselves. This was easily the #1 Benkinian soup I'd had, and it was at least in my top 300 overall.

"You've been all across the universe," Lulu continued. "Are there any leisure worlds you recommend?"

I swallowed the keplach in my mouth before answering. "I was actually thinking about taking a vacation soon, but somehow I doubt you'd be a fan of lava rafting."

"Most likely true." Lulu looked amused as she put a cloth napkin on her lap.

"You ever been to Taito V?" Aarif asked. "They have some seriously amazing art museums."

"I can't say I've ever heard of that world, no." Lulu smiled. "Thank you for the suggestion."

I sighed internally, knowing full well Lulu had no intention of actually listening to anything either of us said on this matter. She knew how different we were and that Aarif and I didn't take lavish trips. She was being polite instead of being straightforward.

"Mother." A girl who was younger, slimmer and taller than Lulu, but nonetheless resembled her, entered the room, her whole body shivering and her voice meek. "Are… are these the thieves you hired?"

"They are indeed," Lulu said. "Now steady your stance and properly introduce yourself."

The girl only continued to shiver, stuttering like an old pig cartoon I used to watch, and looking like she was about to have a panic attack.

Lulu sighed. "P'Ken, meet Yael Pavnick and Aarif Bhatti. Yael, Aarif, this is my daughter."

P'Ken wore a similar dress to her mother's, but hers was a dark shade of green, and in place of a broach she wore a skinny lime-green tie, which matched her even poofier sleeves.

"Nice to meet ya," I said, hopefully not spitting out any of the food I'd been chewing.

"N...nice to meet you too," P'Ken stuttered, her head cast down. "A..an... and thank you."

She took a seat next to her mother at the fourth place setting, but didn't look like she was in any mood to eat.

"Excuse P'Ken." Lulu said. "Life hasn't been easy for either of us as of late, but it's taken an especially great toll on her."

I didn't have a clue what to say to that, so I kept stuffing food in my mouth. Of course I felt bad for her, for both of them, but I'd already done literally everything I could to help.

"I'm so sorry you had to live with a man like your father," Aarif said. "And please don't worry about not presenting yourself well around us. Trust me, even if you were asleep with your face in the soup, you'd still have more dignity in your pinkie than we do in our entire bodies."

P'Ken shut her eyes and giggled. "My face in the soup... that's funny."

I cracked half a smile while still chewing. I was lucky to

have Aarif around to keep me from seeming like a heartless bitch.

"Um, what fragrances do you have on?" P'Ken asked, still looking uncomfortable but now with a small smile. "I haven't smelled anything like them before."

Aarif and I quickly turned to each other and exchanged smirks before looking back at our hosts. I wasn't sure if she was being passive aggressive about our stench or if she genuinely thought we were wearing odd perfume. Either way...

"I'm wearing Alexi Orlinor's "Salty Goodness" and Aarif is sporting the brand new "Old Fashioned Oil," I said.

P'Ken rolled her hands around each other, embarrassed. "I... I'm sorry, I don't know Alexi Orlinor. Is he in?"

"She's messing with you," Lulu said, shaking her head. "Yael is a low-maintenance girl. She isn't the type to spend time fussing over how she presents herself." Her smile glowed. "But I'd be happy to help you fix that in place of our agreed-upon payment."

I laughed internally at the thought of enrolling in this school. I might have found Lulu and P'Ken's unnatural scents pleasant, but it wasn't how I was supposed to smell.

"Thanks, but I'll stick with the gidgits."

"Are you sure?" P'Ken asked. "Mother's an excellent teacher. And I think you'd look wonderful in some proper clothes."

There was nothing "improper" about my clothes. Whatever that meant. It didn't mean anything negative about me that I didn't wear long, fancy dresses as casual wear like the upper-class women of this world. "Again, I appreciate the thought, but if I stayed here, I wouldn't be out there, helping other people out of jams like yours."

"Oh yeah, you steal for people out of the goodness of your heart," Aarif mocked.

I couldn't think of a good comeback, so I just glared at him and continued to eat.

Lulu blew on a spoonful of broth, and only then did I notice we weren't using the same type of spoon. "Regardless of your reasons for why you do your job, I'll always be thankful I bumped into you that day at the ice festival. Even if you don't wish to take advantage of our services, you'll always be welcome here."

Picking up a new client by chance in the middle of an in-progress job, like I had with Lulu, was what we in the business liked to call, "damn convenient."

I chugged back all the delectable blue wine in my glass before slamming it back down on the table. "Thanks, Lulu." I wiped the wine on my face with my fist. "I'll keep that in mind."

"Do you know where you're going next?" P'Ken asked, still not having touched any of the awesome food.

"Well, not to brag, but—" Aarif cut me off by kicking me under the table.

"Don't you think it's safer if they don't know?" he asked, clearly in pain from the impact.

"Getting involved in something dangerous, I take it?" Lulu asked.

"Hopefully not," I burped. "But he's right that it's better if you don't know. Don't want you getting in any trouble."

If Lulu really didn't want to risk getting into any trouble, she never would have hired a professional thief. She would have gone to the local authorities. But as she'd put it when I asked why she was turning to me: "Thieves have more honor."

"Um, what about the story of how you retrieved Mother's heirlooms?" P'Ken asked. "Would that be safe for us to hear?"

I wasn't the best at reading people, but I was pretty sure I could finally see a small smile forming on her face.

"Heh, sure. Why not?"

If Benkin was a world where there was a massive class divide, Trionga was a planet where class was non-existent. If you lived there, you were either an outcast looking to live out the rest of your life as a farmer, or a criminal in need of a place to hide.

Jellz's office was located on a small farm along the southern peninsula. It was one of dozens of offices he had across the quadrant, and in exchange for financial aid when they were struggling, the owners of the land didn't rat him out. Not that the local authorities were anything to worry about, another advantage of the planet, but the Sunrisers were always a theoretical call away. At this point, there was practically no part of the universe they weren't in charge of protecting.

"Oh my goooooood," I groaned as we trudged through the crops. "Why is it so windy?!"

I'd checked the current temperature before leaving the ship, so Aarif and I were at least bundled up in heavy coats, but there was nothing to be done about the wind. I knew vegetables like cracklin corn and c.a.k.e thrived under these conditions, but that didn't make them any more pleasant.

"Still not as bad as his office on Spiguss," Aarif shivered. "We should be glad we aren't being pecked at by birds of prey from Hell."

"*Don't fight back against the birds*," Jellz had told us. "*They just want friends.*" We still had the scars from our visit.

"Gotta keep my eyes on the prize," I said. "If this works out, I could be drinking with Madame N'gwa and Shion the

Librarian before the week is up."

Aarif dusted some cracklin corn specks out of his hair as he replied, "I know they're the most elite group of female thieves in the universe, but they're also all over 50, and mostly over 70. You think you'll have much to talk about?"

"Of course! Sure, they may not be interested in hearing my thoughts on the newest developments in the wrestling world, but there's so much I can learn from them. Like how to weaponize kumquats!"

"You sound way too excited about the prospect of melting someone's bones with citrus."

"Bleh!" I stuck my tongue out at Aarif.

Eventually we pushed through the last of the crops, and a small house entered our sights. It matched Jellz's description exactly, with a burgundy roof, no windows, and just big enough to not be considered a hut. I'd have asked Aarif if he wanted to wait outside, but neither of us wanted to bear this wind longer than we had to. So, cramped we would be.

Walking up to the house, I knocked on the front door with the pattern Jellz had most recently instructed me to use.

"What did the duck say to the platypus?" Jellz asked from inside for his next security measure.

"Go chase a meteor, ya dumb yellow belly," I replied, doing my best impression of a stupid Earthling.

The door opened, revealing Jellz, who had a shotgun pointed at me. I'd asked him multiple times to stop putting guns in my face.

"What was the first drink you and I shared together?"

Jellz's hair was short, black and greasy, he hadn't covered up the burn marks on his pale face at all, and he was dressed in a white button-down shirt, brown trench coat, jean-shorts and hiking boots, all unwashed.

"Trick question. I bought us a bottle of Mafellian vodka and you drank the whole thing yourself."

Jellz continued to aim his gun at me for a few more seconds, before hesitantly lowering it as he bit his lip. "Come on in," he said, turning around and walking further inside. "Shut the door behind you."

Aarif and I walked in behind him and I did as he asked. The "living room" we entered was minuscule, with barely enough room for the sofa and chair inside it. There was an equally small kitchen area and a single door, which likely led into a bedroom.

"So talk to me," I said as we all sat down. "Now that I've got their attention, what do The Order of the Banshee want me to do?"

Jellz crossed his legs, snapped off one of his thumbs and blew into it before twisting it back on. "In two weeks, they're gonna be holding a little shindig. Nothing too fancy, lucky you, just a chance for members to catch up. Not every member is invited, they'd never all gather in one place, but there are gonna be some big shots in attendance. Madame N'gwa, Moonriver, Electric Ellie, etc. And their eyes are all gonna be on you."

As excited as I was by what Jellz was saying, I was also relieved I wouldn't be meeting all my heroes at once. Both because I'd be even more tongue-tied than I was no doubt going to be around a select group of them, and because the fewer people I had to deal with at once in general, the better.

"They're going to be talking to and observing you all night," Jellz continued. "And at the end of the night, they'll vote on whether or not you'll be added as their newest member." Jellz pounded on his stomach three times, and then the fourth time he did so, he coughed up a tablet.

"Nasty," Aarif whispered, repulsed, as Jellz handed me the device.

"That's got a map on it that'll lead you to the meeting site," Jellz coughed. "Don't lose it and don't share it with anyone."

I grinned, looking down at the saliva and blood covered tablet, before looking back up at Jellz. "Thank you so much."

With a thunderous gagging noise, Jellz coughed up a small pistol. "Thing never stays down," he groaned. "Anyway, don't thank me. I'm just a middle-man. Two of their members nominated you and they came to me."

Joy surged up my chest as my grin widened. "Two of them nominated me. Please tell me you know which two. Please tell me one of them was Madame N'gwa!"

"No idea, sorry. I'm sure you'll find out yourself in a week."

I had to know. I had to know now. I had to know if the greatest thief in the universe, who'd forgotten more about the art than I could ever hope to learn, had been one of the women who'd nominated me.

Jellz belched. "Ugh. I swear, if there was a safer way to keep things safe than to swallow them, I'd go with it." He paused. "Since you don't have any more jobs lined up and the party isn't for two weeks, could I count on you for a lift to Momento? The ship I took here is on its last legs… and I know you're always stocked up on beer."

I smirked. "Sure thing. And even if you were 'just' a middle-man, I'm grateful enough that I'll only charge you 66% of our usual passenger fee."

The old man laughed, tilting his head back and letting out another burp. "That's cute."

CHAPTER 4: YAEL

The trip to Momento hadn't been fun in the slightest.

Lasting six days, Jellz's presence on board had proved to be far more annoying than I could have anticipated. He woke us up multiple times singing in the shower, him and Aarif nearly came to blows more than once as they were forced to sleep in the same room, and by the gods did he enjoy telling us every little thing he thought we were doing wrong.

Eventually, I had two options: Be direct with my associate, tell him he was being a disturbance on the ship, and act like an adult about the matter, or steal his robotic teeth while he was sleeping, hide them in Juri's dog food, and promise to only give them back if he agreed to stop being such an ass.

The latter plan had ended up working as well as I'd hoped.

Once we'd parted ways, I was left with eight days to prepare for The Order of the Banshee's party. As a rule, I hated parties, but that was because of a combination of the large crowds and boring conversation topics. With the Banshees, neither of these things would be a problem.

The first thing to do was to find the right outfit to wear. All of the best thieves had a signature look, but I'd never been able to pick one out. I'd spent the six days we were traveling with Jellz giving it deep thought though, and I'd finally narrowed it down to three choices.

Since I'd started out in this business, I'd been inspired by Madame N'gwa, so basing my look on hers sounded cool. My only concern with this idea was that N'gwa would think I was ripping her off, not paying tribute to her, and the last thing I wanted to do was insult my hero.

Outside of stealing, the IUWL was my jam, so I was also thinking about going with a flashy wrestling outfit. It would consist of a sparkly neon blue unitard, and equally sparkly neon yellow boots.

The last option I was seriously considering was to show up in my normal clothes, but with the addition of a silly hat, which I would make up a dramatic backstory for. One of rising from sorrow and defeat and achieving greatness!

The Banshees hated weapons, so no matter what I wore, I'd be going in unarmed, but I would be bringing along a few tricks, just in case.

Once I'd made my choice and my outfit was assembled, my focus turned to practicing my social skills with Aarif. I wasn't worried about having things to talk about with the coolest women in the universe, but my Autistic ass still didn't function the same way their brains did, and so I'd reluctantly agreed to the practice and done my best to learn, regardless of how idiotic and nonsensical I found most of what Aarif was telling me.

Eventually the day came, and we were landing on the fourth moon of Milash. I was 33% excited, 33% nervous, 33% hungry as shit, and 1% ready to throw up at any second.

"You are a strong, badass, independent, queer as Hell woman whose Autism, while sometimes off-putting to those who don't know you, makes you the awesome woman you are," Aarif said. "You are the best thief in the universe, and you are definitely going to be voted into The Order of the Banshee."

I wrapped my arms around Aarif. "That was so fucking sappy, but I needed to hear it, so thank you."

"You can… repay me… by letting go." Only as he spoke did I realize I was squeezing the life out of him.

I quickly unhooked my arms and let him breathe again.

BARK! BARK!

"Thanks, Juri," I said, bending down to scratch her head. "I definitely couldn't have come this far without the best dog in the universe."

I didn't just mean that because of her emotional support. Juri being on death's door was what had brought Aarif and I together, and he was the one who kept me flying. Aarif owed just as much to her of course; if he hadn't run into me looking for help, he still would have been nothing more than the guy who served two years in prison for the most embarrassing crime ever.

"Remember, if anything goes wrong, call me immediately and I'll swing in to grab you," Aarif said, still catching his breath.

"Aye aye," I replied with a little salute. "Wish me luck!"

I turned around and walked off Ricochet, Aarif closing the entrance behind me as I stepped onto the moon's surface.

While the moon did have an artificial atmosphere and artificial gravity set up, it hadn't been terraformed. The meeting spot was a few miles away, as we'd been instructed not to land within seven kilometers of it, so I was in for a long walk through a gray, rocky wasteland. I was glad it was at least fairly warm, especially compared to Trionga and Benkin.

As I walked, my thoughts turned to my parents, of all

people. I hadn't seen them or talked to them in over a decade, but I guessed there was a part of me still wondering what they'd think if they could see me now. They'd been as heartbroken as I was when I'd been rejected by the Sunrisers, and, to make me feel better, they'd offered to train me in the family pickle business. I knew they meant well, but they had to have known that would never have suited me. I needed a job that put my talents to use.

I hadn't woken up one morning and told them, "Mom, Dad, I'm going to become a thief," instead running away without a word, and while that may have been kind of a dick move, I knew they wouldn't have approved of the path I'd chosen. And they definitely wouldn't have approved of all the genetic engineering I'd had done, even if all those surgeries had helped me not die more times than I could count.

Still, if they knew that not only had I survived as a thief, but that I'd thrived, to the point where I could be by far the youngest woman to ever join The Order of the Banshee, maybe it'd be enough to make them proud of me. It wasn't important. This was just another instance of my mind going off on a tangent. All that mattered was impressing my heroes and getting ridiculously rich. Maybe I'd anonymously send some gidgits my parents' way, but I had no serious plans to ever see them again.

Following my map and looking into the distance, I was pretty sure I spotted my destination: a cave shaped like a bear's head. I knew we wouldn't be meeting in a building, and this was exactly as extra as I'd been hoping for.

I continued my hike over to the cave until I was standing right in front of it. The inside was pitch black and I couldn't see a thing, but I knew they were waiting for me.

With a hop in my step, I charged forward into the cave. I

didn't have my night-vision goggles on me and I hadn't had enough money to get my eyes that kind of upgrade when I'd had all my surgeries done, so I was blind. I could hear things though. I could hear my boots crushing every rock I stepped on. I could hear the almost musical sound of the wind blowing through the cave. And I could hear faint whispers.

"Not a gray hair or a wrinkle…"

"Quite muscular…"

"Why does she wear such a peculiar hat?"

I couldn't recognize any of their voices, but a grin still emerged on my face. They were watching me. Now was my chance to make a good first impression. I rolled my shoulders back and did some quick leg stretches before tossing my hat away and up into the air, sprinting forward, and doing a double back salto tucked with two full twists, followed by a double salto with a double twist. Right as I finished, I grabbed my hat before it touched the ground and put it back on my head.

After putting my time on the academy's gymnastics team to use, I performed a kata I'd recently taught myself, with mostly flawless execution, to show off my martial arts skills.

Finally, I tightened a fist and hit the ground beneath me as hard as I could, a massive cloud of dust rising into the air as the ground shook.

"I also have an awesome dog."

Dim lights momentarily blinded me as they flooded the cave, illuminating my surroundings. I rubbed my eyes and, once I could see again, I realized I was standing in the middle of a large circular area of the cave, surrounded by eleven of the greatest thieves in the universe and multiple refreshment tables.

"Welcome, Yael Pavnick," Lioness said.

It took everything in my power not to squeal with excitement. Just like Jellz had said, Moonriver, Electric Ellie, and friggin Madame N'gwa were all here, but among the others there were also Beatrice Nunez, Athena York, and Lilith.

"While physical talents are not what we value most, that was an... adequate demonstration," Lioness continued, stroking her ankle-length hair.

"Thank you," I responded in the calmest tone I could manage.

The greatest thief in the universe, with a bounty of 300,000,000 gidgits, stepped toward me, the bells she wore all over her body making sounds I'd only heard about. A fool might have thought it was counterproductive for a thief to have noisy bells as part of their signature look, but it was something you could get away with when you were the best of the best.

"I am Madame N'gwa, chairwoman of The Order of the Banshee." She reached out her arm, which was covered by a long, fingerless, white glove. "A pleasure to meet you."

My hands flapping, I gripped one of hers tightly and smiled, hopefully not grinning like a complete dork. "It's an honor."

"An honor? That's an odd thing to say to someone you seek to be a peer of."

My heart sank as she let go of my hand. "I'm sorry. I didn't... I meant..."

"I'm messing with you." She grinned, flashing her yellow teeth. I wanted to breathe a sigh of relief, but I was still standing on pins and needles. "When you're my age, you have to make your own fun every chance you get."

No one knew exactly how old Madame N'gwa was, but it was believed she was almost 200. If true, she was one of the oldest people to ever live.

"I understand," I said nervously, nodding.

Madame N'gwa continued to smile. "Many of us have been impressed by your exploits over the past ten years. Monarchs, CEOs, and even Sunriser bases have all fallen victim to your skills. You've caused untold chaos across the universe with your actions and have had long-forbidden surgeries performed on you, and yet you've managed to avoid even having a bounty placed on your head. It is for these reasons Lioness and Beatrice have nominated you for entry into our group."

It was disappointing Madame N'gwa hadn't been one of the ones to nominate me, but Lioness and Beatrice still came in at #8 and #11 on my ranking of the Banshees.

"However, many of us believe that, regardless of your skill level, someone of your age, with such a lack of experience, has no place among us. Knowledge is everything, and new members must possess new information to offer us." Her smile completely disappeared. "Tonight, the eleven of us present shall make a final decision. Enjoy the refreshments, and do your best to convince us you have new knowledge which will aid us in our future endeavors." Madame N'gwa raised one of her wrinkly arms into the air. "Let's party."

My hero snapped her fingers, causing jazzy music to start playing from seemingly nowhere and the lights to turn violet. The mood of the cave completely changed as the older women started either talking with one another, walking over to one of the refreshment tables, or, in Lilith's case, dancing like there was no tomorrow.

Okay, Yael, I thought. You can do this. You can be… social.

"If you find out who nominated you, make sure the first thing you do is thank them," Aarif had told me.

Following his advice, I went over to one of the refreshment

tables, where Lioness was pouring herself a glass of Rikunian brandy. Lioness looked exactly like she did on her wanted poster, sporting amber hair, light skin, and her signature faux lion fur coat. Most thieves had outdated photos of them on their wanted posters, but Lioness annually sent a new picture of herself to the Sunrisers. Like her namesake, she was full of pride, and she wanted everyone to know who she was, and didn't care about any potential risks. She only had the seventh highest bounty among The Order, but she was known to act like she was #1.

"Thank you for nominating me," I said, tapping my heels.

Lioness sipped her brandy before she acknowledged me. She was scowling.

"What? It isn't an honor to have been nominated by me? Only to meet N'gwa? That is so typical."

I swallowed nervously. "Is this… another joke?"

Instead of chomping my head off, Lioness took another sip of her drink, still wearing her scowl. "It was your heist three months ago of the files containing information about the secret operatives on Applitia that really impressed me. Reminded me of something I would have pulled when I was your age." I was terrified looking into her fearsome eyes, but my heart couldn't ignore the compliment she'd just paid me. "I may be biased, but I believe it would serve you well to do more work like that, and less work for any client who catches your fancy."

I couldn't say the wrong thing again, so I tried to think of the least potentially offensive way to respond that wouldn't also make me sound like a drooling idiot.

"I've been thinking about doing more independent robberies. And I have so many questions I'd love to ask you about spacing out the timing between them. I mean, you're the master."

Lioness swung back her glass, chugging down the remaining brandy, before slamming the glass back down on the table. She still wasn't smiling, but her scowl had vanished.

"You can ask me as much as you want if you get in. Right now, I have a few questions for you."

"Anything," I said, trying not to sound too excited.

Finally, we were getting to the good part. The part where I could just geek out about my craft with supremely awesome women and not have to worry about jokes or saying the wrong thing.

"Okay." Lioness popped her lips. "Like I said before, physical ability isn't what we value most. And your lack of experience is what raises the most doubts about your qualifications. But I remember just how much life I lived during the earliest parts of my career. What are the wildest parts of the universe you've seen? What have you experienced that I haven't? While having information that contributes to our group's success is vital, it's equally important you have good stories to share at functions like this. Being a thief isn't just about making money, it's about the adventures one has along the way, and shared stories from others let us experience far more than we ever could on our own. I know all about your greatest heists, so tell me something I don't know."

She sounded so cool the way she was talking. One of the few things I looked forward to about getting older was the extra air of authority I'd carry. I was mildly disappointed she wasn't asking me any questions which would let me show off my mad skills, but I was mostly in awe. I had to think back across the past ten years and pick my most exciting adventure, one which didn't involve my thieving and one which would definitely wow her.

The tale of how I got my genetic enhancements was a pretty grand one, but there were secrets there I didn't want to share, and there was no way to properly tell that story without getting into them. Other ideas which soared through my head included: my first time flying through an asteroid field, the time I traversed the jungles of Qlipandra, the time I helped end a war on Brickoll, and the job which had left me smuggling a dozen monkeys across a dozen galaxies.

After a brief eternity, I figured out what to go with.

"Know anything about Yumel II?" Lioness shook her head."Okay, so there I was on the planet's surface, having just finished retrieving a collection of ancient artifacts for Izu Furuhara. I was pretty pooped, so my partner and I decided to wait until the morning to take off. Now, we were having a good night, slurping some noodles and watching a bad movie, when we heard a sound. Something unlike anything we'd heard before. Aarif, my partner, went down into the engine room with our dog, Juri, to hide, while I went outside to investigate. As soon as I stepped off my ship, a sharp wind brushed past me, cutting my cheek. This was followed by a demonic-sounding howling, accompanied by a repeat of the same sound from earlier. At this point, I was tempted to say "Screw this" and run, but I was too curious as to what was going on. I called out to whoever or whatever was out there, asking it what it wanted. Another gust of wind came, and this time my left knee was cut. Then there was a soft voice, "Invader..." Now I'm not one to believe in aliens or the supernatural, but my first thought at that point was, I'm talking to some old, nationalist ghost. I asked it if I was right, but it just said it didn't know what a "ghost" was. And then it cut me again. I told it I was really getting sick of it doing that, and if it didn't stop, I was just going to leave. I figured if it wanted me dead, it would have just cut my throat, so clearly it wanted to keep me around. And the next words it said were, "My love." That's when I realized I wasn't dealing with a xenophobic ghost, but a ghost whose, most likely equally dead, romantic partner, had also been from another planet. And from the fact he was cutting me, the romance hadn't ended well. I told him I was not his "love" and asked if there was anything I could do for him. I wouldn't normally ask a stranger that, but you know, not everyday you meet a ghost. He asked me for a kiss. That tossed my momentary generosity out the window and I told him to go screw himself. His high-pitched voice pierced the sky and the ground trembled. Not wanting to stick around for what was next, I ran back onto my ship, shut the entrance, and immediately flew us out of there. I called Izu, waking him up, and asked him why it wasn't common knowledge that ghosts or "dead spirits" existed on his world. He had no idea what I was talking about, but before we could delve into the matter further, Izu started screaming and the call cut out. He was found dead the next day. The two things I learned from all this: Never, ever got to Yumel II, and always make sure to get paid ASAP, cause you never know when a client is gonna get killed by a fucking ghost."

Lioness turned her back to me and poured herself another glass of brandy. She took a single sip of it before turning back to me. This time, she was smiling.

"Not bad."

The lights again in the cave once again changed, everything becoming blood red tinted. Lioness's focus turned to the other Banshees, whose eyes were all on one another. Dread and silence filled the air, but I didn't want to risk looking like an idiot by asking what was going on. For all I knew, this was part of the party.

"You traitorous bitch," Electric Ellie growled in my direction. "You sold us out to the Sunrisers."

CHAPTER 5: YAEL

Entropy is chaos. We are extropy.

That was the motto of the Sunrisers, and I couldn't remember a time where I didn't know it. Whenever I'd felt down as a child, I'd repeated it to myself. Joining their ranks and becoming a captain was all I'd wanted from life. But I'd grown up, and now all I wanted was to join the Banshees. Now, however, it looked like both organizations wanted my head.

Outside the cave, ground troops were being deployed, the sound of their combat boots stomping on the moon's surface echoing. And inside the cave, eleven of the smartest and most dangerous women in the universe were staring daggers straight into my eyes.

"I knew we couldn't trust a whippersnapper," Athena York said.

"How very disappointing," Beatriz Nunez snarled.

"I have a granddaughter in the Sunrisers," Lilith hummed. "If you tipped *her* off, I'll at least respect you for going for the heart."

I shook my head and swung my arms around, sweating from every pore. "I swear I didn't call them. This is all just a big misunderstanding. You have my complete loyalty."

Madame N'gwa cocked her head to the side and grinned. "You wanted to be a Sunriser when you were even more of a baby than you are now. Perhaps you made a deal to make your dream finally come true."

A shocking pain surrounded my heart. Those Sunriser bastards had stolen all the trust I'd earned from my idols through years of deceit. Whichever captain was in charge of this operation was going to pay.

Lioness stepped forward, crushing her glass in her hand and sending small shards flying all over the place. "Thank you for sharing your story with me. But I don't think we'll be hearing anymore of them. Rather, I don't think you'll be *living* any more of them."

I ground my teeth and held in tears from streaming down my burning face. I needed to look at the bright side. Things hadn't been screwed up by my own social ineptitude. I'd been doing well with Lioness! They all hated me now, and wanted my head, but if I could prove I was innocent, I could fix all of this.

But that would have to wait. The Banshees no doubt had some kind of escape plan, but I wasn't going to be included in it. And I had better odds for survival with the incoming army than I did staying here.

Grinding my feet into the ground, I spun around and raced back the way I'd come. For the first and only time in my life, I was the dumbest person in the room. But I was also unquestionably the fastest.

"I'm really sorry, everyone!" I called out. "But I promise I didn't do this! You'll see!" I tapped my earpiece. "Aarif, come and get me! The Sunrisers are here!"

"*Ah, crap,*" Aarif replied, chewing on something crunchy. "*On my way.*"

My physical enhancements and years of training in Cykebian Mixed Martial Arts, krav maga, and wrestling had proven capable of handling large mobs of enraged bikers and Cykebian war mechs, but assuming it was a Parallax-class ship the sensors had detected, I wouldn't be able to win in a straight fight. Burnt-orange octagonal prisms that were 1800 meters in diameter, along with the 12,000 officers serving aboard them, Parallax-class ships were home to 30,000 ground troops, ready to be deployed at a moment's notice. No, my only hope was to run as fast as I could and hope Aarif reached me before I got shot too many times.

As I ran, the cave was flooded with a purple gas. From the eggplant-like smell and the way it practically burned my eyes out of their sockets before I could shut them, it was viseph gas. A second layer of sweat coated my body as I was cooked by the signature poison and group dispersal method of the Sunrisers. Without my enhancements, there was no way I would have been able to keep moving.

I raced out of the cave and re-opened my twitching eyes to see a legion of soldiers in full black and orange body armor aiming their laser rifles at me. There must have been about 300 of them. If I was the captain in charge of this operation, I would have left a small number of my troops here to guard the perimeter of the cave to prevent a direct escape, while I deployed the rest of my men to find and destroy the Banshees' ships. It seemed like this captain was using a similar strategy.

"It's the X-factor we were warned about," one of the faceless goons called out. "Identify yourself at once."

"No problem at all," I said, deciding in the spur of the

moment to speak in an old-fashioned Australian accent as I bent my knees. "I'm a flipping kangaroo, ya dingos!"

Unbending my knees, I sprang myself into the air and leaped over the Sunrisers' heads. It sucked their helmets hid their faces, because I would have loved to have seen their stupid, dumbfounded expressions.

None of them came running after me as I continued to sprint across the moon's surface. They could call in other troops to come and get me, but they weren't about to abandon their post blocking off the Banshees to chase after the girl without a bounty.

As I got a little further, there were screams of agony from the cave. The captain in charge of the mission must have sent some of their troops into the cave to take the offensive, but they should have known the Banshees would have traps in place.

The Sunrisers were all hypocritical bastards, but especially their high-ranking officers. They acted like they were the biggest heroes in the universe who everyone should aspire to be like, while looking down on all who made their living through less than legal ways. But thieves like me had never killed anyone, meanwhile they took no issues with slaughtering thousands or sending their own men to die in the name of "peace," all the while sipping wine in their offices.

Some more ground troops raced toward me and fired their blasters, but I cartwheeled around all of the incoming lasers. When they got in close to fight me hand to hand, really, a pretty dumb decision even by their standards if they'd been informed of my earlier jump, I backhanded each of them across the face, sending them flying across the moon's surface.

I'd expected to be swarmed by endless mobs of troops until Aarif showed up, but no more soldiers came after me as I continued to run. However, off in the distance, I could see the silhouette of a woman in an officer's uniform. I couldn't fathom the idiocy or reasoning an officer would have for beaming down to come and face me after seeing how easily I'd dispatched their men, but I wasn't about to complain about smacking one of the uptight, oppressive bastards who'd just ruined my night.

"Yael!" The sound of her voice stopped me in my tracks as I took in the sight of who the officer was. "It's me! *Molina*!"

My powerful knees buckled underneath me, my mouth hung open, and my heart exploded, sending warm, wild sensations through my body.

I couldn't believe my eyes, but I'd know my Moli anywhere. With her dark amber bob cut and matching eyes, flawless skin that was slightly paler than my own, and her adorably stiff posture, there was no mistaking her. And from the look on her face, she was just as mystified to see me here as I was her.

"Moli?" My eyes lit up and a grin spread across my face as I opened my arms and sprinted right at her. "Holy fucking goddamn shit, it's you!"

I wrapped my arms around her, hugged her with all my might, and swung her around, getting her to giggle like we were seventeen again. And as I put her down, she smiled right back at me with equal excitement.

"You're a captain!" I shouted, letting go of her and observing her burnt-orange uniform, black cape and boots, gold epaulets, and the five gold earrings in her right ear. "A goddamn Sunriser captain! At 27 years old!

"I was promoted two weeks ago," she said, visibly holding in tears of joy. "I have command of the Noriker."

"The Noriker." I licked my lips. "Good ship. Gods, you're

even wearing a sword on your belt. I can't believe they actually let you get away with that."

"I try to not take advantage of nepotism, but being the supreme general's daughter has its perks." She bounced on her feet. "And look at you! I didn't think it was possible for you to get any hotter!"

"I eat the impossible for breakfast."

Moli giggled again, and memories of all the times I'd made her laugh throughout our childhoods raced to the front of my mind. Memories of all the times I'd helped her with her sword training, because she'd needed *someone* to spar with, no one else was interested, and I couldn't say no to her. I still couldn't believe this was really happening.

"When I saw you on my monitor, I knew I had to come save you myself. We can explain to the troops you hurt later that you were just reacting to exposure to viseph gas. I'm so sorry about that by the way. All we knew was that a non-Banshee would be present. We had no idea it would be you." She put a hand on my shoulder. "Come on, let me beam us up. We can talk and catch up once we've gotten you far away from those reprehensible thieves."

"Heh, thanks. They all think I called you here and are trying to kill me, and they really don't seem to be willing to listen to logic right now. I'd already be dead if I wasn't so much faster than them."

Confusion overtook Moli's smile. "Wait, you didn't tip off Zenith Command about this meeting?"

"Why the Hell would I have...?" My face fell. "Riiiiiiight, you don't know. Shit."

I'd been so thrilled to see my Moli that I'd forgotten being a Sunriser meant she was a freaking *Sunriser*. And by the sound of things, she was under the assumption I'd been a prisoner of the Banshees, and not an applicant trying to join them.

Her face shifted to match mine. "What don't I know?"

Before I could answer, an explosion shook the ground. Turning around, I could see there had been a cave-in. The Sunrisers wouldn't have wanted that to happen, which meant…

"Commander Bythora, the Banshees must have an underground escape route," Molina called out, pressing down on her com device. "Order all remaining ground troops to beam down to the surface and aid in the search of their ships. They cannot be allowed to leave the moon."

While she was in the middle of talking and not paying attention to me, I sprinted away. My heart was screaming at me to go with Molina and make up some bullshit excuse for what I was doing here so we could talk like nothing was wrong, but I knew going down that path would only land me in a jail cell.

With my superior speed and head start, Moli was never going to catch me. But that was under the assumption she didn't draw her blaster and shoot at my feet, which she did with a fierce determination in her eyes.

"What the Hell, Moli?" I asked, coughing from all the dust which the laser fire had spread around.

"Why were you running away?" she asked as she caught up with me. "And what are you doing here? Because I've been working under the assumption you were captured and experimented on."

As I stopped coughing, I re-donned my grin. "That's hilarious."

Molina was rightfully befuddled. As a kid, I'd been the last person anyone would have expected to become a criminal, let alone willingly work with the Banshees or get illegal genetic enhancements. But things had changed. Hopefully, however, things hadn't changed too much between us.

"Listen, I really do want to catch up, but right now I've got to go. I'll call the Noriker later." I resumed running away, but stopped once more and turned my head around. "Oh, and for both our sakes, I highly recommend not chasing after me again."

Molina clenched her gloved hands, sneered at me, and raised her blaster. "I hate having to do this, but, Yael Pavnick, by the authority of the Sunrisers, I'm placing you under arrest. Please don't make me shoot."

I pouted. "What did I just say?"

I reached into my pocket, swung my arm, and threw a Hercutious lima bean at Moli's feet. A green, gelatinous substance spewed out of it, knocked Moli over, and stuck her to the ground. With how adhesive that stuff was, she wouldn't even be wiggling her arms or legs.

"I'm really sorry!" I shouted, running away from my old best friend. "That gel will dissolve in an hour! Promise I'll make this up to you!"

"Yael! Get back here right now!"

She had to have been having trouble processing everything that was happening. Gods knew I was. The girl she'd known never would have assaulted a Sunriser captain, and definitely never would have assaulted *her*. But shitty as I felt about the latter, staying out of the reach of the law was always priority #1.

But I'd make things up to her. And to the Banshees. I could set things all right. I wasn't sure *how* I'd make things right with Moli, but at least with the Banshees, all I needed to do was find the real culprit.

It was possible one of the other Banshees had sold the

group out and was using this meeting as a chance to pin the blame on me, but I didn't want to believe any of my heroes had betrayed their decades of sisterhood. No, more likely the traitor was one of their employees. With the exception of Madame N'gwa, every Banshee's ship was massive and staffed by either dozens or hundreds.

If it was one of them, however, I had no idea how I was going to narrow things down. And in the meantime, the Banshees would think of me as an enemy. They all hated me. And after what I'd just pulled, Moli probably hated me too.

Molina was probably an amazing captain, but with her out of commission, there was no way the Banshees were getting captured. Which was good, but that also meant they'd be coming after me to try and kill me. Even if they were captured, there were twenty other Banshees who knew about this meeting and who'd want revenge. And that was on top of now being on the Sunrisers' radar after avoiding them for a decade.

As Ricochet appeared in the sky and flew down to pick me up, the choices I'd made over the past ten minutes crashed down on me. My stomach rumbled and a headache split my head in half.

Oh gods. What have I done?

CHAPTER 6: YAEL

There were no words to describe how stupid and awful I felt. Not even my favorite instant noodles and beer were making me any less miserable.

"First the good news," Aarif said, standing in the doorway. "We got away without any problems at all and no ships have been sent after us. I guess with how focused they were on the Banshees, they didn't have time for little old us."

Sitting on my bed, I slurped down all the remaining noodles in my cup and spoke with my mouth full. "And the bad news?"

"It's all over the major channels: They got N'gwa and every other Banshee who was present, along with their crews."

"Blaaaaaaaaaaah," I moaned, throwing my cup and fork across the room into the trash can. "This was supposed to be our big break." I hopped off my bed, jogged over to Aarif, and lightly pounded my fists against his chest. "Tell me what to do."

I knew Aarif didn't always like playing therapist for me and that I could be annoying and whiny, but he loved me enough I figured I could get away with it.

"Well, you have three problems: The Banshees hate you, the Banshees have been captured, and your old friend is probably pissed at you, but is likely more confused than anything else based on what you've told me about her. Way I see it, you can start fixing all three problems by making good on that promise to 'talk later'".

"How so?" I asked, backing up a little.

"Simple. You get that old friendship up and going again, thus dealing with one problem, and then we take advantage of that friendship to save the Banshees before they're dropped off at a Sunriser base, thus solving the other two problems."

Maybe it was because he wasn't pitching an actual plan for that second part, but his words hadn't made me feel any better. I probably did need to give Moli a call, but I hated that this was happening under these circumstances. Unlike my parents, I'd thought about calling Moli or even just looking into what she was doing a bunch of times over the years. I'd always ended up thinking of an excuse not to, but the instant I'd seen her, I'd regretted ever losing touch.

She was as cute and stiff as I remembered, but her uniform and the authority and success she'd achieved had all made my heart go even crazier than it used to. She really was out there living our dream. Even when I'd been rejected from the academy, I'd still hoped that she'd make it, and she'd done so in even less time than I could have imagined. I didn't have a lick of respect for the Sunrisers, but I was damn proud of her.

"We'll need to put more thought into it, but calling her will be a good start," I said as I walked around in circles. "You really think she won't hate me for gooping her?"

"She'll definitely be pissed, but you guys fought when you were kids, right? Try and make up like you used to."

Our fights had been few and far between and I barely remembered most of them, the two of us always making up pretty quickly. Even with our new positions, I had to believe Aarif was right to be optimistic about this.

"All right, let's call her." I grabbed my beer off my bed and walked out of my room, followed by Aarif. Once we were seated in the cockpit, I connected my watch to the ship's computer and sent a hail out to the Noriker.

The Noriker wasn't legendary like the Lipizzian or as powerful as the Karbadian, but it was still a Parallax-class ship, one my sixteen-year-old self would have been honored to serve upon, let alone command. I was shifting around my seat and hopping up and down, each second of Molina not responding killing me.

When we were kids and she took longer than an instant to respond to me, I'd always assumed she was in trouble and needed my help. More than once, this had resulted in me running over to her house and barging into the middle of family fights or other awkward situations I had no business being present for. It was always worth it though. I had to look out for my girl, no matter how much anxiety it caused me.

My computer beeped and blooped and a hologram of Molina's head emerged from my watch. Even just seeing her like this caused my heart to race and butterflies to soar around my stomach. It didn't help that she was sneering, and she was extra cute when she was grumpy.

"Hello, Yael," she said coldly "For the sake of transparency, I hope you remember enough of your training to know that we're tracing this call."

"You can try," I said, hopefully more playful than antagonizing. I wasn't entirely up to date on the Sunriser's tech, but last I'd checked, the software Jellz and I had installed in Ricochet should have been enough to keep that from happening. He was way out of my league when it came to programming know-how, but I knew every detail of how the Sunrisers' systems worked.

Molina elevated her head. "I'm giving you a chance here. Tell me exactly what you were doing on that moon with the Banshees. Tell me what you've been doing for the past ten years. And don't even try lying to me. I know your tells."

A major reason I'd always chickened out of calling her in the past? I'd never wanted to do this.

"Ummmm," I turned to Aarif, who gave me a reassuring nod. "Okay, well, I don't think we really need to cover everything I've been up to. You're a captain, and I'm sure you've got a million other things you need to get to. But, as for what I was doing with the Banshees… I was kinda trying to join them."

"So you really are a thief." I could hear the pain saying that caused her. "I don't understand. You never would have chosen this path and, even if you had, you would have had a bounty put on your head a long time ago."

"Well, uh, I did, and, up until this point at least, I've always managed to stay off your radar. Knowing every Sunriser procedure off the top of my head has come in handy."

Molina bit her lip. "You're the girl who was always even more of a stickler for the rules than I was. The girl who cried hysterically because she thought she would be sent to jail for getting one more scoop of ice cream than she paid for and not returning it. You're lying."

"I thought you knew my tells."

"Quit it with the snark!" she shrieked, leaning forward. There was pain in her eyes, pain I hated that I was causing. But I didn't know how else to talk. "If you're being blackmailed, threatened, or otherwise coerced into this life, then tell me. I can protect you."

I looked to Aarif again. Making up some sob story about how I'd been forced to become a thief and taking her up on her offer would get me onto her ship and closer to the Banshees, but it'd also probably mean having a large security detail placed on me, both for my own safety and to make sure I didn't try anything. I wouldn't be able to save the Banshees like that.

Aarif shook his head, agreeing with my assessment.

"Way I remember things, you were usually the one in need of protection." I tried to soften my smile. "Morphea still a bitch?"

Moli's smile matched mine. "The biggest." As cute as she was when she was grumpy, she was even cuter when she was visibly happy like this. I wanted to give her another big hug and kiss her on the forehead.

"Okay, listen, you have to believe that every word I'm about to say is true," I said. "I'm a thief. A really good one. And in spite of who I used to be, I love the job. But I also still love you, Moli. I'm so sorry I never called to check in and I'm super sorry I used that gelaball on you back there. I've been an idiot and I really need us to be cool. So what do you say: Can we be friends again?"

Molina folded her hands in front of her face, and all softness from it disappeared. "I'm currently en route to drop off eleven of the most wanted women in the universe at Sunriser base 9B-T5. That's five days away from my current position. We weren't able to scan your ship, but I imagine it would take you a few more. Before we arrive, I expect you to either tell me that you'll meet us there, or simply inform me of what's really happened to you. If you fail to perform either of these actions, I'll have no choice but to track you down, place you under arrest for association with The Order of the Banshee, and force you to be honest." Moli lowered her hands. "Us being together again would make me even happier than my promotion to captain. But like for the last decade, you're the one standing in the way of that happening. I hope you make the right choice."

I didn't know what to say to that, so I tapped my watch and ended the call, the hologram disappearing. I leaned back in my chair and chugged my beer.

"Can't say that went great, but at least she doesn't seem mad like you were worried she'd be," Aarif commented.

"No, she just can't accept that I'm not the giant dork I used to be," I replied, finishing up the third beer I'd had since getting back on board.

Aarif smirked. "Was that story about the ice cream true?"

"I was worried a criminal record, no matter how small, would ruin my chances of being fast tracked to becoming a captain," I said, my voice cracking. "It was scary."

"Okay, so you weren't a giant dork, but the *biggest* dork."

"Says the guy who went to jail for selling bootleg movie files."

"*Quality* bootleg movie files."

"Is this your way of trying to be helpful?"

"As a matter of fact, it is." Aarif took my hand and held it tightly. "You know, there's one other person we probably need to call."

"Nnnnnnnngh," I groaned. "Now he's definitely going to be angry."

"What happened down there wasn't your fault. He may be pissed, but he has no reason to take it out on you."

I tightened my hand around Aarif's, taking care not to break it. "Thank you for saying so many sweet and logical things today."

"Just be sure to remember how helpful I am when we're splitting up Banshee-level profits."

Calling Jellz wasn't something I usually did, or was even

capable of, but before we'd parted ways, he'd given me a method of contacting him that would work today, and only today. He'd wanted to know as soon as possible that he was managing a Banshee.

"What the Hell happened?!" Jellz screamed the instant his hologram popped out of my watch. He either had blood or ketchup on his face, but the projection wasn't clear enough to tell. "How did the Sunrisers know about the meet-up?! I specifically told you not to share that tablet with anyone!"

"I didn't!" I shouted back. "And way to assume it was my fault, because it wasn't. I have no idea how the Sunrisers were clued in, but I may have to find out if I'm gonna prove my innocence to the Banshees."

Jellz laughed mockingly. "Yeah, good luck with that. There are 20 other Banshees out there and they all know what N'gwa and the rest were doing today. Won't be long before they're all coming after you."

"Sunrisers are on my ass too."

"Of course they are."

"If it makes you feel any better, we're also trying to figure out a way to rescue the Banshees before they're dropped off at a Sunriser base."

"As a matter of fact, it doesn't." Jellz gripped his face and rubbed his forehead. "Look, you said you wanted to take a vacation before? Go do that. Find some place to lay low. It's too dangerous for you to be out there trying to play detective or hero. I'm gonna try and get in touch with the remaining Banshees and do what I can to help them save their associates. Best case scenario, we succeed and I keep them from murdering you."

"I don't just want them to not murder me, I want to still join them," I whined.

"That ship has sailed," he said through grit teeth. "Think about a new dream while you're hiding out."

The call ended and Jellz's projection faded away.

"Fuck!" I shouted. "This isn't fair! We have to go against what he's saying, right? We have to prove my innocence and free the Banshees ourselves! I mean, I've robbed Sunriser bases before!"

Aarif tilted his head down and scratched the back of his head. I wasn't going to like what he said next. "Sorry, but I have to admit, the other Banshees probably have a better chance of success than we do. Stealing a cube is completely different from freeing prisoners."

"Aarif!"

"I'm not agreeing with him that you should give up on your dream, though. But I think that if we don't need to risk being captured by the Sunrisers, then we should stay out of it."

I leaped up to my feet, bumping my head against the ceiling. "You were just saying before how we could use my friendship with Molina to help us save them."

"And note how I didn't mention an actual plan there."

We stared each other down for a few moments before I looked away, exhaling.

"Molina's still gonna be coming after us in five days. And she's probably good enough to find us anywhere."

"So the best we could do is at least go to the last place she'd think to look." Aarif put his hand on his chin. "Well, it's not much of a vacation spot…but I doubt she'd ever assume you were a welcome guest at St. Shiala's School for Girls. I mean, you two were a couple of dorks, not 'proper ladies.' Unless there's something you still haven't told me."

I lightly flicked his shoulder. "Lulu did say we were welcome any time. And even if Molina did find us there, it wouldn't look good for her to be deploying thousands of foot-soldiers into a prestigious finishing school filled with the daughters of powerful and influential people."

"And since numbers are the only chance anyone has against you in a fight, you might get another chance to talk to Molina without fear of arrest."

I still thought it would be better to take a more proactive approach, but I trusted Aarif to make the more responsible call. Things could still turn out all right for me. I could still be a Banshee and Molina and I could still be friends again. But for now, I had to bide my time.

This was gonna be so annoying.

CHAPTER 7: MOLINA

"Were we successful in tracking their location?"

"No, Captain," Commander Revudan replied. "The encryption software on that ship is the most complex I've ever seen. Either your old friend is a genius programmer, or she has one on board."

I leaned forward in my chair. Both prospects were equally possible. While she very well may have hired someone else to set up the encryption software, Yael would not only be familiar with all our procedures and how to best counter them, but on the practical portion of the academy's entrance exam, she'd received perfect scores in every category, including programming. No one had ever done that before. If only she'd been given the chance, she could have been the best of us.

"Very well." I rolled my shoulders back.

"Would you like to tell us exactly what the situation is with you two?" Kaybell asked. "Because if there's a risk of a conflict of interest here, either I should take command, or another ship should take charge of capturing this rodent."

"Don't call her that," I said, raising a finger at my first officer. "Yael may very well have committed crimes, but I know she has to have a good reason for having done so. A reason we may have to force out of her. As far as explaining our history together, I'll tell you what you need to know when you need to know it. Understood?"

Kaybell pursed her lips and rolled her chin around. She was irritated, I could tell, but while she was my best friend, I didn't feel the need to share every detail of my past with her.

We continued to fly toward Sunriser base 9B-T5, but there was still another job left to do before we dropped off the prisoners. Father had ordered us to interrogate all eleven of the Banshees we'd captured in the hope that we could get the locations of the remaining twenty out of them. As such, once the prisoners had finished being processed, I left Commander Revudan in command of the bridge alongside Security Chief Michaels, assigned two privates to the helm, and led Kaybell down to deck nine. I'd assigned her to interrogate Moonriver, while I'd be handling Madame N'gwa personally.

The interrogation chambers aboard the Noriker were fully customizable, allowing us to set any conditions for the room we deemed necessary. They could be made as hot as the four suns of Jaeger or as cold as a winter on Karlock Prime. They could appear to stretch wider than the ship itself, or they could be uncomfortably cramped. If we thought it could help get us the answers we wanted, we could, and would, make it happen.

For Madame N'gwa, whose birth name was unknown, I'd rendered the air in the room she'd been sitting in for the past half-hour damp and disgusting, intense lights had been interminably beaming down on her, and I'd been making the room spin around at random intervals and speeds. My aim was to take advantage of her age and make her feel as physically and mentally unwell as possible within a short amount of time. Based on the planets she'd been spotted on, it seemed like she took great care to avoid worlds with moist air and especially bright suns, and the spinning room technique had proven effective during past interrogations.

Additionally, for security measures, N'gwa had been stripped naked so she couldn't make use of any hidden weapons or technology, both of her arms and legs, as well as her head and waist, were strapped to her chair, which was firmly stuck to the floor, with titanium alloy restrains, and I'd be entering the room alongside a team of four armed security personnel. It was impossible to get in or out of one of the interrogation chambers without both a Sunriser's thumb scan and vocal command, but with the Sunriser's #8 most wanted, all precautions were warranted.

We did still have standards, of course. While there were certain cruel methods we had no choice but to implement, directly beating prisoners, outside of self-defense, was against the law, as was the use of any torture devices. And beyond that, there were certain things I was against even if they weren't necessarily illegal. For instance, I'd denied Kaybell's request to force Moonriver to strip down in her cell and walk through the ship in the nude as a form of humiliation.

"That isn't the Sunriser way," I'd told her.

"No, but it is the *royal* way," she'd countered. "And as Princess Kaybell Kose Bythora, daughter of Stephen and descendant of Leon, first emperor of Cykeb and founder of the Sunrisers, future ruler of The Holy Cykebian Empire, that's the only way I should do anything."

With all preparations having been completed, I stepped into interrogation chamber A-2, bracing myself for confrontation with a, hopefully weakened, evil mastermind. The bright lights and moist air were conditions I also couldn't stand, but I couldn't allow myself to show that for a heartbeat. She'd sense the weakness and use it against me. If I was going to break her, I had to appear stone cold.

"Captain Langstone," Madame N'gwa addressed me, her eyes tightly shut and her teeth clenched in a grin. "What a pleasure to meet the future of the Sunrisers."

I wasn't shaken by her words. The fact that she was familiar with me meant nothing. The promotion of the supreme general's daughter to captain had been all over the news. Despite the confidence she was trying to display, she knew nothing about me that the general public didn't.

"Madame N'gwa, are you familiar with the list of crimes you're being charged with?" I asked as I stepped toward her, hands clasped behind my back. "It's quite extensive."

N'gwa chuckled. "I'm sure there are parts of my record from over a century ago which I don't recall, but I believe I have a general idea of it, yes." She tapped her nails against the arm of her chair. "Is this the part where you offer me leniency in exchange for information?"

"Not at all." I circled around the deceptively frail old woman. "You will spend however many years you have left of your life trapped inside a cell. There's nothing you can do to stop that." I paused as I stepped back in front of her. "But if you were to give me the current whereabouts of just one of your fellow Banshees, I could do quite a lot to make your remaining days far more comfortable. Make sure you're fed quality food and not protein paste, get you any books you want… I could even let you keep your bells."

N'gwa's face didn't change at all, nor was she making any effort to move. She was perfectly still, with her eyes still shut and her mouth still curled. Unless I was reading her wrong, my efforts to disorient her had been ineffective. She still possessed great confidence. She still believed she was going to be free again.

"Come now, there must be at least one of these twenty women who you aren't especially fond of. One whose freedom means less to you than the amenities I could provide you with. There are certainly plenty of officers I've served with who I'd sell out were our positions switched."

That was a lie. As much as certain officers I knew had irritated me or failed to live up to my standards, they were still my comrades. Much as I loathed my little sister, I wouldn't even sell out Morphea. Unlike thieves, our honor was more than a visage.

"I've met your father once or twice," N'gwa said, her grin only widening. "Back when he was a captain, Drenian chased me all across the universe. I let him get close so many times, only to escape his grasp. From his perspective, he'd always just missed me, but it always went perfectly according to my plans. After a year or so, I wanted to talk to him face to face. One disguise and a distress call from a barren desert planet later, I had him eating out of the palm of my hand, and escorting me to my "home world." It was so much fun toying with him, while he was completely ignorant to the fact that he could have captured me at any moment, that I pulled the same trick on him again two years later. It was hilarious. And I say all of this as someone with a moderate amount of respect for the man. After all, he didn't need his father to make the rank of captain."

I sneered. Father had never told me these stories, which meant either she was lying, Father had been too embarrassed to ever share these experiences with me, or he had no idea that this had ever happened. As for her last words, she had no idea what she was talking about. I would have risen through the ranks just as quickly as I had regardless of who my father was.

"Is there a point you're trying to make?" I asked.

Madame N'gwa stuck out her tongue, pointing it at me, before slowly circling the circumference of her mouth with it. "You stand above me in your perfectly pressed uniform and polished boots, while I sit here naked as the day I was born. You command this ship, while I am your prisoner. You have thousands of soldiers you can give orders to in an instant, while I only have ten close friends who I have no way of communicating with. You enjoy your creature comforts while forcing me to endure harsh conditions. But none of this matters." Finally, her eyes peeled open. "I am Madame N'gwa. And I always win."

No matter how she boasted, no matter how much she believed what she was saying, I knew she was wrong. On her own, she had no method of escape. If her allies attempted to attack my ship and retrieve her, I'd destroy them. And while Banshees had succeeded in stealing from Sunriser bases in the past, no one had ever managed to free one of our prisoners, let alone one who was under level-6 lockdown, as N'gwa would be. Her confidence was nothing more than a performance.

"If you're so sure of yourself, then why not tell me your plan?" I proposed. "Surely victory over an opponent who knows exactly what to expect would taste even sweeter."

Madame N'gwa giggled. "Dear, I have no plan. How could I? I'm in no position to deal with the security measures you have in place."

"Then why all the bravado?"

N'gwa closed her eyes and, for the first time since I'd entered the room, her smile faded. "Because unlike the rest of my family, I don't believe that your old friend is responsible for our capture."

My heart pounded. She had to have been talking about

Yael. Nothing else made sense. She'd mentioned that the rest of the Banshees mistakenly thought that she'd betrayed them and that they were trying to kill her, but N'gwa shouldn't have had any idea about our past. If Yael had been trying to join the Banshees, the last thing she would have told them was that she'd grown up dreaming to become a Sunriser alongside her best friend. But if she'd done research on Yael prior to meeting her, then it was possible she knew everything about her childhood and, by extension, me. And as frightening as that prospect was, it did give me a new avenue to explore.

"Let's talk about Yael," I said. "Was she really on that moon attempting to join you?"

"In her own words, it was an 'honor' to meet me. I'm her hero." Were it not against regulations, I would have smacked her across the face. "While I normally don't believe anyone under the age of 40 has a place among the Banshees, she was nominated by Lioness and Beatrice for admittance and, based on her accomplishments, I was willing to give her a chance."

"Her accomplishments," I echoed. "So she's committed many crimes then?"

"A far greater amount than most thieves her age, with most of them on the level of a thief with decades more experience."

I bent over and put my face inches away from N'gwa's, sneering as harshly as I could. "I don't care how much research you've done on her, you don't know Yael Pavnick as well as I do. She would never have genuine respect for the likes of you, and while she may have crimes she needs to pay for, she never would have chosen this life willingly."

I'd repeated that sentiment several times now. And my faith in its validity remained stalwart.

"You've been out of touch with her for nearly a decade. A

lot can change in that time. Dreams, people… the universe itself. Are you the same person you were ten years ago?"

I narrowed my eyes. "You must think I'm pretty stupid if you think I'm gonna let you start asking the questions."

"No, you aren't stupid at all. Simply out of your league." She curved her lips to the left. "Now, Captain Asparago may have been a worthy challenger."

I stood back up straight and shut my eyes for a brief moment before reopening them, trying to ignore her mention of my old captain. She was pushing my buttons and it was working. My heart was racing, my thankfully hidden hands were shaking, and I was failing to get answers out of her. I had to take control immediately.

"Let's say hypothetically I'm wrong. Yael chose to become a thief without any coercion. When, how, and why? And what are the most serious crimes she's committed? Answer me about this, and I'll give you the same deal I was offering before for the whereabouts of a Banshee."

Madame N'gwa giggled again. But this time, the giggle erupted into a bursting laughter which echoed throughout the chamber. "I don't think you'll like the answers to those questions. Are you sure you want to know?"

It was possible the answers would hurt, but no benefit would come from living in ignorance. I needed as much information on Yael as I could get before I found her again.

"Tell me."

N'gwa's eyes opened again, this time slightly bulging out of her face. More disgusting genetic engineering. "When? Immediately after she left Cykeb, two months following her rejection from the Sunriser academy. How? She made use of her training and studies to commit several simple heists, and used the money from them to get herself a ship and have herself outfitted with enhanced strength, speed, and senses. Why?" Her grin returned in full. "Because she realized everything the two of you believed in was complete and utter nonsense. It was a moment of self-realization, nothing more, nothing less."

I hadn't noticed any of Yael's tells during our earlier conversation. And I couldn't see any signs that N'gwa was lying now. But I had to be missing something. Yael had been in a depressed slump following her rejection from the academy, but that one setback couldn't possibly have warped her values so completely.

"As for her crimes, there are so many delectable ones to choose from. She's stolen the royal jewels from the ruling family of Hudrup and framed one of the noble houses of the world for the theft, hacked into several intergalactic corporations to steal classified information, and, of course, she's stolen a cube containing weapon schematics directly from a Sunriser base."

It took all of my power not to physically react to that. Internally, I was screaming.

"Oh yes, she's infiltrated your impenetrable fortresses before. And with how much she looks up to us and wants to be a Banshee herself, I have no doubt she intends to do so again."

I turned my back to N'gwa so I could let some of my frustration and confusion bleed out onto my face. If there truly weren't extenuating circumstances for Yael's actions and there were no signs that she was capable of rehabilitation, then she could be looking at the same life sentence as the Banshees. If I was going to prevent that from happening, I was going to need to remind her of who she truly was. Capturing her wouldn't solve anything. I had to convince her to turn herself in.

"I'm sure you're dying to talk to Yael about this," N'gwa

continued. "And, if I may offer you a suggestion, since you're clearly in dire need of help, it would be in your best interest to capture Yael before dropping us off at a base. You'll still need to contend with the rest of my family, but they will be willing to play the long game. Yael possesses the impatience that comes from youth and will attempt to rescue us very, very soon."

Did she really think I would listen to any suggestions she gave me? This was another way she was messing with my head. She was telling me to go after Yael first, which meant she was most likely trying to use reverse psychology. But at the same time, it was possible she just wanted me doubting myself. I was in no condition to find out right now.

"Congratulations, you've earned your rewards," I said, walking away from N'gwa. "We'll talk again later."

I scanned my thumb and input a voice command, getting the doors to slide open.

"Why do you wear that sword, Captain?" N'gwa asked before I could exit the room. "For protection? Or do you look to ancient heroes for inspiration rather than modern ones? I wonder what reason the daughter of a supreme general would have to do that. Do you have a—?"

"Shut up!"

As soon I shouted, my mind filled with regret and shame. I could feel the smile N'gwa was shooting my way. She'd gotten me. Without giving her another chance to speak, I walked out, followed by the security personnel, and shut the doors behind us.

"Don't give her any food or water, and only take her back to her cell once she's passed out," I ordered my officers as I stomped away from them.

If Madame N'gwa and Yael had one thing in common, it was that neither of them took me seriously as a threat. I may not have been able to keep them out of my head, but that was one advantage I possessed. It was what would allow me to beat them both.

CHAPTER 8: YAEL

For the first time in a long time, I woke up in a soft, comfortable bed.

Lulu had been completely understanding of my current situation, minus some details I'd left out, and had welcomed me back to her school with open arms. Three days after we'd made contact with her, we were landing on Benkin and were greeted with another magnificent feast. Lulu was seemingly doing everything she could to make herself my favorite person in the universe.

Because we'd be staying in the school and not on Ricochet, I'd brought Kidney along with us so the poor little guy didn't starve to death. So far he'd seemed to be getting along well with Juri, but Lulu and P'Ken had both been disgusted by him. I didn't see the problem so many people had with rats; they were adorable.

Over the course of our meal, Aarif had volunteered us both to do some work around the school, as a way of saying thanks. I'd tried to protest, but he'd said it was the polite thing to do, and, like usual, I assumed that he knew what he was talking about. So after breakfast today, I'd be dusting bookshelves and performing other such boring chores.

For now though, I was enjoying myself in a way which

I usually only got to while on vacation. While I disagreed with Aarif about how crucial relaxation was to an enjoyable vaycay, I absolutely appreciated a good bed. Unfortunately, my normal, less than comfortable bed was built into Ricochet, so the only way to get a new one would be to get a new ship, and that wasn't happening.

Apart from the delightful bed, the rest of the room wasn't my jam at all. Everything was so formal and delicate and there were even fucking doilies. I knew the school's students were nobles, but they were still kids and teenagers. They couldn't possibly have liked how stuffy it all was.

After lying awake in the marshmallowy bed for a good half-hour, I got up, did my minimal hygiene routine in the bathroom attached to the bedroom, which was just as overly fancy, and got dressed.

As I was about to head out, there was a knock on the door.

"Good morning, Yael," P'Ken greeted me, her gloved hands clasped in front of her. She seemed to be in a chipper mood.

"Um, g'mornin. Was about to come downstairs for breakfast. What's up?"

P'Ken tilted her head down slightly. "Um, well, I'm really happy to have you here, and I know I'm a teenager and you're an adult, but I was wondering if you'd like to go shopping with me when we're both done with our work for the day."

I smirked as I rubbed my eye. "Shopping, huh? What kind of shopping?"

"For new clothes. If you're going to be staying here, you should have appropriate attire. And I still think you'd look excellent in high fashion."

While I had no interest in dresses or shoes, some new, heavier clothes would be helpful for dealing with the planet's low temperature in the long term. Plus, the wild and crazy hat I'd picked up for my signature look had given me an appreciation for extravagant headwear, so I wasn't opposed to buying a few more.

"Sure, why not?" I clapped my hand against P'Ken's shoulder as she smiled brightly. "But you're paying for dinner."

With my plans for the afternoon made, P'Ken and I walked down to the dining room, where Lulu, Aarif, Juri, and Kidney were already present. While Juri was eating fish and, as a result of much begging, Kidney had been given an apple, the spread for us humans consisted of raisin bread, Cykebian molasses, fresh coffee, a variety of cheeses, and some weird fish-like stuff I'd never seen before. All in all, it equated to a very happy Yael.

Once we were all done eating, Lulu went to her office, P'Ken was sent to go sit in on a leadership class, Aarif was asked to fix a few malfunctioning heaters, and I was put on book shelving duty in the library.

Most of the universe had gone strictly digital a long time ago, but there were a few places left that still valued musty old paper and ink. Unsurprisingly, the school's library was humongous, probably the 3rd largest I'd ever been in after the academy's library and The Xyconia Library on Pilan 7. There were clearly identified sections for books on Cykebian history, the sciences, military strategy, politics, and numerous other subjects.

Notably however, just like the academy's library, there didn't seem to be a single work of fiction present. Even back when I'd been a Sunriser-loving dork, I'd found that disappointing. Were it within my power, I'd have made every teenager across the universe read *Yuno* by Richtor Nilsson. That book had saved my life following my humiliating rejection, and while there were very few physical copies left in the universe, it was easily accessible from a tablet.

According to Lulu, every student had a class first period, which explained why, save for one elderly librarian who had looked at me like I wasn't worth stepping on, the place was empty. That was fine by me. Tedious chores were annoying enough without having to deal with other people.

As I got to work, without the distractions of a nice bed or delicious food, my mind turned back to focusing on Molina and the Banshees. I hadn't heard anything from Jellz or any updates on the news for the past few days, which meant no rescue attempt had been made yet. Molina would be arriving at her destination soon, and I had to hope they'd take action before that happened. While a prison break from a Sunriser base would be awesome, none had ever been pulled off successfully. When I had the chance to see Madame N'gwa and the others again, I would do whatever they asked me to do to prove my loyalty, save for letting them kill me.

The idea I would volunteer, when given the chance, would be to personally find out who was really responsible for giving up the location of the meet-up spot. Jellz may not have wanted me "playing detective" while Molina was on my case, but once I'd solved that problem, I'd be free to investigate.

And when it came to dealing with Molina, I had an idea in my head for how I wanted the situation to play out. After giving her some time to mentally recover from having failed her mission, I'd tell her where I was staying. Not wanting to flood the school with ground troops, she'd come inside either on her own or alongside a few of her bridge officers and, while I loved the idea of opening her eyes the same way mine had been opened all those years ago and getting her to come be a thief, I didn't think that was too realistic. So instead, I was gonna go all-in on the best friend card. No matter how much she believed in "peace" and "order," she'd never want me to spend the rest of my life in a cell. I'd get her to cover up for me, I'd be back to being an unwanted woman, and, hopefully, she'd be open to staying in touch. Being a Banshee was my dream, but what I wanted most right now was to be with my cute little Moli again.

"Who is that?"

"And what is she wearing?"

Evidently I'd been working long enough that the first classes of the day had ended and students were now coming to the library. And based on what they were saying and how they were saying it, I was quickly reminded of the bitches I'd had to deal with all throughout my time in school.

I took a deep breath in, and exhaled as I whispered, "They're Lulu's students. Don't break their arms."

I stepped down off the ladder I was on and turned around to face the two students who were smirking at me with amusement. One was tall and lanky with one of the longest necks I'd ever seen, while the other was only slightly taller than Molina and a bit chubby. Both were wearing the school's uniform, a black and silver dress that was less fancy than the dresses Lulu and P'Ken wore, but still possessed an air of snootiness.

"May I help you with something?" I asked as my foot tapped against the wooden floor, doing my best to imitate Lulu.

"Yes, we were wondering when Headmistress Amatyn started hiring slum rats to work here," the tall one said before they both snickered.

My teeth chattered as I forced myself to smile. I'd been bullied for a lot of reasons, ranging from my stimming, to my loud outbursts, to the amount of time I spent studying, to my face, which everyone always said made me look like a chipmunk. But I'd never been made fun of for being poor, both because my parents' pickle business did pretty well, and because poverty in general didn't exist on Cykeb.

Classicism persisted throughout the rest of the empire, however, so I wasn't too surprised by the girls' attitude, but the fact that they felt comfortable trying to bully an adult about their status made me question what exactly Lulu was teaching here.

"I'm not a 'slum rat,' in fact I'm not even from this planet, and you really shouldn't talk to people like that." I would have added, "You never know how people will react," but they seemed like the types of girls who'd react to that by instantly snitching to Lulu that I'd "threatened" them.

"If you aren't poor, then you must be blind," the chubby one laughed.

"And our fathers are counts. We can talk to the *help* however we want."

I continued to force a smile, the grinding of my teeth getting louder and louder. There was now another good reason for me to get new clothes besides the cold weather: they would help keep me from strangling every kid here.

After eight hours of agonizingly boring work and putting up with the most insufferable people in the universe, with only a 30-minute lunch break as a respite, I briefly hung out with Aarif to give Juri some play-time before meeting up with P'Ken and heading into town.

I'd explored Wedgerock when I'd first come to Benkin to steal the town's treasured crystal staff at their annual ice festival. St. Shiala's School for Girls was just a short hike away, and the town seemed to revolve around the school. Pretty much everyone who lived here owned a small business that catered directly to either the needs of the faculty or the students. For every store selling designer clothes and ludicrously expensive accessories, there was one selling affordable and sensible suits. For every steakhouse that would shoo you away for having the best dog in the universe with you, there was a burger joint that appreciated good doggos. And for every spa and salon, there was a bar.

If P'Ken wasn't a minor, we'd definitely be heading for a bar.

"What are your favorite colors?" P'Ken asked as she led me into one of the numerous boutiques. "I'm sure we'll be able to find some outfits you like in them."

"Bright blues and yellows," I told her. "And I don't want anything too frilly."

"Not too frilly, got it."

We proceeded to wander through the casual dress section of the store, and while I normally wouldn't have called any of the dresses available "casual," compared to the utterly ridiculous formal dresses available, I could see the distinction clearly.

After rejecting over a dozen options presented to me by P'Ken, we finally found one I was willing to try on. It was two-shades of yellow, one close to the color of my bed sheets and one significantly darker, it went down to the floor and had slightly less poofy shoulders than most of the dresses for sale, it didn't look like it would squeeze my stomach too hard, and P'Ken had already found some gigantic pearl necklaces to go with it.

I hopped into one of the changing rooms and, as I put the dress on, P'Ken spoke. "Yael, I have to be honest with you. I really do want to help with your wardrobe, but I also had an ulterior motive for bringing you out here. One I didn't want to risk Mother overhearing."

"Normally I'd guess you were out to kill me, but since you were serious about the shopping part, I guess I can rule that out." I was smiling and doing my best to create a light-hearted mood, even if she couldn't see me, but P'Ken sounded as shaken as when we first met. "What's going on?"

"I… well…" She paused. "Ummmmm."

"It's okay," I said, thinking back to the patience my parents always had with me. "Take your time."

She took a series of deep breaths, and then it sounded like she slapped her hands against her cheeks. As I struggled to get the dress on properly, P'Ken resumed speaking. "Ever since I was little, Mother has been training me to one day take over the school. No other alternatives were ever presented to me. It was just a fact that, like my mother, my grandmother, my great grandmother, and every other eldest daughter in my family for six generations, it was my role to play. And that was something I was more than okay with. It was something I looked forward to. Even when Father got… angry, I could just think about the fact that one day I'd be the headmistress of one of the most prestigious schools in the universe."

"And that's changed?" I asked, my teeth grit. The dress was far tighter than I'd thought it would be.

"I… I think so," she answered. "And before I say the alternative on my mind, I want you to know that it isn't a flight of fancy I've decided on a whim. I've been giving it serious thought since we first met."

"Hit me," I belched as I finally got the dress on properly. I draped the pearls around my neck and, I hated to say it, but I didn't look half bad like this. "Or actually, let me hit you first." I pulled open the curtain, puckered my lips, and struck a dramatic pose, but instead of praising me for how I looked, P'Ken said something else, her eyes on the floor.

"I... I want to be your *apprentice*."

My jaw dropped and my eyes bulged out as far as they could without enhancements like Madame N'gwa's. I couldn't have possibly heard that right.

"Oh, wow," she said, smiling like a very confused angel. "You look lovely."

"Thank you, but let's go back a second. What are you talking about?"

Her face fell. "You don't approve?"

"No, no, no," I said, really not wanting to upset her. "I just don't understand. Where did this idea come from?"

"When you were telling us the story of how you retrieved our jewels from Father," she perked back up. "And then afterward when you got a little drunk and were willing to tell us a few other stories. Every one of them sounded exciting and remarkable in their own unique way. Mother has always controlled every aspect of my life, dictating exactly what I can and cannot do, while you do whatever you want. You travel all across the universe having amazing adventures and even occasionally helping people who have nowhere else to turn. Compared to that, a life of sitting behind a desk and helping those who already have everything just... I don't think it's for me."

Under normal circumstances, I would have been ecstatic, nay, honored, to have inspired a new thief. But I wasn't looking for an apprentice, and P'Ken didn't strike me as the type who was cut out for the job. She was so damn eager though, and I had no idea how to handle this without making her cry.

"P'Ken, listen, I believe you that you've thought about this a lot and that you'd put all your heart into the job, but I'm just not sure this path is compatible with the upbringing you've had. I mean, I grew up training to be a Sunriser, and that resulted in me being skilled in hand to hand combat, stealth, programming, and every other ability a Sunriser needs to have. You… know how to be a teacher."

P'Ken crossed her arms, but this time, her smile didn't fade. "I know a lot more than just how to run the school. While I only possess basic self-defense training, I've won several prominent gymnastics competitions, and my education is on par with the Cykebian nobility. Of course I'd still need training from you, but I don't believe there's any job I'm unqualified for."

For such a shy and nervous kid, she had a Hell of an ego. "Okay, let's say you're right and you can easily prove yourself. I'm still only 27. Hardly old enough to be a mentor."

"If age was that important to you, you wouldn't talk all the time about wanting to join The Order of the Banshee."

I cocked my head to the side in confusion and, in response, she nervously scratched the back of her head.

"I… may have hired someone to hack into subspace relay net negative four so I could do more research on professional thieves before I saw you again," P'ken continued.

She had a valid point and I appreciated that she'd taken the time to do her research. The first crime I'd ever committed was hacking into subspace relay net negative four myself. She could possibly have potential, she had initiative, and, thinking about it further, if she could get Lulu's approval, I could earn some extra gidgits in exchange for training her.

I put a hand on P'Ken's shoulder. "I may be here for a while. So I'm gonna think on this, and I'll have an answer for you before we leave."

"That's all I can ask. Thank you, Yael."

My mind was already mostly made up. The only thinking I had to do was about how to tell Lulu that her daughter didn't want to follow in her footsteps, and sell her on this idea. I was definitely gonna need to talk to Aarif about it.

"Come on," I said with a smile, taking my hand off of P'Ken. "Let's go find some shoes to go with this dress that *won't* make my feet bleed.

CHAPTER 9: YAEL

Seeing as I was currently staying in her home and said home was part of my current plan to not get arrested, the last thing I wanted to do was piss Lulu off. And yet as I'd considered all the ways to tell her, "Your daughter wants to be my apprentice", over the past few days, there wasn't a single outcome where I didn't see her kicking me out of her house.

If Lulu wasn't willing to pay me in exchange for mentoring P'Ken, I'd still be able to profit off of the kid by sending her out on small jobs I didn't have time for, but after how sweet she'd been to me, I really didn't want to screw her over. If worse came to worse, I probably would, but it was worth at least trying to be a good person when possible.

Before I talked to Lulu and risked burning that bridge, however, I had to make certain that this arrangement would be a good idea for both P'Ken and I.

"You... live here?" The way P'Ken's face scrunched up in disgust as I brought her aboard Ricochet was about what I'd expected. Even average people who weren't brought up in elite schools had described the ship as "repulsive," "putrid," or "an affront to the gods."

"Yup, and I love it. Quick tour: Engine room's downstairs, kitchen and bathroom are to your right and left respectively, bedrooms and cockpit are upstairs. If you move in, depending on how our current situation shakes out, you'd either get a sleeping bag and share my room, or we'll get a new bedroom installed for you."

P'Ken walked further into the ship, her high-heels clanging against the metal floor, and her eyes moving in all directions. She turned back to me and put on the same polite, fake smile she always wore at meals.

"When I was doing research about thieves, I read about this amazing group of women called The Order of the Banshee." I'd have given her points for good taste, but *every* thief respected the Banshees. Or rather, every thief except for the lame-ass men who hated the idea of an all-female organization. "Some of them have ships like the Night Terror and the Cat's Claw, massive, *clean* crafts with dozens of crewmen. With you being as amazing as you are, why don't you have a ship like that?"

A part of me wanted to call her privileged and snobby, but the Banshees probably would have said the same thing had they seen Ricochet. While I was mostly just attached to the old hunk of junk, I could still fill her in on some details.

"Despite what someone may think from my new wardrobe, I like living a low-maintenance life," I said as I walked toward P'Ken. "A life where I don't have to deal with a lot of people every day. It's much preferable for me only having Aarif and Juri as opposed to a full crew I'd have to talk to and order around, no matter how large a ship they'd allow me to fly or how clean they'd keep it. You get me?"

"Not entirely. I greatly enjoy spending time with others, even if I do sometimes struggle with speaking up."

As I closed the distance between us, a thought shot to the front of my mind. "Since I've gotten here, all you've done is eat, work, study, and spend time alone in your room. Which people do you enjoy being with?"

P'Ken stared down at the floor and clasped her hands in front of her. "Mother, primarily. I also sometimes talk with some of the students between classes. They can be a bit mean, but we laugh together and they... they..."

Holy shit, this poor girl didn't have any friends.

"But that's why I need to come with you!" she shouted, looking back up at me. "So I can meet all sorts of new people. See all new things." She bit her lip and her energetic smile became more nervous. "Be friends with you."

She may as well have punched my heart with a steel covered boxing glove. As a kid, no matter how much I'd been bullied, I'd always had Moli. My parents never really got me and, as polite as Lulu and P'Ken were with each other, I hadn't picked up on much warmth. And then there was her father who I knew had been an abusive piece of shit, but that was a bag of worms I wasn't even going to begin to touch with her.

The point was, I felt for the kid.

"P'Ken, regardless of whether you become my apprentice or not, I'd be glad to have you as a friend," I said with a smile. Instantly, her face lit up like a menorah and her whole body seemed to become more energized.

"Thank you."

Moving slowly enough so as to not startle her, I put an arm around her shoulders and led us both toward the staircase. "Now, I don't make new friends too often, so I'm no expert, but I think this is the part where we learn more about each other. You know

I'm a thief, and I know you like fancy clothes and want to be a thief, but that's just scratching the surface." We reached the top of the staircase and I forced myself to make eye contact with P'Ken. "What do you do for fun? When you're alone in your room?"

"Knitting, mostly," she said, still filled with excitement. "Knitting and reading."

I pursed my lips and narrowed my eyes. "Those sound like the kinds of hobbies your mother would want you to have. Do you really enjoy doing that stuff?"

"Absolutely. You opened my eyes to how much more is out there than the school, but there are still plenty of parts of my life that I value." She giggled. "Joining your crew won't make me start dressing improperly like you usually do."

"Awfully presumptuous of you to be saying you're joining my crew while insulting my clothes."

P'Ken's face fell. "I'm so sorry. The other girls have told me that friends tease one another. Were they lying?"

I belted out a hearty laugh. "No, no, there's a good chance snobs like them were using that as an excuse to be mean, but it is something friends do. I was just teasing back." I looked up at the ceiling. "Guess neither of us is too good with humor."

Another thought popped into my head, this one being a potential additional reason to bring P'Ken aboard. "You wanna see one of the things I do for fun?"

"I'd love to," she answered, nodding.

Grinning at the idea of having someone new to geek out about my special interest with, I took P'Ken's hand and walked us over to my room.

"Pop a squat on my bed while I set things up," I said.

"Oh, are we going to be watching something or playing a

type of game?" she asked, looking at my bed nervously. "I'm afraid if it's the latter, I don't have much experience with games."

This kept getting more depressing.

"Aarif and I do have regular board game nights, which we'd be bringing you in on, you'd be amazed how many games are less fun with only two players, but we're not playing anything now," I said as I picked up my tablet. "No, I'm going to introduce you to the wonderful world of wrestling."

"Wrestling?" Her face curled up again. "Isn't that something barbarians and neanderthals partake in?"

"Heh, not at all." I sat down on my bed and P'Ken slowly followed. "Wrestling is, well, it's an art form. Two strong personalities clashing against one another, both making use of a full arsenal of moves as they tell a gripping story through their battle. It's all scripted, so the winner is pre-decided, but the skill is real. And when you look into the real people behind the personas they put on for the show, the line between reality and fiction becomes slim, and makes it all even more fascinating."

P'Ken didn't look like she was following what I was saying, but I was sure she'd understand once she saw how awesome top-tier matches were. The only question was: Which match would make the best first impression? Ideas which sped through my head included: Reality Check vs Ice Pick, Gary Fortx vs Ivanna Untero, Weyver vs Humberto Rodriguez, and The Great Terra-Rex vs Cara Blade. All of those ranked among my top 30.

Ultimately though, I didn't go with any of them. There was a match which would show her the light better than any of those.

"Here, lemme show you an example. This is 'Pearl Knight' Marshall Cape vs 'Sword Breaker' Dragonius. A classic battle of good vs evil. Dragonius, a human/dragon hybrid, has already defeated most of Marshall's allies, and if he can't stop him, the only member of his team left will be the youngest member of The Knights of Stone, Lazuli."

P'Ken still seemed confused as I pressed play, but I knew she'd be won over soon. The match was filled with classic moment after classic moment. Marshall Cape pulling out the Canadian destroyer, Dragonius burning off half of Pearl Knight's face while taunting him about how he "killed" The Ruby Knight, Pearl Knight pushing through the pain and becoming the first person to lay a major smackdown on Dragonius, and Dragonius calling in his servants to cheat and win at the last moment, leaving Lazuli as the only one standing between him and the championship. It was all an absolute treat.

"So, what did you think?" I asked.

"Very violent," P'Ken groaned. "But also surprisingly emotional. Dragonius was scary, and I felt so bad for poor Marshall. He gave it his all, but it still wasn't enough. And while I may not care for violence itself, the physicality involved was incredibly impressive." Her eyes widened. "Does Lazuli end up managing to stop Dragonius?"

My grin stretched from ear to ear. I'd converted her into one of us.

"We'll watch that match another time. You should see the rest of Dragonius's matches first so you have full-context." I hopped up to my feet. "Which of the moves was your favorite?"

P'Ken raised a finger to her chin. "I think if I had to choose, I'd pick the one where Marshall grabbed Dragonius, turned him upside down, and drove him head first into the mat."

"The piledriver. A classic move." I put my tablet back down on my desk. "You know if you want, I could teach you how to perform one."

P'Ken's jaw dropped. "You know how to fight like them?"

"You bet!" I pointed a thumb at my face. "When I was a kid training to be a Sunriser, I studied Krav Maga and Cykebian Mixed Martial Arts, but after I got into wrestling, I made it a point to integrate all of my favorite moves into my fighting style. Many, or, more accurately, everyone I've talked to about it has questioned the practicality of doing so, but dammit, it works for me."

"Wow."

I hadn't been looking for an apprentice, but the advantages to having one were really piling up. I'd be bringing a new thief into the universe, I'd get to make some extra gidgits, I'd get to help out a poor girl in need of friends, I'd have someone to watch and talk about wrestling with, we'd have someone to join us on board game nights, and it was pretty awesome to have someone look at me with complete awe.

"Wait, you trained to be a Sunriser?" she asked, her face filled with bewilderment.

"Embarrassingly, yes," I answered as I played with one of my fidgets. "Joining them was my dream as a kid, but I ended up realizing what a stupid dream it was, and I chose to be awesome instead." I was embellishing what had happened just a bit, but she didn't need to hear the full story. "An important thing to know when you're a thief: the Sunrisers suck, and they don't at all represent the ideals they claim to."

"Really? I've always thought they seemed so heroic."

"Oh yeah, they're good at giving off that impression, but when it comes down to it, all they really care about is their image and control. Don't get me wrong, they do some good work, stopping wars and keeping people from getting killed, but they only fight in the name of 'peace' and 'order' because that's what they've found gets a positive response. A lot of people don't know this, but spreading those ideals wasn't even their initial mission statement. Emperor Leon founded the Sunrisers with the intention of forcing all other worlds to adopt what was, at the time, the mandatory religion to follow on Cykeb, AKA, worshiping *him*."

"Yes, I believe Mother's told me about that," P'Ken said, standing up. "St. Shiala was one of Emperor Leon's closest advisors. We've both always found it a little strange that the school was named in the honor of someone with such outdated views, but it was never deemed appropriate to change it."

Yet another example of the Sunrisers' hypocrisy. They so often fought against bigots and religious zealots, but they also paid tribute to their founder, who was a bigot with a god complex. The nobles who held the highest ranks in the organization all thought themselves to be evolved and beyond prejudice, while at the same time indulging in rampant classicism. And they hunted down criminals while being willing to kill and implement more than a little cruel imprisonment methods themselves. Molina really should have seen it by now.

"That's enough about buzzkills," I said, putting my fidget down. "Why don't we take a look at all the gadgets and tools that aid me in my awesomeness?"

DEWDEWDEWDEWDEW. DEWDEWDEWDEW.

"Whoops, looks like I'm getting a call." I walked out of my room, but quickly turned around. "Please, please don't touch anything."

"Yes, ma'am."

I pointed a finger at P'Ken. "Never call me that again."

My watch's ringtone continued to sound as I made my way

to the cockpit as quickly as I could in the low-heels and long dress I was stuck in. When I got there, I saw that the call was from Jellz, so I connected my watch to my computer to hide my location, before answering.

"Got news for me?" I asked.

"Not good news," he answered, scratching his chin. "Shion the Librarian led a rescue attempt of Madame N'gwa and the other Banshees. It involved taking command of multiple Utozex battleships, a fake distress call, nanomachines, and a team of officers they'd bribed to betray the Sunrisers, but it didn't work, and along with the Banshees they already had prisoner, they also captured Greka Vyra. All 12 of the captured Banshees were successfully dropped off at one of the Sunriser's bases." He spat. "This Captain Langstone must be something else."

"Um, yeah," I chuckled nervously. "She must be." I swallowed. "So, does Shion have another plan? Could they use my help?"

Jellz sighed. "It seems they've decided not to take any further actions until they've restored their ranks with new blood. They don't want to risk another attempt resulting in them all getting captured and The Order being killed forever. And no, they do not want you as one of their new additions."

This was such bullshit! I hadn't done anything wrong, and yet my heroes didn't have any trust in me whatsoever. When I got my hands on whoever really had given the Sunrisers the location of the meet-up spot, I was going to tear them apart.

"So they're just going to let everyone rot in a Sunriser base for who knows how long?"

"That's precisely what's happening. And you're going to stay where you are and not do anything either. I can see in your eyes that you want to do something and I am ordering you not to.

You hear me? If the Banshees and I couldn't pull off the rescue, neither can you. And if you try to pull some stunt and get yourself captured, you will never hear from me again."

Jellz was looking out for his own safety, and I couldn't blame him, but at the same time, if the Banshees weren't going to save their own, then I had to. It was the right thing to do *and* a chance to prove myself.

"Okay, I promise I won't get captured."

"Your wording there worries me. Again, you are not to try *anything*! After everything I've done for your career, you owe me this. Now promise you will not even attempt to stage a jailbreak."

There was an honor among thieves that didn't exist among the Sunrisers or most other groups. I couldn't lie to a fellow thief. But Jellz was a businessman who worked with thieves, not a thief proper. "I promise I won't even attempt to stage a jailbreak," I lied, using his exact words.

Jellz nodded, and turned his head all around to make sure no one was sneaking up on him. "By the way, what the Hell are you wearing?"

"Goodbye, Jellz."

I hung up and disconnected my watch from the computer. Molina was still going to come and find me, but now making things cool with her wouldn't be enough. I had to use our friendship in a way which would allow me to free Madame N'gwa, Lioness, and everyone else. Aarif may not have had an actual plan when he'd made the suggestion of doing this earlier, but now I had no choice but to formulate one. And after several minutes of standing on my hands, nearly managing to focus on just this one task, with only minor worries that P'Ken was touching my stuff distracting me, an idea began to take shape.

Molina hadn't failed her first mission, so she didn't need any time to mentally recover. With that in mind, I put step one of my new plan into action and sent her a transmission.

CHAPTER 10: MOLINA

I'd had to face a series of trials and tribulations to get my prisoners to their new home, but in the end, we had triumphed, and even managed to capture additional criminals in the process.

I was proud of myself, but I couldn't have accomplished the mission without my entire senior staff. I'd dealt with the battleships that had tried to threaten us, Security Chief Michaels and Commander Revudan had put a stop to the sabotage attempt by the crewmen the Banshees had bribed, and Kaybell's technological knowledge aided our head of engineering, the middle-aged and excessively hairy Commodore Pen, in stopping the nanomachines that had infiltrated our systems from freeing the Banshees.

With twelve members of The Order of the Banshee safely under level-6 security, their crews under level-3 security, and the crew members who'd betrayed us awaiting their court martials, we'd received new orders to focus on tracking down Shion the Librarian and capturing her before the Banshees could recruit new members. I planned on accomplishing this mission just as I had my previous one, and to kill two birds with one stone, since she hadn't come to the base like I'd told her to, I planned to find a lead on her by tracking down Yael.

I still hadn't been able to tell the crew what my connection to her was, but I was able to truthfully tell them that we'd be tracking the woman who'd gotten away from us on Milash's moon. I'd find her, get her to turn herself in, and make her give me information on where to find Shion.

We may have been in for a long and difficult search, but shortly after we began looking for Yael, I received a transmission from her. She'd somehow ended up on Benkin and was staying at the St. Shiala School for Girls. Hearing that had made Kay nostalgic for her schooldays, but I was confused as to what the most slovenly girl in the universe was doing at a school for nobility. As a tactical location, it made sense; she knew I couldn't beam down a platoon of ground troops without frightening the students, and facing the political ramifications of doing so. But how she'd managed to acquire housing there was confounding. She'd given me an exact date, time, and location she'd wanted to meet, and I'd sent her a reply stating that I'd be there.

Two days following the initial transmission, I was beaming down to the town of Wedgerock, flanked only by a small team of security personnel. The sky was dark, the air was freezing, and snow littered the ground, but I wouldn't be out in the open for long, so none of these factors presented an issue.

The restaurant Yael was no doubt waiting for me in was down the block and, just as her current housing situation was puzzling, the fact that she'd chosen a steak house to meet in as opposed to any of the more casual restaurants or bars made me wonder if her being a criminal wasn't the only thing about her that had changed.

With a raised hand, I signaled my officers to wait outside while I walked in. The interior of Pietro's Steak House was like many of the places I ate at when I wasn't on duty. The walls and floor were made from fine, polished wood; crisp, white tablecloths covered every table; and the waiters were all dressed in tuxedos with white gloves. At several tables, I could see elegantly dressed teenagers enjoying lavish meals and laughing, but all the way in the back was the reason I was here.

If I hadn't been looking for Yael, I may never have even recognized her in the gorgeous but completely uncharacteristic yellow dress she was in. At least there may have been some difficulty had she not also been chugging back a beer without using her hands like she always used to do with soda.

"Moli." Yael's face lit up with the same joy it had on Milash's moon as she set her beer down on the table and stood up to greet me, her hands flapping like the wind. "I'm so glad you came. This should, uh, be a lot more comfortable than talking over a holo-call or while I'm trying to avoid getting killed and you're trying to arrest people."

The cadence of her voice and the way she spoke were identical to how she'd talked when we were younger. I believed that I'd grown and changed for the better in that area over the past decade, but this was one area where Yael hadn't changed at all. If I was going to get Yael to do what I wanted, I needed her to trust me. And more importantly, I *wanted* her to trust me.

Only a little afraid, I opened my arms up for a hug. "Try not to crush me this time, please."

Her eyes slightly watering, Yael tightly, but not too tightly, wrapped her arms around me. In turn, I put mine around her. When we'd hugged on Milash's moon, I'd been too caught up in the moment to fully appreciate it. Now though, being in her arms again, feeling safe and protected, a single thought overtook my mind. Or rather, a single desire.

"Do you think we hug too much?" I'd once asked when we were thirteen.

"I mean, if you're getting tired of hugging, we could always try kissing," Yael had replied.

I'd blushed and tugged at my long hair. "Are you... are you being serious?"

She'd narrowed her eyes. "Am I?"

We'd always just been best friends. Some conversations we'd had in our teenage years may have been construed as flirting, but neither of us had ever had the courage to make a move. Now though, we were adults. I was a Sunriser captain who regularly faced life-threatening danger and other high-stakes situations, and I was sure the life of a thief hadn't been easy for Yael. And it was possible the feelings that had always resided just under the surface in both of us were still there. I couldn't let myself get too carried away, and my first priority had to be getting Yael to turn herself in so I could get her leniency, but once that was settled, I needed to figure out how far my feelings went.

We pulled back and, looking her in the eyes, she truly was stunning. A beauty that no one else but me had ever appreciated. "So... where should we start?" I asked as I sat down, trying to keep my voice firm.

"Not sure," she answered as she followed my lead. "I have so much I wanna tell you."

"Believe me, the feeling's mutual." I eyed Yael up and down. "Why don't you tell me why you're dressed like that, and what we're doing in a steakhouse?"

Yael laughed. "The dress is because this planet, as you may have noticed, is more than a little cold, and because I didn't want to stick out. The steak house is because I figured this was the kind of fancy-schmancy restaurant you ate at regularly now that you're a captain."

"Well, that isn't false," I said. "But it's less so because of my rank and more because of my friend."

"Oooh, the person you replaced me with," she mocked, crossing her arms. "Tell me about them."

My face curled. "It isn't fair for you to put it like that. You're the one who left and never called."

"Sorry." Still smiling, she nonchalantly raised her hands. "But come on, I really do wanna hear about them."

A waiter walked up to the table, placed a glass of ice water in front of me, and handed me a menu that matched the one in front of Yael, before giving a small bow and walking away.

"My best... the person who has been my best friend since the academy is actually Princess Kaybell Bythora. She's, well, she's a lot, but underneath all the pomposity and aggressiveness, she's trustworthy and funny, and an incredibly capable Sunriser."

Yael had a hand over her mouth and appeared to be laughing.

"What's so funny?"

"What isn't funny?" The volume of her laughter increased as she put her hand down. "Me leaving apparently led to you becoming besties with the future ruler of the universe. You must spend your shore leaves having high tea or riding horses or whatever else royalty does for fun."

As often as I'd wished Yael had never left Cykeb, it was true that my life would be completely different if she hadn't. It was possible I may never even have met Kaybell, let alone become friends with her. Yael being in my life for the past ten years would have been amazing, but I wouldn't have wanted to trade away all the experiences I'd had in that time.

And Yael wasn't wrong about the type of things we did for recreation.

"And you're satisfied... doing what you're doing?"

My grip on the menu tightened. "Is this the part of the conversation where you say I shouldn't be a Sunriser? That I'd be happier if I was a criminal like you?"

"I'm not telling you to break the law." She looked back up, but her eyes were on the ceiling, not me. "And I really do think what you've accomplished is impressive. But the fact is, you're too good for them."

It was astounding how she could simultaneously compliment me and insult my very way of life in a single, short sentence.

"Perhaps I didn't make myself clear, but I serve right alongside Kaybell. She's my first officer. And if, as you put it, "the future ruler of the universe" isn't too good for the Sunrisers, then no one is."

"I meant morally," she groaned. "And I know you're probably friends with a lot of them, but take it from someone who's spent the last week working in a school full of them: Cykebian nobles are a long way off from being the pinnacle of morality."

Were anyone else saying this to me, I would have become furious. But I knew who Yael had once been and what she'd once believed in. And I knew what was truly bothering her.

"'I can't imagine what it's been like living with all this pain and hate," I said, looking at my friend with the deepest of sympathies. "It could make anyone choose the wrong path. But if you're going to get your life back on track, you need to move past your rejection from the academy."

Yael shut her eyes, and her lips curled as she bit her lip. "I won't deny that my rejection left a major impact on me. That it hurt like Hell at first. But what I ended up taking from it was a realization about the Sunrisers not being who I thought they were, not 'pain and hate.'"

"Just because you weren't qualified—"

"Wasn't qualified?" Her eyes re-opened and widened. "We both know there's never been anyone more qualified than I was."

"When it came to the theory and practical portions of the exam, you blew everyone else to ever take it out of the water," I said in the most assuring, calm tone I could muster. "But every single psychologist they had you talk to agreed that you were mentally unfit."

"Mentally unfit," she echoed, scoffing. "You know what that ruling was? Bullshit. Bigoted, spicy bullshit. They couldn't stand a mind that worked differently from others, no matter how efficiently it functioned. So despite training and working and studying all my life, my Autistic, ADHD ass was called 'mentally unfit.' The Holy Cykebian Empire claims to be the greatest empire the universe has ever known, with no prejudice of any sort, and the Sunrisers claim to be the ultimate peacekeepers, but all I see is a whole bunch of classist and ableist fuckheads who claim to hate crime and inhumane conditions, but subject people to executions and life in prison."

This was even worse than I'd thought. Her hate had completely blinded her to reality. When Yael had turned out to be a thief, I'd assumed she must have been threatened, blackmailed, or otherwise coerced. But now I was almost sure that there was something genuinely wrong with her. And if that was true, then my first duty as both a friend and a Sunriser captain was to get her the help she needed.

"That feel good? To get that all out? Have you had the

chance to vent like that before?" Yael shook her head as she chugged back some water. "I hope it was relieving. And your feelings aren't irrelevant. But here's a fact you're ignoring: I'm Autistic too, and none of the psychologists had any issue with me."

Yael rolled her eyes. "Yes, you're Autistic, but you aren't ADHD, and our symptoms have always been different. Did the psychologists even know you're Autistic? Is it common knowledge on the ships you serve on? Does your dad even know?"

I took a deep breath in and, as I exhaled, I breathed out, "No."

"And you're happy serving an organization that looks down on you because your mind works differently?"

"Yes, as a matter of fact I am," I said, crossing my arms. "Because the Sunrisers have always been evolving, and I know that one day, they'll change to the point where they no longer make mistakes about people like you. And in the meantime, I can still do my part in making the universe a safer place. What's far more unbelievable than me being satisfied with my life as a Sunriser is you being satisfied with yours as a thief." I took a deep breath in and shut my eyes. "You know, your parents and I were worried out of our minds when you disappeared. We thought you were *dead*. Nearly every day before it was time for me to go to the academy, I was at your house, trying to comfort them as we all cried together. I was in therapy my entire time at the academy, and I think your parents are *still* getting help."

Finally, some guilt made its way onto her face.

"I'm sorry I didn't say anything before leaving. That was *really* shitty of me, and if I could go back and do things differently, I would." Her guilt disappeared and made way for a smile. "But you're not the only one who's happy with her life. For friends, I've got my engineer Aarif who has a brilliantly creative mind and who's willing to put up with all my BS, the best dog in the universe, Juri, and I even just made a new friend who might end up becoming my apprentice. And as far as the actual thieving goes, if I was a Sunriser officer, I'd almost always be up on a dull, black ship. With this life, I get to constantly see new worlds and have all kinds of crazy adventures. I really could talk your ear off about them all day. But, because I know it's what's important to you, I'll first mention that I do help people sometimes. Not often, but… sometimes."

She spoke with such passion and enthusiasm. Clearly she wasn't just deluded about the world, but herself as well. To protect itself from the pain and emptiness of the life of a criminal, her mind had made itself think that such a life made her happy.

"I would love to hear any stories you have about helping people," I said. "And trust me, I have plenty of stories to share, myself. But the past can wait a little longer. Right now, we should talk about the present."

"In the present, we're two old friends catching up over a meal and having some disagreements," Yael snarked.

The waiter returned and Yael told him, "Two medium rare Romanian tenderloins, please. Extra caramelized onion on one of them," ordering for both of us, and getting the waiter to walk back away.

"Yes, we are," I said. "But you're also in danger. The only reason there isn't already a wanted poster of you is because I haven't reported you, and I've also kept my officers from doing so. But I can't protect you forever. Once you're in the system, I'll have no choice but to bring you in, and if what Madame N'gwa told me about the crimes you've committed is true, then you'd be looking at a life sentence."

Yael put her water down and spun her wrists around, each crack of her bones audible. "You'd really do that to me?"

"It's the last thing I'd ever want to do," I said truthfully. "But if we're going to avoid that outcome, we need to work together. Like we always used to."

Her wrists stopped moving and her eyes pierced mine like daggers. "What did you have in mind?"

This was my one chance to make my case. I'd hoped to have a less bumpy conversation before getting to this point, but it was where we'd landed. I had to make her see that if she didn't trust me now, she'd be dooming herself. I had to open her eyes to the new life she could lead, just by saying "Yes."

"Come with me and turn yourself in," I began. "You'll confess to your crimes, and I'll make a case for you that you haven't done any of this while in your right mind. We'll get you a psychologist, one you can really trust, not any of the ones from the examination, and get you on medication, and after a few years, once you've shown that you're completely recovered, you could be free to go." I lightly tugged on my hair. "And then... then we could think about us. About how we feel about each other. Explore some things that I know we both always felt... but were too afraid to."

Yael shined a toothless grin. It was beautiful, but it also filled me with concern. It didn't seem like the kind of face someone would make when admitting they have a problem.

"That last part sounds really great," she said. "Every time I thought about calling you, I always wondered, 'what if?'" Yael shook her head. "But none of the rest of that junk is happening. Because, apart from a possible addiction to beer, there isn't anything wrong with me."

Dammit, I thought, clenching a fist under the table.

"You're welcome to try and catch me, but just like on Milash's moon, I'm warning you not to. Because clearly, for reasons I can't fathom, you're still dedicated to your job, and I'd make you look really bad."

I scowled, no longer able to hold in my frustration. "You always did think you were better than me," I growled. "But what happened on that moon was a fluke. While you've been gallivanting across the universe stealing and having heinous medical procedures performed on yourself, I've continued to train and gain experience. I have a crew of 42,000 at my disposal, while you have an engineer, an apprentice, and a dog. Yael, I'm telling you this as a fact: You won't be able to escape me. And once I have you, I'll do whatever it takes to make you turn yourself in, get help, and bring us back together."

Yael picked up her beer and seemingly chugged back everything left in the bottle before slamming it down. I could feel us being glared at by the nobles.

"Sorry, Moli, but that's not happening. See, I'm gonna be leaving this planet soon, and I'm gonna free the members of The Order of the Banshee you captured so they'll let me in."

The nerve of her to say that to my face. She really *did* think of me as an unworthy opponent, just like Madame N'gwa. I was a Sunriser captain and she was a thief. I would not be talked down to like this.

"We can't do anything about you right now," I said, barely holding in my anger. "From what I've seen of your physical abilities, a handful of troops wouldn't be enough to take you in, and an army would frighten the nobles. So I'll wait on my ship until you're ready to leave. And that's when I'll catch you."

I stood up, dusted myself off, and turned around to walk

out, but before I could get far, Yael asked, "Where are you going?"

I turned back to her with narrow eyes. "Back to my ship. Where else?"

Yael looked at me like I'd just said my ostrich was pregnant. "Back in your seat. Our steaks are coming and, if we can avoid shop talk, I'll even let you treat me to another beer."

"You... you can't be serious."

"I promise I won't talk about any of my heists and I'm sure you have things to talk about that don't involve the Sunrisers. We've got plenty else to discuss. Like your sword training. How's that been going?"

"I... I don't understand. How can you be so casual?"

"Cause I love ya," her voice cracked. "Don't get me wrong, if the Sunrisers were some fascist group rounding up neurodivergent people and putting them into 'reeducation camps' or some other shit, we would not be having this conversation. Nah, they're just discriminatory jerks who you've allied yourself with because you believe in their greater mission, which, even if I don't like it, I do understand."

That was all so easy for her to say, but what about me? She could see why I'd made the choices I had, but all I saw was a clearly mentally unwell criminal. Someone who had just told me a major crime she was going to commit that I would have to stop. Someone I would never share a meal with.

No, that wasn't right. I should have been objective, but I could still see Yael. I could still see this beautiful, annoying and snarky, but charming in her own way woman. This person who thought she was so much better than me, but who would also break the arms of anyone who'd ever insult me. I saw my best friend. I saw the woman who, regardless of what kind of feelings they really were, I loved more than anyone else.

And so I sat back down.

"Okay, let me tell you about the sword I'm wearing right now. Because it's pretty awesome."

CHAPTER 11: YAEL

After a tense start that had made my stomach tingle in all the wrong ways, Molina and I had managed to have a meal and conversation which had made my stomach tingle in all the right ways.

I wasn't sure what had made me happier: the fact that, once we'd moved past our differences, we were able to banter and laugh and yammer about our special interests like old times, or the fact that she was open to the idea of us getting together romantically. I'd never been with anyone in that way, but there had never been anyone I'd wanted to be with more than Moli. I'd just never thought she saw me that way. The delicious steak also helped to make the experience amazing. Easily one of the top 10 steaks I'd ever had.

When it had been time for us to part ways, Molina had made things awkward by reminding me of what would happen when I tried to leave the planet, but I'd still made sure we said goodbye on a good note by giving her another hug. All in all, while it would have been nice to have lured Molina away from her shitty job, things were still mostly going according to plan. Unfortunately for me, the next part of my plan involved more talking, and I was already socially exhausted. Still, it had to be done.

"Yael, did you have a nice night out?" Lulu asked as I walked into her study.

The study wasn't too gloomy, still pretty dark but partially illuminated by a couple of dim lamps. There were several massive bookshelves and a coffee table with a fancy tea set sitting atop it, and paintings of Lulu's ancestors and a Cykebian flag were proudly displayed on the wall.

I was wearing my yellow dress, which was slowly growing on me and which I really hoped Molina had found me cute in, while Lulu had changed into a long-sleeved, floor-length silver evening gown with black floral highlights, and a matching head wrap. She was seated in a large, comfy-looking recliner, and had a thick book in her hands.

"I'd say so," I said, sitting down across from Lulu. "Listen, there's something that's been going on that I need to talk to you about."

Lulu shut her book, set it to the side, and smiled directly at me. "Whatever's the matter?"

I typically went into conversations either with no idea what to say or with every single word meticulously planned out. I knew what reaction I was hoping to get out of Lulu, so I'd spent the morning thinking this through. At least the parts of it where I hadn't been focused on seeing Molina again. It helped that I'd already been thinking about how to talk to her about this subject for a while, but instead of trying to convince her to let her daughter come with me, I now had a different goal in mind. "It's P'Ken," I started. "We've been spending a lot of time together and she's opened up to me about a lot. One thing in particular stood out to me and I felt you should know about it."

"Is something wrong?" The fear and concern in her voice

was instantly apparent. "Has she gotten herself into some kind of trouble? Is she sick?"

"Nothing like that," I assured her. "No, she's been thinking a lot about her future. And she isn't sure if taking over your school is what she wants to do."

Lulu laughed the same way I often heard noble girls laugh in the library. "Nonsense. P'Ken has never wanted anything but to inherit my job. She spends nearly all of her time working and studying so she can become worthy of doing so. Now, if my baby is feeling insecure about whether she'll be ready to take over for me, that's something I can talk to her about. She certainly isn't ready now, but I know she will be when the time comes, and I'll say that straight to her."

I shifted around in my seat, hopping up and down. "That's definitely an option, but there's something else. She told me what she does want to do with her life."

Lulu bent over, grabbed the teapot and poured herself a cup, sipping the herbal scented drink before speaking, a calm smile on her face. "Let me guess: She wants to avoid having to work at all by marrying a powerful noble. As a child, she dreamed of marrying a prince, but I imagine her fantasies have become marginally more realistic."

"Actually... she wants to be my apprentice."

The middle-aged woman beamed skepticism into my eyes. "Excuse me?"

"She decided she wants to be a thief and she wants me to train her. And while I wasn't sure at first, I've been won over. So if you're okay with it—"

"Absolutely not!" she cut me off. Lulu set her tea down on a saucer before sitting up perfectly straight and glaring at me.

"I do not blame you for this. You simply are who you are, and I'd assumed my daughter was mature enough to not be influenced by you. But if what you're saying is true, I'm going to have to ask you and Aarif to leave first thing in the morning. I cannot allow P'Ken to abandon her duty for the first new thing that catches her fancy, no matter how grateful I am to you. I'm sorry."

I hopped out of my seat and put on the same kind of fake, polite smile P'Ken wore a lot. "No need to apologize, I completely understand. This is why I brought the matter to you." I pouted and shifted my body to seem more concerned. "But what if P'Ken gets mad at you for denying her her new dream?"

"Pish posh," Lulu smirked as she stood up. "I assure you, once you've been gone for a week, maybe two, she'll realize how silly she's been and never think about living your kind of life again."

I really did like Lulu, but especially with Molina breathing down my throat about my career, I could definitely have done without the condescension.

"Well, thanks for letting me stay for this much time," I said, reaching out a hand.

"It's been a pleasure," she replied, shaking my hand. "Thank you again for being straightforward with me and for understanding."

The conversation had panned out just as I'd planned. Tomorrow, we'd leave Benkin. And after that, Lulu would definitely be out to kill me.

The preparations Aarif and I had needed to make took longer than I'd expected, so neither of us had ended up getting any sleep, just like the previous night. Before leaving Ricochet, we'd both put our certified caffeine plans into action to deal with this,

Aarif chugging down three cups of black coffee while I drank a Querlious energy shot. Aarif didn't like me drinking them since the side effects could get really weird, but I figured I drank them infrequently enough that I didn't need to worry.

When we got back to the school to collect Juri, Kidney, and all of our stuff, I made a detour and stopped off at P'Ken's room.

"Good... good morning, Yael," she said, standing in her doorway, her head downcast. "Mother t...told me what's happening."

I knew the feeling her face and body were screaming all too well. It was the same way I'd been following my rejection from the academy. And while the dream of mine that had been crushed had been present all my life and P'Ken's new dream had only been present for a couple weeks, I was sure for her, it felt just as awful.

"Yeah, Lulu didn't take the news well and we'll be out of here in less than an hour. Don't know when we'll be back either."

Tears streamed down her face, smearing the makeup she'd probably just finished putting on, before she wrapped her arms around my waist. I liked connecting with people on my own terms, not being touched by them without warning. But for once, I'd let it slide.

"Hey, hey, don't cry," I said, gently pushing her away and smiling. "I never said I wasn't taking you with me."

P'Ken let go of me as her eyes widened. "What are you talking about? Mother said I wasn't allowed to train with you."

"And part of being a thief is not doing what anyone tells you," I said, putting my hands on my hips. "Except for me. As your mentor, always listen to me."

"I... I don't understand."

"Do I have to spell it out for you?" I laughed. "I'm inviting you to come fly around the universe and train under me, and I don't care what your mom has to say about it. So are you in or what?"

She was no doubt still filled with conflict about leaving her mom and her entire life behind. But if she'd put as much time into thinking about this as she'd said, and this was what she truly wanted, then she wouldn't let anything stand in her way. P'Ken looked all around, in every direction her head could move in, and when she turned back to face me, her face had lit up.

"Thank you."

I patted her shoulder. "Go wash your face and pack your things. And remember, we don't have much room." P'Ken wiped her eyes as she nodded vigorously, before walking back into her room. "And be quick about it!"

At this point, I was looking forward to teaching P'Ken. I was still only 27 and there were some lingering doubts I had about her, but like she'd said, if I was fit to be a Banshee, I was fit to be a mentor, she'd already proven that, if nothing else, she'd be fun to have around on the ship, and getting her away from a life with a controlling mother and no friends was the right thing to do. But before she'd act as my apprentice, she'd first serve as a domino.

Once P'Ken was finished cleaning up and packing, taking two large luggage bags with her, I snuck her around the school, intentionally doing a bad job of it so that a few students spotted us together, and brought her back to Ricochet, where Aarif and our pets were already waiting. Lulu had tried calling P'Ken on her watch while we were walking out of the school, no doubt wondering why she wasn't at breakfast, and to keep her from saying the wrong thing, I'd told her to not answer, and to continue to not answer no matter how much she called.

BARK. BARK.

As we stepped onto Ricochet, Juri charged forward and

tackled P'Ken to the floor, furiously licking her face.

"Ahh! Ahh!" P'Ken screamed. "What's happening?!"

Aarif and I laughed, looking down at them.

"She can smell that you're the newest member of our crew," Aarif said. "And that means you get dog kisses."

"I like animals, but I don't like this!" P'Ken cried. "Please get her off!"

Still laughing, I picked Juri up, while Aarif helped P'Ken up to her feet and closed the entryway to the ship.

"I didn't realize dogs could be so heavy."

DEWDEWDEWDEW. DEWDEWDEWDEWDEW.

"Is that my mom again?" P'Ken asked as my watch rang.

"Yup, and I'm still not ready to talk to her, so I'mma let that go to voice mail," I said, tapping my watch. "All right! Let's get out of here! P'Ken, go unpack your things in my room, Aarif, you're with me in the cockpit, Juri, go eat your breakfast."

We all mobilized and got ourselves ready to take off. Lulu kept trying to call both P'Ken and I, but to no avail. Once we were airborne, Aarif went to go make sure Juri was eating, and I left the ship on autopilot to go and make sure P'Ken wasn't vomiting all over my room. Fortunately, despite this being her first time flying in a spaceship, she seemed to be in pretty good shape, and the only problem she was having was finding room for all the clothes and makeup she'd brought.

Before long, we were back in space, and that meant it was time to call Molina. Returning to the cockpit, I connected my watch to the ship's computer and hailed the Noriker, which Ricochet seemed like a flea next to. A minute later, it wasn't a projection of Moli's cute little face coming out of my watch, but the face of an angry looking woman I didn't recognize.

"Who the Hell are you?" I asked.

The grumpy looking woman made her face look even angrier. "I am Commander Kaybell Kose Bythora, daughter of Stephen and descendant of Leon, first emperor of Cykeb and founder of the Sunrisers, future ruler of The Holy Cykebian Empire. And you're under arrest."

A few thoughts sprang to mind in rapid succession. First was amazement at the fact that this woman's ego was so big that it seemed like this was the normal way she introduced herself. I knew how rich and powerful she was, but it was still weird to witness. Second was that I couldn't imagine Moli getting along with her at all. She'd said that she was a trustworthy friend underneath all her pomposity and aggressiveness, but I wasn't getting that vibe at all. She just seemed like a major bitch.

Finally, I was left wondering where Molina was that she hadn't been the one to answer my call. Either I'd timed my call wrong and she was doing work in her office or something, or she'd decided she couldn't bring herself to capture me personally, and so she'd delegated the task to her cronies. The unexpected situation wasn't ideal, but I could still make it work.

"Oh yeah? And how do you plan on arresting me?"

The commander continued to scowl. "Through whatever means necessary. We've already run a full scan of your ship. It has no weapons and its maximum speed is light-years slower than ours. You have no chance of escape. Hand yourself over peacefully, and no harm will come to either you or your crew." Her lips curled into a sinister smile. "But by all means, try and get away."

"Is that your way of saying you're prepared to fire upon me?" I asked, leaning back in my chair. "Because I'd really rather you didn't."

"I'm afraid the opinions of criminals are irrelevant."

"Are they though? Because before you fire at me and destroy my ship, you should probably know that your captain loves me and would be crazy pissed at you for killing me."

The princess flexed out her hand, showing off nails which matched her eyes and hair. "I don't know what Captain Langstone feels for you, but it certainly isn't love. As for your fear of death, we don't need to kill you to cripple your engines and life support."

If they'd already run a scan of Ricochet, then they knew we had systems that prevented anyone but Aarif and I from beaming aboard. And if they couldn't beam troops aboard, then what she was describing was their primary option of capturing me if I didn't come willingly.

"This is a pretty old ship," I told her. "It's not too sturdy, the shields barely function... if I know Parallax-class ships like I think I do, a single missile or second of laser fire would wipe us out. You're too powerful to simply take out my engines."

The commander's eyes narrowed and her mouth opened, but before she could say anything, I said, "Aaaaaaaand, before you bring up your tractor beam, there's something you should be aware of." I smirked. "I have a hostage."

Ms. Grumpy Face rested her head against her fist. "There are only three human life signatures on your ship. That lines up with what you told the captain last night. You, your engineer, and your apprentice. You have no hostage."

"Oh, but I do. See, my apprentice didn't quite get her mother's permission to come with me, so I kidnapped her. And if you use that tractor beam to reel me in or attempt to fire on me which, again, I wouldn't recommend, I'll cut her fucking throat."

She was definitely holding in rage, now. I knew the forced

rigidity of a Sunriser anywhere. As for my threat, it was a complete bluff. Hurting P'Ken, let alone killing her, would be like kicking a puppy, and I felt pretty good about never having ever killed anyone at all. But I knew how Sunrisers thought. In their eyes, all criminals, no matter how non-violent, were capable of the most heinous of crimes.

"Why should I believe that they aren't with you willingly?" she asked.

As I'd thought, that was the part of the bluff she was questioning. And I was fully prepared.

"As the princess of The Holy Cykebian Empire, I'd wager you studied at St. Shiala's School for Girls. Give your old headmistress a call. Seeing as I kidnapped her daughter, she should be pretty pissed, and will tell you her daughter never would have come without permission."

Ms. Grumpy Face showed her teeth. Finally, I was getting an emotion out of her other than frustration and disgust: anger. "Don't go anywhere," she said, before ending the call.

While she went to go talk to Lulu, I took advantage of the break by heading to my room and scarfing down a delicious apricot muffin I'd been saving, alongside a beer. P'Ken had started "cleaning" my room, which was something I'd have to fix later, but what was important was that she was distracted and had no idea what was going on. I didn't need her to start freaking out on me. Not yet, at least.

A couple minutes after I returned to the cockpit, this time joined by Aarif, my watch rang. And this time when I answered, I saw the person I was actually hoping to see.

"I apologize for not being present earlier. I was practicing that new move we talked about." As she spoke the second half of her sentence, Moli's voice became quiet, garbled, and all around embarrassed. "Yael, you can bluff my first officer, but not me. I've learned enough about this new you to believe that you'd kidnap a girl to use as a bargaining ship, but I don't believe that you'd actually kill her."

I grinned. "You look like you always did right after gym class. Sorry I didn't give you time to shower."

"Yael," she growled.

"Sorry, sorry, not the time for flirting, I guess," I giggled. "Look, I absolutely do not want to kill this girl. But you're the one who forced me into this position with all your talk of making me turn myself in so I could 'get help' or whatever. You already know from your scan that my ship is completely unarmed. We are no threat to you. But if you fire at us or use your tractor beam, if you decide to be the aggressor, then you'll be dooming an innocent kid. Alternatively, you can save her by standing by and letting me go free the Banshees."

Molina shook her head. "I don't believe that you're that far gone, and you know I can't let you do that."

If she wasn't in the mood for being friendly, then I had no reason to prolong this conversation. "Well, you know where I'm going and I won't kill the girl unless you actually try something, so you're welcome to follow me and try to come up with a new solution to this little dilemma of yours. Should be fun."

I ended the call, hoping Molina wouldn't hold this against me too much, and looked up at Aarif, who had the smuggest look on his face.

"All according to plan."

CHAPTER 12: MOLINA

Yael Pavnick was not a murderer.

Yael Pavnick was *not* a murderer.

It was a possibility I refused to acknowledge on a personal level, but one I was forced to from a tactical position. If there was even a chance that making a move would endanger an innocent girl's life, then we couldn't make it. But if Yael thought this was a problem for us, she was wrong. We would follow her right back to Sunriser base 9B-T5, and give two day's notice to the security staff that she was coming. The best thieves in the universe couldn't perform a prison break from a Sunriser base even with the element of surprise on their side. Without it, she was hopeless.

She'd be caught, Headmistress Amatyn's daughter would be returned home safely, her engineer would be locked up, and I'd use my authority as a captain to have her brought into my custody. Yael was as crafty as any Banshee, and I could see why they'd been interested in her. But no thief was a match for the power of the Sunrisers.

"Kay, set a course for Sunriser base 9B-T5 and don't let that ship out of our line of sight."

Turning my head to the side, Kaybell appeared to be in an especially bad mood. I wasn't sure exactly what had been said during her conversation with Yael, but I could imagine my old best friend getting under my current best friend's skin very easily.

"Something on your mind, Commander?"

Kaybell crossed her arms. "What is your relationship with this trash? I'm not asking a question as your friend, but demanding information that I believe is imperative for everyone on this bridge to know."

I turned my head away from Kay and looked around the bridge. Sure enough, Commander Revudan also had her eyes on me now. It was possible I had put off sharing what was going on with Yael for too long and left my officers in a state of confusion. I'd had my reasons not to share everything with them when this had all started, and the idea of telling Kay everything still bothered me, but it was clear from the looks on everyone's faces that my secrecy had been troubling them. And if Sunrisers were supposed to be one thing, it was selfless.

"Okay, listen up," I began, my eyes on the floor. "First off, Kay, don't call Yael trash, or any other derogatory terms you may have for her. Second... Yael Pavnick is one of the most important people in my life."

I proceeded to give the majority of my senior staff a brief rundown on my history with Yael. From the time we met on the first day of Pre-K to all the time we spent playing and studying together to Yael's incredible grades and performance in all scholastic areas to her rejection from the academy to the present, I covered every major point I was aware of. There were definitely many things I still didn't know about the last 10 years that I couldn't cover, though, and I went out of my way to avoid saying anything about what I'd been like as a kid or how I still had feelings for Yael.

"Captain, if everything you're saying is true, then I must

agree with the assessment Commander Bythora made following our first encounter with Ms. Pavnick," Revudan said. "There is a conflict of interest here and she should take command. Especially if we consider the possibility that Ms. Pavnick still has a card she hasn't played yet."

A part of me knew that Kaybell had been right back then and that Commander Revudan was right, now. But at the same time, no one knew how Yael's mind worked better than I did. And no one else would understand that what Yael needed was the aid of a mental health professional, not decades of jail time.

I returned to looking at Kaybell, who now had her hands clasped behind her back and a calm look on her face.

"When I attempted to take command previously, it was because I had no idea as to what was going on between you and this girl," Kaybell said. "Now that I know everything, however, I don't believe I have anything to be concerned about. You've moved up a long way in the universe since you and this girl were friends, and while I don't understand why you'd still have any sense of attachment toward someone like this, I know you, and I know that these feelings of nostalgia within you aren't strong enough to interfere with your strategic-thinking or sense of duty. You were chosen to be captain over me for a reason."

I donned a small smile as I made myself more comfortable in my chair. There was a reason Kay was my closest friend and it warmed my heart to hear her support me.

"We will succeed. I promise."

We'd been trailing Yael for two days, and still, she hadn't taken any unexpected actions or attempted to contact us again. I was dying to talk to her more, to chat like we had at dinner, but I couldn't risk any of my officers, or even any of the ground troops overhearing me having a casual conversation with the enemy.

And if speaking with her was unacceptable, then telling anyone that I'd been dreaming about her was unthinkable. The dreams had us in a variety of locations, be it a rose garden, a dojo, or the roof of Zenith Command. In all of them, we were engaged in sword combat. She did her best, but I always won. And then as a prize, she'd give me a kiss.

The only dream where these events hadn't played out was the one most similar to the dreams I'd had as a kid. They featured the two of us, together on the bridge of the Noriker, commanding the ship as a team and stopping a war together. I knew that even in the best case scenario, it was unlikely that Yael could ever become a Sunriser, but it was the future we'd always dreamed about, and it was the future I still wanted to make a reality.

"Captain, Ms. Pavnick's ship has changed course," Revudan reported. "I can't seem to identify any likely destinations."

"Continue to follow her and raise shields to 50%."

"Yes, Captain."

While precautions were necessary, I had a good feeling about this. Whether it was fear or reason which was driving her, Yael had seemingly made the sensible choice to not attempt a foolhardy prison break. That scenario ended with her being brought into my custody as well, but things would be so much easier and simpler if she surrendered now. Knowing Yael, she was probably taking the time to think of a way she could surrender without making it seem like she'd accepted defeat.

We continued to chase after her for another three hours, all of which I spent on the bridge, only occasionally getting up to stretch my legs. I wasn't going to risk not being present when Yael attempted to contact us again.

My patience rewarded me when, as we entered a barren, unpopulated system, we received a transmission from Yael. Up to this point, she'd been making holo-calls, not sending transmissions. It was possible she was having trouble processing her feelings and didn't want to have a conversation right now, but I couldn't be sure.

"Play it."

Instead of Yael's beautiful voice, my ears were greeted to the grating sound of static. It was like listening to a million swords scratch against a million rocks. Eventually, the static ceased, and it was replaced by an unfamiliar voice.

"Hello! My name is P'Ken Amatyn! I'm currently being held hostage by two really mean thieves and I'm really scared. They've been trying to lure you into some kind of trap utilizing the properties of the nearby moons. They're asleep right now though, and I've taken the wheel. I'm going to be landing on the planetoid located at 32Z by 7R. Please save me!"

As the transmission ended, I leaned forward and folded my hands in front of me. Yael wasn't making this easy on herself after all.

"Commander Revudan, run scans for any unusual properties in any of the celestial bodies in this sector and for viruses across all systems and set a course for the coordinates she gave us." I turned my head to my first officer. "Kaybell, how much of her story do you believe?"

Kay smirked and put her hands on her hips. "She isn't a very good actress. That was not the sound of someone in genuine danger. Either she was forced to send that message by the thief, or she's working with them as I initially assumed. Regardless, it would seem they've decided to take us on."

"If there was something about this system they were going to use to their advantage, why would they have told us that?" Commander Revudan asked. "Maybe she thought it would distract us?"

"No," I said. "She's well aware of how many tasks a Parallax-class ship can perform simultaneously."

"If my assessment is correct, then they're currently attempting to lead us into a trap. But as far as they're concerned, they've just told us that sending down troops to the coordinates they gave us won't cause the thief to kill her potential hostage."

I cracked my neck. "Then we'll walk into whatever trap she has set."

I'd beaten the Banshees. Despite how difficult and stressful it had been, I'd successfully imprisoned 12 of them and fended off the rest. No matter what clever plan Yael had brewing, it wouldn't be enough to stop me.

By the time we reached the coordinates we'd been given, both of Commander Revudan's scans were complete. So far, no unusual compositions had been detected in any of the system's planets, moons, or planetoids, and no viruses had been found in the transmission.

"The criminal ship has landed on the surface," Commander Revudan said. "We have their location. How should we proceed?"

"Send down 10,000 ground troops. Arrest everyone on board, have them all placed in level-6 restraints, and annihilate their ship once everyone has been taken into custody."

No matter how smart Yael was, no matter how strong her enhancements made her, while she was stuck on the ground, there was nothing she could do against 10,000 trained soldiers dressed head-to-toe in top of the line, lightweight battle armor and helmets equipped with night vision and gas masks, and armed with Excalibur-class assault blasters, smoke grenades, flash grenades, viseph gas cannons, and stun batons.

Additionally, regardless of the hostage's true status, she had her engineer and dog to worry about. She could potentially survive everything we had to throw at her, but they most definitely could not.

"Scan complete, Captain," Revudan reported. "There are no unusually composed bodies in this system." Had it been a bluff? Potentially. I'd get answers to all of my questions soon enough. "Ms. Pavnick's ship has been surrounded by 1,000 ground troops and more are beaming down as we speak."

"Have them all stand by. I don't want any moves made until all 10,000 of them are present. Once they are, have them break into the ship and make sure they know their first priority is to secure the hostage."

The seconds passed, each one feeling like an hour, as I waited for all the troops to be deployed. Yael, and the future I desired, was within my grasp, and I wasn't going to let it slip through my fingers.

"All assigned troops are on the planetoid and have surrounded the criminal's ship," Kay said. "They've already successfully cut through the ship's shields and made their way inside."

This was it. After ten years of her running away, Yael would be mine again. Her ship was small. Pathetically small. It would take mere moments for it to be fully searched.

"Captain, the troops have secured the hostage, as well as a dog, but there doesn't appear to be any sign of Yael or her engineer."

My heart plummeted. This couldn't have been happening. This wasn't possible. There was nowhere she could have gone. Her ship had no beaming capabilities.

"Commander, run a scan for human life signatures on the planetoid," I ordered nervously. "Are there any underground tunnel systems?"

The Banshees on Milash's moon had tried to get away through an underground escape route, but if Yael was attempting to imitate her "heroes" then she should have known not to try the same trick that had already failed on me once.

I was nervous and taken aback, but I still felt like I was going to win this. And then all the lights on the bridge went out.

"What just happened?" I growled as the emergency lights came on.

"We've suffered a complete system failure," Commander Revudan said, confusion in her voice. "Shields, weapons, life-support... everything is down."

"How is that possible?" Kaybell snarled. "There's no way that rat could have done this. Are we at least still in communication with the ground troops? Are we still capable of beaming down to the planetoid?"

"Negative on both counts, Commander. And it seems like whatever caused the system failure also damaged the emergency life support. We have less than an hour before we're out of oxygen."

I clenched my fists and slammed them against the armrests of my chair. Whatever she'd done, Yael was now playing with over 30,000 innocent lives.

Maybe she *was* a murderer after all.

CHAPTER 13: YAEL
EARLIER

"So here's what's happening," I said to Aarif, having sat him down on my bed. "Please pay attention, because I don't want to repeat myself."

"Yeah, *I'm* the one who needs reminders to pay attention."

I stuck my tongue out at him before I resumed speaking, pacing back and forth across my room.

"Right, so, I've got a plan to beat Molina and rescue the Banshees, but I'm gonna need you working overtime to pull it off. Being real with you: We're probably gonna miss at least one night of sleep."

"If this ends with us getting rich, I can live with it. Go on."

I nodded. "I just sent a transmission to the Noriker and gave Molina an exact time, date, and location to meet me. She'll get here and realize she won't be able to deploy an army of soldiers to take me in, but I'm gonna tell her at the dinner I have planned for us that we'll be leaving the next day."

"And once we're in space, what exactly will stop her from either shooting us down or catching us in a tractor beam?"

"P'Ken." I grinned. "She wants to come along and be my apprentice, but the first thing I'm gonna have her do is play the role of a hostage. I'll threaten to kill her if Molina makes any attempt to capture us and to really sell the idea that she was kidnapped, I'm gonna tell Lulu in advance that P'Ken wants to join us, which she'll definitely be against, so that I can tell Molina to call Lulu and verify that I kidnapped her daughter if they don't believe me."

"Wow." Aarif's eyes widened. "Bitch move."

"We do what we've gotta do." I sighed. "Anyway, I'll then tell Molina that we're gonna go to Sunriser base 9B-T5 to rescue Madame N'gwa and the others. We'll let them follow us for a couple days before, suddenly, we'll change course. Then, we'll have P'Ken, pretending to be terrified, send a transmission to them, telling Molina that we've gone to sleep and that we were planning on taking advantage of some unusual substances in the system or whatever, just something to make them look in the wrong direction and not do anything more than a basic virus check after they hear our message, so that they don't catch a program that will allow us to access their transport system via our watches. When P'Ken lands the ship and Molina comes after us, we'll no longer be on board, but right in the heart of the Noriker. I'll take out whatever security officers they have on duty, and, using my knowledge of how Parallax-class ships are laid out, I'll get you straight to the engine room, where you can cripple the ship in a way only you can fix. Then, we'll—"

"Stop," Aarif cut me off, raising a hand at me. "I have a feeling I get where you're going with this. We demand that they free all the Banshees from their prison and allow us to go free in exchange for me fixing their systems and keeping them all alive, right? Good plan, except I don't have the slightest clue how we're even supposed to get over there! Hiding a program in a transmission that will allow us to use their beaming technology through our watches? I don't know how to do that! And last I checked, neither do you."

"Come on, Aarif, don't be like that," I said, bouncing up and down. "Like I said, we'll probably miss at least one night's sleep, but I'm sure we can figure it out if we put our heads together. With my programming knowledge and your engineering know-how? It's a cinch!"

Aarif scratched his head. "Okay, and what about the part where I have to disable their systems in a way none of their elite engineers could? How am I, alone, supposed to do that?"

I sat down next to my friend and slapped him on the back, knocking the wind out of him. "Dude, you're the guy who put Juri back together and made her go from being *one of* the best dogs in the universe to the *best* dog in the universe. You can do this."

Aarif pounded on his chest and coughed as he regained his breath. "Alright, fine. Not like I've got any alternative ideas for how we pull off a jailbreak." He smirked at me. "Let's do it."

NOW

As I stood in the Noriker's engine room with Aarif, surrounded by unconscious security personnel and engineers, back in my normal clothes, and having just caused a complete system failure, the thought occurred to me of how completely screwed all my fellow criminals would have been had I become a Sunriser.

Sure, I was only pulling off this current job because of my inside information and because I had Aarif with me, but the fact that things were going so well at all spoke volumes about my awesomeness. Molina was definitely gonna be pissed when I explained what was going on, but at the same time, I was really hoping she'd be impressed.

Not too long after we'd finished working, a team of ground troops arrived in the engine room and aimed their assault blasters at us. Even with their body armor and weapons, I was still pretty sure I could beat these guys up, but they couldn't do what I wanted if they were out cold.

"Oye," I said, deciding in the moment to speak in an old-fashioned Cockney accent. "If you want to live, take us to the bridge."

The troops turned to each other. With their communications systems down, these poor guys actually had to think for themselves for a change. They weren't entirely on their own, as Molina had likely given them orders to come down here, but there was definitely a little voice in their head telling them to kill me now.

"Move," one of them said with a high-pitched voice. "Make one wrong motion and we'll shoot."

Aarif and I grinned as we walked forward, our arms hooked around one another's, and allowed half the troops to walk in front of us, and the other half behind us, as we made our way through the many, many decks of the Noriker, up the hundreds of steps we were forced to use since we'd shut down the elevator system.

Eventually, the now-exhausted Aarif and I arrived on the bridge, where Moli was standing up perfectly straight, and looking adorably rigid and furious.

"You insolent little—"

Before Ms. Grumpy Face could growl anything else, Molina shot her a harsh stare, getting her to shut up.

"What could you have possibly been thinking with this?" Molina asked as she turned her head to face me, the soldiers in front of us stepping aside. "Do you even realize what you've done?"

"Course I do. Pretty cool, right?"

"Cool?!" Her right eye twitched uncontrollably. "You've endangered tens of thousands of lives!"

"Yeah, but no one will die so long as we can make a deal. And I'm sticking to it being cool. Aarif and I, together, are probably the only people in the universe who could have pulled this off."

"Hi, I'm Aarif," he said with a small wave of his hand. "As the only ones to ever be best friends with this wonderfully wild woman, I feel like we have a lot to talk about when this is over."

While Molina and Ms. Grumpy Face still had nothing but anger on their faces, the other bridge officers just appeared confused.

"You people cannot be real," the helmswoman said.

Molina pointed her face down and squeezed her forehead repeatedly before looking back up at me. "There will be no deals made. My engineers, engineers who actually graduated the academy, will figure out what you did and get our systems back online, and once that is done, you will be brought to a holding cell, where you will remain until you agree to turn yourself in."

"You still want me to turn myself in," I said, pointing a finger at Molina. "You're still looking out for me. After all this? That's love." With how red Molina's face already was, it was hard to tell if I'd gotten her to blush. "Anyway, that's not gonna work. With my knowledge of how your engines work, and Aarif's mechanical genius, we took out your systems in a way only we can fix. I mean, your engineers probably could fix them if given enough time, but we've got less than 50 minutes before we're out of oxygen."

"And in exchange, you'd want to be let free… and have the 12 captured Banshees released from their imprisonment as well?"

"Now you're getting it."

Molina spun around on her heels and walked toward the

helm, her hands clenched behind her back. This was the part where she considered all of her alternative options. Most likely, she would think inside the box and consider either sending out a distress call or work to have the doors to the shuttle bay manually opened so she could begin an evacuation. But we were too far out in the middle of nowhere for any ships to reach us in time, and even if they could get an evacuation going, they didn't have nearly enough shuttles to save everyone.

Molina turned back around, the fire in her eyes having been replaced by ice. "And what if I were to threaten to shoot Aarif in the head and splatter his brains across my bridge if you don't fix the ship immediately?"

That certainly hadn't been what I'd expected. Even if she was bluffing, just making that kind of threat against an unarmed man violated protocol. Either one of the captains she'd served under had taught her to take more drastic actions when faced with a crisis, or I'd gotten even more under her skin than I'd expected.

It also may have had something to do with the influence of her first officer. Right as Molina made her threat, a large grin had appeared on her face.

"We both know you aren't going to do that, Moli," I said. "I'd never shoot a defenseless man in the head, so you sure as Hell wouldn't either. And even if I did think you'd do it, it wouldn't accomplish anything. You'd just be dooming us all."

As Molina's body shook, the ice in her eyes melted and her face went cool. "Suggestions?"

She'd thought of her potential sensible options and tossed them out, and her illogical attempt at an extreme measure had failed. Now I had to hope none of her officers had any bold ideas.

"We could transfer all emergency power into the thrusters

and attempt a manual landing on the planetoid," Ms. Grumpy Face said.

"It's been eight years since I performed a manual landing of a Parallax-class ship and that was just a simulation at the academy," the helmswoman said. "I'm not sure I could pull it off."

"The scans we performed reported that the planetoid is composed primarily of Miranite, and the atmosphere has a density of 2.0 kg/m^3," a woman with long braids said. "Even the smoothest landing would still result in catastrophic damage."

The option of manually landing the ship had completely gone over my head. I hadn't run any kind of scans on the planetoid's composition or atmosphere and, for all I knew, Molina could have had a top-notch pilot who practiced manual landings regularly. I'd dodged that bullet by complete luck.

"Alternative idea then," Ms. Grumpy Face snarled. "I believe we should get the shuttle bay open and begin a rapid evacuation of all officers on board. The ground troops who would be left behind would gladly give their lives to ensure that dangerous criminals stay where they belong."

Molina unclenched her hands and allowed her arms to hang at her sides. She looked all around the bridge, at each of her senior officers, before looking back at me.

"To clarify your terms, you want me to transfer our emergency power to the communications systems, and order the release of the imprisoned Banshees, with the reason given to General Snype that the lives of my entire crew are at stake, and, in exchange, you'll restore all functions to the ship, beginning with life support?"

I giggled. "Don't forget the part where you let me go free too when I'm done. Oh, and I also want the Banshees to know

I'm the one responsible for their freedom, as well as the release of their crews."

Molina walked toward me until she was mere inches away. Her face was no longer cool. It was sad. "Give us some privacy. That's an order."

The senior officers didn't seem like they wanted to go anywhere, but they ultimately relented and walked off the bridge, the equally confused troops following their lead and taking Aarif with them. Once they were all gone, Moli put her right hand on my cheek. It had more calluses than I remembered from when we'd hold hands as kids, but it was still wonderful on my skin.

"Please don't make me do this, Yael," she begged, her eyes watering. "You'd be destroying my career." She swallowed. "I'll let you go. I'll give you back your ship and allow you and your crew to get as far away from here as you want. Just please don't make me free the Banshees."

This would have been so much easier if I were just screwing over some random, loser captain instead of Moli. Destroying their career might have actually been downright enjoyable. But despite the peppy front I was putting on, I knew how much this must have been hurting her. In formulating this plan, I'd compartmentalized my feelings. I'd thought that I'd save the Banshees now, and make things up with Molnia later. Looking at her now, however, I wasn't sure if there would be any coming back from this if I didn't manage to say the right thing. And I was terrible at doing that.

"Moli, I'm really sorry you were assigned this mission. I would have beaten anyone your dad pitted against me, but having to do this to you—"

"Stop acting like you're better than me!" she screamed, interrupting me. "You've always done this and I hate it. And it makes no sense that you're doing it now. I am a Sunriser captain and you are nothing!"

I turned my eyes away from her. "I'm sorry," I said truthfully. "That's something I was working on when we were younger, but I'm... I'm out of practice."

Looking like she was holding back tears, Moli took her hand off my face and gripped my hands with both of hers. "If you make me do this, you'll ruin my chances of ever becoming a general, let alone supreme general. Do you really want to do that to me?"

I tightened my hands around hers. "If you think there's no chance for progressing as a Sunriser, then why not come with me? You don't have to work with me, as fun as that would be. But I'm about to be rich. I could spoil you even more than your noble friends probably do."

Molina shook her head furiously as she pulled her hands away from mine to wipe tears from her eyes before they could stream down her cheeks. "Your life is not better than mine," she growled. "And it's a life I want no part of. If I offered you a full pardon and guaranteed acceptance into the academy in exchange for fixing the engines, would you take that deal? Both scenarios would bring us together, but only one would put us on the right side of the law."

I tilted my head back. "No. No, I wouldn't accept that." I looked back at Moli and tried to think of something, anything, to make her feel less miserable. "I could knock you out? Your first officer would take command and then she'd have to be the one to make the call to have the Banshees freed."

Molina grit her teeth and gulped. "I will not be part of any deception, nor will I sacrifice my friend's career to save my own." She walked forward a few steps so that our shoulders were horizontally adjacent. "Yael, if you go through with this, we will never have another lovely night like we did at that steakhouse. We will never casually spend time together again in any way. And I will make sure you spend your life in a cell. Do you understand me?"

I stepped back so I could see her eyes. This had to be another bluff. I couldn't live with Moli hating me, and I knew she'd never want to make me suffer for decades to come, no matter how mad she was. No, I had to believe that I could make this up to her. When this was all over, I'd buy her every sword she could possibly ever want.

"I understand. Now, do we have a deal?"

Molina lowered her head and put her hand over her face as she sobbed. I wanted to physically comfort her somehow, but I felt like she wouldn't take that well right now.

"Yes, Yael. We have a deal."

It took Aarif and I half an hour to bring all of the ship's systems back online. Once we were finished, Molina sent us down to the planetoid, without even saying goodbye or waving back at me, to be reunited with P'Ken, Juri, Kidney, and Ricochet. We stayed put until we received confirmation that Madame N'gwa and the others had all been released from Sunriser base 9B-T5. I sent Molina an apology transmission and tried holo-calling her before we left, but she didn't respond to either.

Aarif was completely wiped out, both mentally and physically, so he went to take a nap as soon as we were airborne, while P'Ken was filled with a rush of excitement that she'd helped our plan succeed, although she had been pretty scared by all the soldiers.

Not long after we left the planetoid, I received an encrypted transmission from Madame N'gwa, which included a brief thank you message, as well as a map to a new meeting spot.

"You've carved out a bright future for yourself," were the words the transmission had ended with.

I'd done what I'd set out to do, my crew was safe, and no one had gotten killed. By all rights, this was a complete victory. And yet I felt like the universe's biggest piece of shit.

CHAPTER 14: MOLINA

I'd never been more humiliated in my life. I'd been completely outsmarted and suffered an absolute defeat, a defeat that would ruin me and make my father the most disappointed he'd ever been, and all at the hands of the woman I treasured more than anyone else.

After I'd put myself through the agonizing pain of having to make the call to Sunriser base 9B-T5 and order the release of the Banshees, I'd gone to my quarters so I could deal with my feelings of pain and embarrassment in private. It wouldn't have been appropriate to allow any of my officers to see me doing so.

I wasn't given too much time alone, however, as while my order was still being processed, Kaybell had come to me and argued that maintaining honesty wasn't worth allowing all of these criminals to roam free again, and that I should cancel the order and capture Yael. As tenacious as she was, I was able to hold my ground.

When everything was finished, and Yael's ship was no longer on our sensors, I needed time to lie down, so I'd put Kaybell in command of the bridge. I still needed to write my report of everything that had transpired, but that could wait until after I'd processed everything and considered what was going to happen to me.

As much as Yael had hurt me, as much as my heart still ached, I couldn't think of anything I could have done differently. I'd walked right into her trap, but I'd done so by following procedure to a letter. And even if I'd strayed from procedure, like I'd briefly done when I'd threatened to shoot her friend, there was little that could have changed what had happened.

As much as I hated to admit it, Yael had been right. She would have beaten any Sunriser captain.

Yael. Awkward, shy, head-in-a-book Yael. Always protecting me from Morphea and the both of us from other bullies, Yael. Prom date Yael. Now, armed with more knowledge of Sunriser technology and procedure than anyone else, and a genius level intellect, potentially one of the most dangerous criminals in the universe.

And it was my fault. She'd made the choice to become a criminal, and made choice after choice to stay on that path, and that was on her. But maybe if I'd been a better friend, maybe if I hadn't gotten into the academy either, then she never would have made those choices. Maybe she hadn't had as fulfilling a time at dinner as I had and that had made her feel like our friendship wasn't as strong as it once had been. Maybe she'd just been putting on an act. Maybe she didn't love me as much as I loved her.

I'd always had some problems with her attitude. Her unbridled, if earned, confidence in her abilities and the way she'd brag. But perhaps she had problems with the way I'd acted too. It was possible that after I'd been accepted to the academy, I'd been a condescending bitch to her without even realizing it.

Yael belonged in a cell. But I needed to know that she

didn't hate me or blame me.

DEEK!DEEK! DEEK!DEEK!

My monitor signaled me to an incoming video call, and there was no doubt who it was on the other side. I quickly brushed my hair, dusted off my uniform, and stood in attention before answering. To my utter horror, as if this couldn't get any worse, my father wasn't alone. Standing at his side, with a grin full of sadistic glee on her face, was Morphea.

"Captain, I assume you know why I'm calling?" he asked in a stern voice.

"Yes, General," I replied, trying my hardest to maintain eye contact and not focus on Morphea's haunting smile.

Father folded his hands in from himself as his lips curled downward. "The tip that allowed us to capture eleven members of The Order of the Banshee was a once in a lifetime opportunity. Most likely the Banshees will find out who ratted them out and will ensure that they can never do so again. These criminals will more than likely all spend the rest of their lives free and harming others."

Any excuses I had were pointless. It didn't matter if this would have happened to any Sunriser captain, it had happened to me. And I had to face the consequences.

"All I can do is apologize and promise to do better in the future, sir," I said. "I hope the fact that I was able to successfully capture the assembled Banshees in the first place, as well as the fact that I fended off an assault from the remaining Banshees and captured another one in the process, shows that you didn't make a mistake in giving me this command."

"Nothing you did previously matters," Morphea's shrill voice squeaked. "Your efforts have amounted to nothing but a waste of time, money, resources, and, as the supreme general already stated, an incredibly valuable opportunity. And that's without even getting into how you've humiliated the entire organization. News channels and broadcasts across the universe are already calling into question our effectiveness."

"How can they be telling people what happened when I haven't even turned in my report?" I questioned, not entirely succeeding in keeping my voice calm.

"Unless your report doesn't include you being manipulated into freeing twelve level-6 criminals, I'm afraid it won't change anything," Father said.

This was going about as poorly as I could have expected. But if excuses wouldn't fly and my previous victories meant nothing, then I only had one card left to play. I elevated my head and made sure I was looking right into my father's eyes.

"Supreme General, please allow me to capture the criminal truly responsible for the release of the Banshees, Yael Pavnick. She is highly dangerous, has complete knowledge of all of our technology and procedures, and, as you'll read in my report, left me with a choice of either making the call to free the Banshees or allowing tens of thousands of people to die. I will find her and arrest her, and then I will capture not only the Banshees I was forced to release, but every other one as well."

Neither Father's expression nor his posture changed at all, but Morphea's lips curled even further up her face, making her resemble the Cheshire cat.

"Yael Pavnick? As in the same Yael Pavnick who was inseparable from you when we were kids?"

"Yes," I answered, holding in a scream. "But, again, as you'll see in my report, none of the actions I took that resulted in the release of the Banshees were primarily motivated by any personal feelings I still have toward her."

I wasn't lying, but it still felt like I was. Several actions I'd taken, from beaming down to "rescue" her personally back on Milash's moon to having dinner with her, while playing no role in my defeat that I could see, had been motivated by my personal feelings.

"I find that difficult to believe," Morphea said. "Captain, are you sure that you—?"

The supreme general raised one of his hands, making Morphea instantly silence herself.

"I will not make any judgments about your relationship with this woman until I've read your report," he said. "That's only fair. However, given the circumstances, I cannot allow you to pursue her, nor go on a wild goose chase after the Banshees in the name of redeeming yourself. That isn't how we operate. Once I've read your report, I will decide who to send after Ms. Pavnick, and the teams in charge of monitoring potential Banshee activity will continue to proceed with their duties as usual. As for the Noriker, you are to stand by and await further orders. You will respond to any distress calls you pick up, but apart from that, you have no present mission. Do you understand?"

Not being given a mission and only responding to distress calls… those were the kinds of orders aging captains received when it became clear they were past their prime and never going to advance in rank. And here I was receiving those same orders not even a month after becoming a captain. I wanted to start crying again, but I managed to keep my emotions bottled up.

"Yes, General. I understand."

Without saying goodbye, or even saying that he was eagerly awaiting my report, my father ended the call. A part of me had hoped that my pleas to Yael hadn't been entirely true, that my career was still salvageable. But it was becoming more and more apparent that my thief of a best friend had stolen my future.

As difficult as writing my report was, informing the senior staff of our new orders had been more painful. I hadn't managed to bring myself to even do it in person, instead sending messages out to each of their watches. It was cowardly and disgraceful, but I couldn't bear to do anything else.

Every time I closed my eyes, I saw Morphea and Yael's smiles taunting me. One of them may have hated me and was glad to see me suffer, while the other claimed to still care about me like I did about her, but right now they both brought me nothing but pain.

By the time my report was done, it was late, and I was starving. I could have had food brought to my quarters, but staying in them would have only been a further act of cowardice, so I ventured out to the senior officers' dining room. When I arrived, I found that, already seated at the table, eating a plate of alligator meat and chili peppers, was Kaybell. As I walked in, she didn't even bother to look at me.

Out of the entire senior staff, Kay was the one I least wanted to see right now. She had even less experience with failure than I did, and absolutely no experience with punishment.

"Captain Langstone to the kitchen," I said, pressing down on my com device as I sat down at the head of the table. "Please bring one sashimi platter and one beer to the senior officers' dining room."

Kay shook her head, still not turning to face me. "Do you really think you deserve that?"

I leaned back in my chair and crossed my legs. "I know that you're angry, but do you think I shouldn't be allowed to eat?"

"I think you shouldn't be eating your *favorite* meal."

"It's artificial food from the ship's kitchen," I groaned. "It isn't as if I'm flying a shuttle back to Cykeb and having Toshiki Kubota himself prepare me a meal."

Kaybell scoffed. "As if you could even afford to eat at his restaurant without me."

I slammed my arms down onto my chair's armrests. "Kay, if you have something you want to say to me, then please just go ahead and say it. I'm really not in the mood for games."

Finally, Kaybell looked up at me, a sneer on her face.

"I should have been made the captain of this ship. Not you."

I'd been expecting her to say something like that. But while I may not have been able to stop myself from being dressed down by my father, I wasn't going to be talked down to by my subordinate.

"You had your chance to take command and you turned it down," I told her. "You agreed that I was capable of completing the mission."

"Yes, because I love you and I trust you, but you *lost*, Molina, not only bringing shame to all of us aboard this ship, but to the entire organization. Any and all crimes those thieves commit are now on your head."

I sat up straight and folded my hands in front of me on the table. "There was no way for us to beat her. Any captain would have lost. Even you."

"I *told* you my idea for how we could have prevailed—"

"And that idea involved sacrificing thousands of good troops."

I cut her off. "It was out of the question."

Kaybell skewered a large chunk of meat with her fork and blew on it before putting it in her mouth and slowly chewing on it.

"There was another move we could have made," she said, dabbing at her mouth with a napkin after she'd swallowed. "But I thought you'd be more likely to go with that one." I tilted my head to the side and waited for her to elaborate. "We could have killed Headmistress Amatyn's daughter as proof that we really would kill the thief's engineer if she didn't cooperate."

The doors to the dining room slid open, a cadet walking in and handing me a beer. They gave a respectful nod before walking back out.

"Have you considered that maybe I was promoted over you because I don't have the values of a princess interfering with my values as a Sunriser?" I asked as I cracked open my beer. "Because I don't see my life as worth more than those around me?"

"My life *is* worth more than anyone else's on this ship," she snapped. "The life of a princess is more valuable than the life of a noble, the life of a noble is more valuable than the life of a commoner, the life of an officer is worth more than the life of a ground troop, and the lives of everyone aboard this ship are worth more than the life of any criminal."

I took a large chug of beer before slamming the bottle down on the table. "Nobility and hierarchy exist for good reasons. Nobles have the breeding and education necessary to properly lead society and hierarchy is required for a massive organization like the Sunrisers to function, but no one is more entitled to life than anyone else."

Kaybell shook her head as she sipped wine from her goblet. "I have always been patient with you, but you have *never* respected my beliefs. Everything about my very being and how I view the universe, you see as me being snobby and self-centered."

"That's not true."

"And it's not *just* me. You've judged every other noble you've served with."

"As if they didn't all judge me for being a commoner."

"My ancestor *founded* the Sunrisers, and yet you think I don't know what the organization stands for."

"Your actions—"

"Well you know what, Molina, I don't need to deal with the self-righteousness of a captain who can't even see that *her* morals are the reason the careers of every person on this ship are over, and why people across the universe are going to suffer."

"My morals may have jeopardized the mission, but I at least I *have* some."

As soon as the words left my mouth, regret shot up my spine.

Her face showing nothing but anger, Kaybell took her napkin off her lap and threw it down on the table, getting up and walking toward the doors, leaving her food behind.

The two of us had had disagreements about our different views over the years, and we'd joked about Kay's ego, but I'd never realized she felt so offended by how I saw things. I'd never realized how much I'd hurt her. And I'd never said something so stupid to her before.

"Kay, wait," I said. "I'm sorry." She kept walking. "That's an order, Commander!"

She continued to ignore me as she exited the dining room, not paying me another glance.

I picked my beer back up and chugged it. It was bad enough that I'd ruined my career and had no chance left of a future with Yael, but now my best friend hated me too.

Yes, the beer in my hand would definitely not be the only one I'd be having tonight.

CHAPTER 15: YAEL

"Yael Pavnick, you bring my daughter back home this instant!"

Even from the hologram I was looking at, I could see veins bulging out of Lulu's forehead.

"Sorry, but no can do," I said. "She wants to stick with me for now and I'm pretty excited about taking her under my wing."

Before we made the several-day trip to the coordinates Madame N'gwa had given me, P'ken had insisted on calling Lulu and letting her know what was going on. She hadn't even started her training yet and she was already making better decisions than I had.

"I'm so sorry for upsetting you, Mother," P'ken said, seated next to me in the cockpit. "But please try and understand that being trapped in the school for the rest of my life isn't what I want. I want to be free, I want to go on adventures, and I want to see the universe. I want to be a thief."

Lulu's rage didn't fade at all. "P'ken, you are 16 years-old. You don't know *what* you want. Your mind has been polluted by the ideas of a toxic woman who I made the mistake of trusting, and the longer you stay with her, the more polluted your mind will become."

"Yael hasn't done anything of the sort," P'ken protested. "She's simply opened my eyes to things I never saw before."

"Yeah!" I added in enthusiastically. "What she said."

I was still grateful to Lulu for the shelter she'd provided me with and all the food she'd filled my stomach with, but I had little appreciation for those who'd try to control the lives of others. And she seemed to have it stuck in her mind that if P'ken didn't become a boring headmistress, then she was throwing her life away.

Lulu tapped her watch and, next to the hologram of herself, appeared a hologram of my new wanted poster. Unfortunately, the only semi-recent picture of me the Sunrisers evidently had was one from a meatball eating contest I'd won the previous year, so I'd need to pull a Lioness and *send* them a new picture to use. More positively, my bounty was a whopping 150,000,000 gidgits.

"Do you see this P'ken?" Lulu asked, the pitch of her voice going up an octave. "Your new hero is a wanted criminal with an inordinately large bounty. Not only the Sunrisers, but every bounty hunter in the universe will be coming after her, and if you're with her, aiding and abetting her crimes, then I won't be able to protect you!"

"Yael can protect us *both*, Mother," P'ken said, the admiration I loved that she had for me showing. "She's a genius."

"She is a *single* woman!" Lulu screamed. "I don't care how smart she is, she can't overcome the most powerful paramilitary organization to ever exist, and if you don't have her bring you home, you will spend years of your life in jail! Do you hear me? Jail!"

The glow from P'ken faded and her face softened. I thought Lulu had gotten to her and I was about to step in, but before I could say anything, P'ken spoke for herself.

"I promise I'll come home eventually, Mother. And when I do, I'll have all sorts of wonderful stories to tell you. Then you'll understand why I had to do this."

Lulu continued to seethe for a few seconds, but eventually her face fell and her shoulders relaxed. "Please take care of yourself, sweetheart. I love you."

P'ken nodded, her eyes watering. "I love you too." She tapped my watch and ended the call.

The kid looked pretty shaken, so I patted her on the back while I disconnected my watch from the computer. She was making better choices than I had, but mine had been much easier. Calling Moli like this after I'd left and having to see her be sad and angry with me would have fucked me up.

I then remembered that I'd literally *just* caused Moli to feel both of those emotions by completely screwing her over, and suddenly I was craving the same amount of alcohol that had knocked me out the previous night.

"Are you kidding me?!"

As P'ken and I walked out of the cockpit, we found Aarif climbing out of the engine room and screaming at his watch.

"What's the problem?" I asked. "Something wrong with the condor coil again?"

"No, everything down there is fine," he groaned. "It's my bounty. They finally posted it, and it's only 30,000,000! You wouldn't have been able to free the Banshees, or even get *close* without me, and yet it isn't even a *fourth* of yours. Talk about being undersold."

"Heh, at least your photo looks good," I said, having pulled up his poster on my watch. "I find it difficult to believe that they really didn't have anything but the meatball pic for me. I mean I'm *proud* of having eaten 55 meatballs in 10 minutes, but it's not what I want to be known for as a thief."

As I walked toward the staircase, my sleeve was tugged on.

"Yael... am I selfish?"

I turned around to face P'ken and put my smile away. "What are you talking about?"

P'ken cast her head down. "By leaving my mother and the school, by not fulfilling my duties and hurting her, all so I can do what I want... is that selfish?"

"Uhhhhhh," I groaned as I tried to figure out what to say to that. "I guess when you put it like that, it *is* selfish. But being selfish isn't always wrong."

"How can being selfish ever be the *right* thing to do?

I put an arm around P'ken and resumed walking toward the staircase, the kid turning her head up at me.

"Being selfless is usually the right thing. I'm usually selfish and most people would say my job solely consists of doing the wrong thing. But if you only ever do the selfless thing, then you're living your life for other people. And that isn't healthy. You've got to live life for yourself. So I guess, be considerate of the people you care about, like your Mom, but don't blame yourself if they're upset because you're doing what will make you happy."

I wasn't sure if I was qualified to be giving advice like this or if what I was saying was too influenced by my own experiences, but regardless, my words put a small smile on P'ken's face. If I could keep doing that like I had been and eventually get around to teaching her a trick or two, I'd make a half decent mentor.

Electric Ellie had the Night Terror, a ship ten times the size of Ricochet with a crew of 50 people. While it lacked any traditional weapons, it possessed an EMP capable of taking out any enemy ship's primary systems without affecting itself, and it was rumored it could move at speeds equal to a Parallax-class ship.

Shion the Librarian had the Dagda, named after a god from Celtic mythology. It was even more gargantuan than the Night Terror, with a crew of approximately 250, and it contained a massive library filled exclusively with one-of-a-kind, irreplaceable texts. Being hired by Shion to take care of her books was considered by many to be an honor, and she certainly paid better than any of the handful of remaining libraries.

Madame N'gwa's ship wasn't like either of those, or like any of the other Banshees'. Her ship wasn't her home, but a simple, single-passenger ship that enabled her to get around. No one knew where she truly lived, but I'd always theorized that she had mansions and castles all across the universe.

Because she didn't have a ship to transport us onto, we were to meet on another moon, this one being the sixth moon of Tigyius. I wasn't sure what she was trying to say by choosing it, but it was nearly identical to the moon we'd met on previously. It was just as gray, it possessed the same amount of artificial gravity, and it was even about the same temperature.

She only wanted to meet with me, so when we landed, I once again set off on another hike by myself, leaving the others behind on the ship. P'ken was watching wrestling videos in our room, while Aarif was waiting to hear from me in the cockpit, in the unlikely event that this meeting didn't go as well as I was hoping, and I needed another rescue.

In spite of the definitely unhealthy amount of alcohol I'd been drinking to try and forget about her, I couldn't stop myself from thinking about Molina as I walked. Nearly every night since we'd first reunited, I'd seen her in my dreams. A few times she'd appeared in a sexy wrestling outfit, in a couple dreams we were just snuggling, eating noodles, and playing board games, and only once, things had gotten kinda kinky. If I could ever get her to leave the Sunrisers, I'd definitely want her to keep the uniform.

I'd prioritized helping and getting into the Banshees over bringing Moli and me together, but alcohol could only help my heart ignore what it really wanted for so long.

After half an hour, I arrived at a massive crater, one large enough that Ricochet could have fit inside it. And sitting over the ledge of it, dressed in her signature bells, robe, and white gloves, was the greatest thief in the universe.

"Yael Pavnick," she said. "Welcome."

"It's good to see you again," I said, walking closer to her. "Not an honor, because I hope to be your peer, but it is nice."

Madame N'gwa slowly stood up, each crack of her bones echoing and mixing with the sound of her jingling bells. Once she was on her feet, she turned around to face me, revealing her eyes to be closed and her grin to be wide.

"You didn't break into a Sunriser base and free us all directly, but what you accomplished was still remarkable," she said. "We are all incredibly grateful."

I wanted to fangirl at her praising me so badly, but I knew I had to exercise restraint here, so I just scratched the back of my ears.

"Thank you," I said as calmly as I could. "I hope that any thoughts that I was the one who gave away the meeting spot are gone, and if you still need me to prove myself, I swear, I'll find whoever was responsible and punish them appropriately."

Madame N'gwa cackled. "That won't be necessary."

"You mean you already know who was responsible?"

"In a manner of speaking." Her eyes opened and slightly

bulged out of her head. "*I tipped off the Sunrisers.*"

My arms fell to my sides and my face froze up. "Whaaaaaaaaaaat?"

"As I said when we met before, I was skeptical about someone so young being inducted into The Order. Nothing you could have said to me at the party, nor any amount of support from my sisters, would have been enough to win my confidence. But, since Lioness and Beatrice believed in you, and you did have an impressive record, I elected to set up a test for you. Without telling any of the other Banshees, I arranged for us all to be captured, and put you in a position where your only option to prove to everyone that you weren't a traitor was to break us free." N'gwa put a wrinkly hand on my shoulder. "You didn't go about things as I expected, but what matters is that you got it done at all."

I should have been angry at her for setting me up like this and for being the reason Moli and I had been pitted against each other, but at the same time, an elaborate trick like this was super cool and, without her, I'd have never seen Moli again at all.

"What if I'd failed?" I asked nervously. "What would you have done then?"

"Any member of my family incapable of breaking out of a simple jail cell never belonged among us in the first place."

I nodded. Of course they were never in any real danger. The Sunrisers were nothing to them.

"So... what did you all decide about *me*?" I cringed a little as I asked, but I needed to know.

Madame N'gwa took her hand off of me, clasped her hands in front of her, and retracted her eyes back into her head. "I informed the other ten members of The Order of my gambit. Once I was finished, we took a vote about you. And it was unanimous."

N'gwa raised one of her hands. "Welcome to The Order of the Banshee, Yael Pavnick."

She'd really just said those words. She'd really just said those words! She'd really just said those fucking words!"

"Thank you so, so much," I said with my lips curled all the way up my face. "I promise that I won't let you down."

We put our hands down and N'gwa resumed speaking. "As a member of The Order, you will attend all of our virtual meetings, at which you will be encouraged to share advice that will help the rest of your new family with our current jobs, as well as ask for any advice you need about your own jobs. You will be invited to certain in-person gatherings, you'll have access to an entire new realm of clientele, and, as per tradition, you will be granted a welcome gift of gidgits equal to your current bounty."

All of that sounded absolutely amazing. But as much as I looked up to the Banshees, I was most tantalized by the last thing she'd said. They were going to give me 150,000,000 gidgits. I was officially rich.

"This is everything I've ever wanted."

Madame N'gwa snickered. "Well, we both know that isn't *entirely* true, but I understand the sentiment." She tilted her head up at the star filled sky. "As you should recall, the Banshees crave information and stories above all else." Her head fell back down. "We'll be having a virtual meeting in a week, and we don't want you to leave out any details from the story of how you saved us."

"Of course," I said, finally unable to keep myself from bouncing on my heels and flapping my hands. "I'll make sure to tell it in as juicy a way as possible."

The conversation continued for another few minutes, during which time N'gwa informed me of a few more rules, and advised me to take a new job from one of their exclusive clients soon, as well as to pick up a cloak for my ship as soon as possible. I would do both of those things, but with all the excitement going on in my brain, I felt like I could do anything, which meant there was something I needed to do before anything else.

"150,000,000 gidgits," Aarif softly echoed the good news I just shared. "We're rich!"

"I didn't know criminals could make so much money," P'ken said in awe. "That's incredible."

"Oh man, Jellz is gonna lose it when he hears about this," Aarif laughed, filled with just as much excitement as I was. "You gonna finally call him now?"

I smirked. Jellz had been trying to contact me since the news about the prisoner release had broken, no doubt eager to get back on my good side and apologize. And now that I was a Banshee, I was more valuable to him than ever.

"No. Not yet."

But after the way he'd spoken to me, I was gonna let him sweat for a while.

Aarif wrapped an arm around P'ken's shoulders. "Alright kid, we're *definitely* going on vacation now and, since you're one of us, you get a say in what we do. Where do you most wanna go?"

P'ken shook her head. "I don't want to go on vacation at all. I'm here to study and learn and explore, not relax."

"Yael, talk some sense into your mentee," Aarif said, taking his arm off of her. "Tell her she'll have plenty of time to do all that after we take *our* much deserved break."

"I've already been waiting for days to get started," P'ken said. "I don't want to wait any longer."

I shook my head as I turned around. "Sorry guys, but I'm

not ready to do either of those things just yet. You see, I've got money and prestige and I've got my ship, my crew, and the greatest dog in the universe. Now?"

I spun back around to face my friends and dramatically flipped my hair.

"I need to get the girl."

CHAPTER 16: MOLINA

"Your lightspeed processor shouldn't give you any more trouble," I told the Larakian ambassador over a holo-call.

"Thank you so much for your help, Captain Langstone," the bald man with an enormous mustache replied. "The people of Larak IV owe you an enormous debt of gratitude."

"We were just doing our jobs. Would you like an escort for the remainder of your trip?"

"That's much appreciated, but I believe we'll be fine from here on out. Safe voyages, Captain."

"For you as well."

The call ended and I leaned back in my chair. Without us, Larak IV's ambassadors would have missed out on an important meeting of delegates that would decide the future of the Dra-Tar system, and without representation at the meeting, the people of their world could have lost everything. But thanks to our actions, they'd have a proper chance to speak for the needs of their planet. It was *almost* fulfilling.

"Well done everyone," I congratulated my officers.

"Thank you, Captain," Commander Revudan said, sounding like an emotionless robot.

I looked up at my first officer and smirked. "I suppose the results of this meeting don't really matter. After all, the worlds in this system will eventually become a part of The Cykebian Empire, right Kay?"

She didn't look back at me. "That's correct, Captain."

I gripped the armrests of my chair and bit down on my lip. For the past week, I'd been made to feel isolated on the bridge of my own ship. Kaybell was furious with me, my crew no longer believed in me, and no matter how many distress calls we answered, the atmosphere didn't change.

"I'll be in my office," I said as I stood up. "Commander Bythora, you're in command."

"Yes, Captain."

I walked off the bridge, my whole body tense as I did so. With Kaybell wanting nothing to do with me, the bulk of my free time had been spent either in my office, reading *The Deckon Defense* by Ceturio Dekcon, or training with my sword in the gymnasium. The book, which told the author's life story, leading up to him developing the technique he was famous for, was informative and exciting, and I always enjoyed my training, but they were solitary activities, and I was growing increasingly lonely.

I wasn't sure how the rest of the crew saw me, but I was fairly sure they'd all lost faith in me as well. Everyone had continued to do their jobs, department heads had continued to turn in their reports on time, and my orders remained followed to the letters, but I'd received over a dozen requests for transfers to other ships, the departments heads were as cold with me as my senior staff, and I was far from the only one who found it difficult to take pride in any of our recent accomplishments.

There wasn't an iota of morale to be found aboard the

ship, and I had no idea how to fix that. Captain Asparago had been assigned the duty of capturing Yael, and Yael being put in prison would potentially raise the crew's spirits, but not nearly as much as if we were allowed to catch her ourselves.

If anyone could succeed where I'd failed, it was Captain Asparago, but I still doubted her chances. As smart and experienced as she was, Yael was completely unpredictable, and like no opponent she'd ever faced before.

What I feared more than Asparago failing was that she'd resort to lethal force to bring Yael down, and simply blow her ship apart. If Yael died because I wasn't capable enough to save her from her deteriorating mental health, I'd never be able to forgive myself.

Maybe it was stupid or even unhealthy to still care about Yael so much after what she'd done to me, but I couldn't help how I felt. And I knew that deep down, underneath the amoral criminal who'd jeopardize the lives of thousands in order to rescue a group of notorious criminals, was the same perfect girl I'd grown up with.

I entered my office, which was mostly similar to the office I'd had aboard the Mangalarga. The only differences were that it was slightly larger, and that I'd hung a fourth sword up on the wall. As captain, I'd felt I could get away with spoiling myself a little more.

I sat down at my desk, crossed my legs, and opened up my book to where I'd left off, the start of chapter six. It wouldn't fully take my mind off of my problems, but it'd at least distract me for the next hour.

The chapter told the story of the time Deckon's master ordered him to climb to the peak of Mount Polyphemus on the planet Triton, and retrieve a sword he'd planted there when he was a young man. Deckon thought that the task would be fairly easy to accomplish, until his master clarified that he could wear warm clothes in order to not freeze to death, but he was not allowed to use any tools or equipment to aid him in his climb, nor bring along any food.

Deckon thought what his master was asking was impossible, the mountain being 8,000 meters tall, but he was told that if he wanted any further lessons, he'd do as he was told, and that he knew what he was asking was possible because he'd done it himself.

Deckon didn't believe his master's claim, but, with no other choice if he wanted to continue his studies, he traveled to Triton and began his climb. For page after page, he described how it was one of the most difficult things he was ever forced to do. As the days went on, the strain on his muscles, the sub-zero temperatures, and the lack of any sustenance other than water all became almost unbearable.

More than once, Deckon thought about giving up. However, each time a thought like that would emerge, he would imagine the sword that his master had claimed to have planted at the peak, and put all his attention on proving that his master had lied, and that he was working toward a goal no one else had accomplished before.

After nearly a week of pain and struggling, Deckon had run out of water and he was on death's doorstep. However, he knew that he was almost at the peak of the mountain, and so despite his lack of energy and a raging blizzard, Deckon made one final push, imagining his master's non-existent sword the entire time.

By the grace of the gods, Deckon just barely made it to the peak before passing out. When he awoke, the blizzard had ceased and there was indeed no sword to be found. Instead, Deckon saw his master pouring him a cup of tea.

"Negative emotions can harm the soul," Master McDaid said. "But spite can also be a powerful motivator."

As the two sipped their tea together, the master explained that while he'd lied about scaling the mountain in the past, he'd never ask his student to accomplish something he couldn't, and so over the past four days, he'd forced himself to endure the same conditions and hardships as Deckon.

The lesson Deckon learned was more than just about spite. He wrote about the effect the mind has on the body, and how, when properly driven, you can accomplish physical tasks that *should* be impossible. And to close out the chapter, he wrote about the mental imaging that which had aided him in his climb.

"If you can block out all other thoughts and focus on a single image representing your goal, nothing can stand in your way."

I slammed the book closed.

Was I capable of doing that? Of blocking everything else out and focusing on a single goal? I'd always thought I was, but now I wasn't sure. Had Yael beaten me because was more intelligent? Or did she win because a part of me wanted her to?

I could have deployed ground troops to capture her from the start. It would have been damaging for me politically, but politics had never been my priority. Maintaining peace and capturing dangerous criminals always came first in my eyes, but as the supreme general's daughter, all of my actions reflected on him. And Father hadn't gotten where he was by prioritizing anything above politics.

But there were other reasons I didn't deploy ground troops. We didn't know the limits of Yael's physical enhancements, and for all we knew, she could have been capable of tearing apart each and every one of them, and their blasters could have had no effect. And while she hadn't killed anyone yet that we were aware of, we didn't know what she'd do when pushed into a corner.

While the moment in which I'd frozen up had been embarrassing and a failure on my part, I saw nothing wrong with minimizing risks when lives were on the line. One of the first proper calls I'd made as captain had resulted in twenty casualties. I would make any decisions I had to in order to keep myself from repeating that mistake.

Still, Yael was a highly intelligent and dangerous criminal. As much as I respected her, Captain Asparago would face difficulties in apprehending her, and it was likely she'd fail just as we did. With my knowledge of how her mind worked, I could potentially find her first. Find her, capture her, and take the first step toward redeeming myself and my crew. The first step to earning back everyone's trust and respect.

What I was thinking of doing would get me relieved of duty in the best case scenario and court martialled in the worst case scenario. The outcome would likely depend on whether or not I was successful in catching Yael, but either way, I'd be disobeying my father's direct orders. The idea was almost unthinkable, but at the same time, the only thing at risk would be my career. And unlike the lives of my crew, that was something I *was* willing to gamble with.

CHAPTER 17: YAEL

"You buy a collection of notable swords and send them to her one by one with romantic letters attached."

"You kidnap her and make her see how much happier she is living with you. I've read several romance novels where things like that happen."

"No and no. That first one could take too long to be effective, and P'ken, I don't care how well-written a book is, there is nothing romantic about kidnapping someone."

For over a week now, I'd been having Aarif and P'ken pitch me ideas for how to win Molina's heart while we ate dinner, but so far we hadn't found the right one. And while some of their ideas sounded okay, others made me think that they were messing with me.

"Okay, how's this?" Aarif started. "We get enough money to buy the Sunrisers, dismantle them, and leave Molina with no reason not to be with you."

"I... think that would take far longer than your last idea," P'ken said, nervously staring down at her beans and swirling them around. She still hadn't quite gotten used to how we ate around here.

"Uggggggggh," I groaned as I set my can down on the counter.

With how badly I'd already hurt Moli, I knew I couldn't afford to screw up whatever plan I went with, so I had to wait until I found the right one. But having to wait so long to find that right idea so I could kiss her adorable face was super annoying.

"P'ken, come stand on your hands with me!" I shouted as I flipped myself out of the kitchen and onto my hands.

"Um... what?"

"I usually only do this when I'm alone, but it sometimes helps me think. And if you can think *like* me while still providing a different perspective, we might be able to get somewhere."

P'ken looked up at me. "I... I can't. I mean, I can, but I'd need to get changed first. I can't do a handstand in a dress."

"Got it. But you can finish eating first if you want. Food comes first."

"No, no it's fine," she said, eagerly putting her can down. "I'll go get changed right away."

P'ken walked out of the kitchen, carefully made her way around me, and went into our room. When I brought Molina on board, I'd definitely need to have a new room installed for P'ken so Moli and I could have some privacy.

"You know, I can't do a handstand, but it'd be cool if I could," Aarif said, chewing on a mouthful of beans. "Maybe I could join P'ken in whatever physical training you're planning on putting her through so I can get buff."

"Heh, good one," I laughed, doing some handstand push-ups to shake off my arms.

"I'm serious!" he shouted, pointing his spoon at me. "We're putting all this time and effort into helping you get a girlfriend. Why not help get my body beach ready so I can impress some ladies?"

"Aarif, if you were serious about getting into shape, you

could have done so during your two years in jail. Remind me how you spent your time instead again?"

My friend crossed his arms, embarrassed by how much time he'd spent writing fanfiction. "I don't wanna talk about it."

"Look, dude, you're probably one of the top ten engineers in the universe," I said. "You don't need to be ripped to get the kind of girls you're attracted to."

"You don't know that," he said, eating another spoonful of beans. "Maybe I want a girl who's shallow and only cares about looks."

"I don't know if you're joking or not, but regardless, the idea of you with muscles freaks me out. So why don't you just—?"

Before I could finish that thought, I was knocked on my ass as Juri and Kidney came running under me and into the kitchen, Juri charging toward her dinner, and Kidney making a bee-line for P'ken's leftover beans.

Looking down at me, Aarif was smirking.

"Alright, maybe I can get you abs," I groaned as I rubbed my head. "But no bicep training! I like your noodle arms too much."

"Heh, I'll take it."

A few minutes later, P'ken returned, now wearing a sparkly silver unitard with matching athletic shoes. The site of it took me back to my days on my high school's gymnastics team. Every planet was different, but some things were consistent across the empire.

"What prestigious competitions did you say you'd won again, kid?" I asked, leaning against the counter and nursing a beer.

P'ken's face lit up. "The Benkin Global Games, The Hekatay Interplanetary, and the under-18 division of The Cykebian Olympics."

I put my beer down and smiled at her. The only one of those competitions I was familiar with was the latter, but I hadn't even been good enough to qualify for it when I was her age. I probably could have been, but my heart had never really been in the sport. I'd only joined the team because the Sunrisers required applicants straight out of high school to have been a part of at least one extra-curricular activity. Had it not been for that stipulation, I would have spent all that extra time either studying or hanging out with Moli.

"Very impressive," I said, walking over to her and patting her on the back. "Now come on, on your hands."

P'ken nodded and the two of us flipped ourselves over. But as just as soon as we'd stretched out legs into the air, an alarm blared, causing us both to fall over. We were being hailed.

"Twice in, like, five minutes," I groaned, rubbing my head again. "Should really get some carpeting." I hopped up to my feet. "Okay, idea pitching will resume later. Right now, everyone who isn't an animal to the cockpit."

My friends nodded and followed me up the staircase and into the cockpit, Aarif sitting down next to me and P'ken standing behind us. Before I'd even played the transmission we'd received, I could tell who was contacting us just by looking out the window.

"Yael Pavnick, Aarif Bhatti, P'ken Amatyn, this is Captain Tiffany Asparago of the Sunriser ship Mangalarga. You are all under arrest. We have run a complete scan of your ship, and found that you possess no weapons, minimal shields, and engines incapable of outrunning us. We are fully aware of how you defeated Captain Langstone and will not be falling for the same tricks. We will not answer any holo-calls, nor will we listen to any transmissions you send. You will disable the program preventing my troops from beaming aboard your ship so that they may take you into custody. Any other action will be taken as hostile, and we will respond by destroying your ship. You have five minutes."

As the transmission ended, I leaned back in my chair and popped my lips.

"Okay, so I definitely shouldn't have put off getting a cloak. My bad."

P'ken appeared nervous. "That was a joke, right? You must have a plan."

"Uh, no," I said, standing up. "I think we might be screwed."

As I led the three of us out of the cockpit, P'ken continued to freak out. "Why doesn't the ship have weapons?! Surely a ship that frequently gets itself into trouble needs at least some lasers."

"Yael never wanted any weapons because the Banshees don't like them," Aarif answered. "Plus, even when I looked into the possibility of adding some on my own, I found that nothing decent by modern standards was comptabale with the ship's systems. Same reason our shields suck."

"Maybe if I had time to think," I sighed, tugging at my hair. "But this bitch is only giving me five minutes. I can't think of a way out of this with only five minutes." I spun around and pointed at Aarif and P'ken. "We can't fight them, we can't run away, we can't hack them, we can't even talk to them to get in their heads or make a deal, and I could hear in the captain's voice that she wasn't bluffing about being willing to kill us. I need pitches for how we get out of this, and I need them to be better than the pitches you've been giving me for the last week."

Aarif and P'ken turned their heads in different directions as they got to thinking. I really needed them to come up with something, because the tone of Captain Asparago's voice wasn't the only thing that made me sure she'd really kill us. She'd been a Sunriser for longer than I'd been alive and, in that time, she'd amassed the second highest body count of any Sunriser in the last hundred years. In most parts of the universe, she was still known as "The Butcher of Brotadak V."

"The closest inhabited world isn't far," Aarif said. "We could transfer all power to the thrusters and try to hide out in a highly populated area. At the very least, they wouldn't be able to blow us away once we were off the ship."

I shook my head. One of Moli's senior officers had recommended transferring all power to thrusters as part of a plan to counter the strategy I'd used against them, and the association made me think this wouldn't work either.

"What if we allowed some of their troops to beam aboard and then took them hostage, like you pretended to use me as a hostage?" P'ken proposed. "Surely she wouldn't kill her own men."

"I think she just might, actually," I groaned. "P'ken!" I snapped my fingers. "Hands!"

P'ken looked confused for a few moments, before remembering what we were doing when we were interrupted, and went into a handstand.

"Come on, Aarif!" I shouted, lightly pounding my hands against his chest. "See what I'm not seeing."

"I'm trying, but I'm not seeing any way we win here," he sighed. "We're cornered."

Snarling, I turned around and walked away from Aarif and P'ken.

This was so frustrating. I knew I was smarter than Asparago, but she wasn't giving me a chance to think clearly. She'd read the report Moli had written of her defeat, and, just like she'd blocked me off from talking to her at all, she'd limited the amount of time I had to strategize. She knew exactly how I operated and had put appropriate countermeasures into place. If I was going to get us out of this, I needed inspiration to come and slap me in the face. I needed an idea I hadn't implemented against Molina.

And that's when Juri came running up the staircase and nuzzled her head against my leg, asking for head pats.

I bent down to meet her request and gazed into her big, adorable eyes. I knew what we had to do.

"Aarif, we—"

"No!" Aarif shouted, cutting me off. "I know what idea just popped into your head, and we're not doing it."

"Dude, we have no other options," I said, turning back around and looking up at him. "I know it's risky, but it's our only chance."

"It's *too* risky!"

"Um, what are you two talking about?" P'ken asked, walking backwards on her hands to maintain her balance.

"We'll explain later," we said in unison.

As Aarif and I continued to lock eyes, Juri walked away from me and nuzzled her head against Aarif's leg. Not taking his eyes off of me, he bent down and gave her some head pats.

"If we don't try, we're gonna end up in cells for the rest of our lives, or dead. But I won't do it without your consent. She was *your* dog first."

Aarif bit his lip and stared down at our doggo. "You know how the Sunrisers do things. If we were captured, what would they do with Juri?"

My brain screamed at me to lie and tell him that, as the pet of criminals, Juri would be put down. That would definitely get him to go along with my plan. But if he ever found out I'd lied about this, he'd never forgive me. Meaning I was forced to do the boring thing and tell the truth.

"Odds are she'd be sent to a shelter or, at worst, a pound," I answered. "If we surrender, she could still have a shot at a good life."

Aarif lowered his head. "Not sure if you can call a life where the two of us are separated good for either of us. Plus, I don't want you in jail for the rest of your life. And the kid certainly doesn't deserve to do any time." He looked back at me as he hugged Juri tightly. "Alright, Yael. We'll do it."

I nodded and shot Aarif a small smile.

As relieved as I was that he was giving my plan the green light, I was still worried about my plan's effectiveness and about Juri herself. We'd never tested what we were about to try, and it could potentially end horribly, but no other options had presented themselves.

"Tell me what's going on!" P'ken cried.

"First, get back on your feet," I told her. "Second, I promise I'll fill you in soon. Right now, I've got less than two minutes to disable our anti-transport shields, and it's a much more complex process than pressing a button. Both of you go downstairs!"

As P'ken flipped herself up straight, I walked past everyone and sat back down in the cockpit. The program that kept anyone from beaming aboard Ricochet was far more complex than anything I could code on my own, and Jellz and I had spent several sleepless days cranking it out together. We'd intentionally made turning it off difficult, with over a dozen steps that needed to be followed in a specific order, and with how distracted I was at the moment, I nearly got the order wrong. With probably less than 30 seconds to spare though, I pulled it off. Just as soon as I'd finished, shouting came from downstairs.

"Both of you on the floor!"

"No sudden movements!"

I took a deep sigh as I stood up. I'd just allowed the enemy on my ship, and now I had to hope that hadn't been a giant mistake.

The second I left the cockpit and exposed myself, the troops downstairs pointed their blasters at me. Aarif and P'ken had already been laser-cuffed, and Juri was being held by two of the Sunrisers. P'ken was scared out of her mind, while poor Juri seemed more confused than anything else.

There were about fifteen soldiers on board, all dressed in body armor and equipped with the standard Sunriser weapons and tools. I probably *could* have beaten them up and taken them hostage like P'ken had suggested, but that wouldn't have gotten us anywhere.

"We surrender," I shouted, putting my hands up as two troops came up the staircase to secure me. "However, as you can see, we have a dog. As such, I invoke Sunriser article 83-C, paragraph four, which states that any animals owned by captured criminals shall be properly taken care of by the crew that has captured them until the time a proper home for the animal can be found."

The two troops who were cuffing me looked at each other, no doubt trying to remember if that was a real rule or not. It certainly wasn't one that was brought up often, but I wasn't bullshitting them here.

"Very well," a deep voiced troop said as they shoved me forward. "Your dog will be taken care of."

The troops led me downstairs and lined me up next to Aarif and P'ken, while the rest of the troops spread out across the room.

"Prisoners are ready for transport," one of them said, pressing down on the side of their helmet.

The next thing I knew, my molecules were being disassembled, something that always made me queasy, and reassembled in a dark, dank cell, Aarif and P'ken still right next to me. The cell was barely lit, maybe twice as large as Ricochet's cockpit, and the only furnishings were two "beds" and a toilet. A forcefield separated us from the adjacent corridor, and outside the cell stood two armed security personnel.

"Yael, I can't wait any longer!" P'ken shouted. "Tell me what's going on!"

"Shhhh!"

I understood that she'd never been through anything like this before, but I didn't need her annoying me right now, I definitely didn't need her giving away that we had a plan, and I couldn't tell her what was going on without potentially tipping off the guards to what we were doing. The best I could do was not shout at the kid and tell her to shut up.

"Are we good to go?" I whispered.

"The soldiers may still be looking around Ricochet," Aarif replied just as quietly. We should give it a few minutes."

As we waited in silence, my mind drifted back to Molina, wondering what she'd think when she read about what we were about to do. Odds were she'd be horrified and disgusted with me. I was probably going to be a little disgusted with *myself*. But it wasn't my fault. I just wanted to steal shit; it was the Sunrisers who forced me to perform more serious crimes.

I also wouldn't have had to do this if I'd taken Moli's offer to fix her systems in exchange for entrance into the academy. I could have lived out my childhood dreams and been the most effective Sunriser of all time, right alongside my favorite girl. But I never could have accepted that. Living that life, I'd never be able to be myself.

"All right, they should all be back by now," Aarif said softly. He closed his eyes and exhaled before whispering, "Juri...*cripple*."

The silence resumed for a few more moments, before it was ended once again by the sound of eardrum bursting alarms, accompanied by flashing lights.

"Hey, what's going on?!" one of the two security personnel asked as they turned to face us.

I snickered. "All I'll say is you boys might want to get out of here and fast."

The two looked at each other nervously before turning back around and raising their blasters. Oh well, they couldn't say I hadn't warned them.

"Alright, P'ken, you want to know what's happening?" I asked, turning to her. She nodded furiously. "Right, well, remember how Juri's a *lot* heavier than a normal dog? Well, the reason for that is that she's kinda, sorta, a cyborg."

Shock overtook P'ken's body. "Cyborgs have been forbidden even longer than genetic engineering."

"It's a long story, but the short version is it's what was necessary to keep her alive," Aarif groaned. "And while Yael and the Banshees may not like weapons, I wanted to make sure no one could ever hurt her again."

P'ken turned to Aarif. "Wait, did you just telepathically communicate with Juri and tell her to attack the Sunrisers?"

"Not telepathy," he replied. "She's still just a dog. But we have chips in our brains that allow me to always know where she is, and for her to always be able to hear me."

Along with that chip, Juri was equipped with lasers in her retenas, rapid-fire laser cannons which popped out of her sides, extra long and sharp titanium-alloy claws, and shields capable of withstanding any handheld blaster fire, while also being significantly faster than any non-genetically enhanced human. With the element of surprise on her side, Juri would tear her way through the crew of the Mangalarga, and while I'd done some programming to make sure she didn't intentionally kill anyone, she would "cripple" the ship's systems figuratively, and its personnel literally, and the injuries she left could definitely result in death. Once that was done, we'd get Juri to come break us free, and we'd return to our ship, Captain Asparago no longer in any position to pursue us.

The downsides of this plan were that it was possible Juri's rampage would damage the transport systems, meaning we'd have to waste time fixing them after we were released from our cell, and, more importantly, we had no idea what kind of toll using her weapons would take on Juri's body.

"Attention all security personnel and ground troops, this is Commander Davis," a booming voice said over the ship's intercom. "A cybernetic monster has been brought onto the ship and was last reported laying waste to the lower decks and everyone in them. You are to find it and shoot to kill it on sight!"

Aarif lowered his head as fear overtook his eyes. There was also the risk that, even with the insane job Aarif had done putting her back together, Juri's shield would momentarily malfunction and a lucky shot would kill her.

I moved behind Aarif and gripped his cuffed hands with my own, squeezing them tightly. "She's the best dog in the universe. She can do this."

Aarif gripped my hands back. "Yeah. Yeah, I know."

Turning to P'ken, I wasn't sure what was going on in her head. The first time my life had been in danger, I'd at least had a decade and a half of training to prepare me for it, I hadn't been imprisoned, and there was no cyborg dog in play. Hopefully she would at least be able to grow from this, assuming we got out of here.

The sound of the alarms changed as the flash lights ceased and a red tint overtook everything, indicating that the ship was now on emergency power.

"The forcefield should keep them inside," one of the security personnel said. "Should we go after this thing?"

"There are thousands of people on this ship more equipped for combatting a dangerous threat than us," the other one replied. "No, we stay here and make sure these criminals don't escape."

They *really* should have listened to my warning.

"*The cybernetic monster is on the bridge!*" the commander shouted over the intercom, screams of agony also being picked up. "*I repeat the monster is on the—*"

The commander was cut off mid-sentence, presumably having just had his hand chopped off or his tongue cut out.

"Systems are down and the bridge has been disabled," I said, shocked at how well this was going so far. "Time to go."

Aarif nodded and let go of my hands before whispering, "Juri... *fetch*."

It took another few minutes for her to find us, but when she did, Juri fired lasers through the kneecaps of the security personnel guarding us, and trotted right in front of the cell. I'd never seen Juri like this before, with her glowing red eyes, razor sharp claws, and cannons as big as her. I still thought she was super cute.

"You're doing amazing, Juri," Aarif said, sadness in his eyes. "We just need you to get us out of here, and then you can go back to normal, okay?"

BARK! BARK!, she sounded as her cannons spun.

"You two should get behind me," I said. "If a stray laser or two fires at us after she's gotten through the forcefield, I should be able to take it."

My friends did as I said as Juri blasted away at the forcefield, the sound of her lasers clashing against it ear piercing. Like I'd worried about, a few lasers did come over the cell's threshold once the forcefield had been penetrated, leaving me with a few nasty burns. I'd heal, but they hurt like Hell.

Aarif and P'ken stepped out from behind me, and I could see tears in Aarif's eyes. "All right, girl, now our cuffs, please."

We turned our backs to Juri and, sure enough, she was able to use her lasers to cut the cuffs off of our wrists, freeing our arms which, at least in my case, had completely fallen asleep.

"Alright, that's it Juri, you're done," Aarif said, his terrified voice tinged with relief. *"Power down."*

Juri's eyes returned to normal and her cannons and claws retracted into her body, and I felt as guilty as I could as I watched it happen. Her barking and growling was as loud as ever, and between that and the look in her eyes, it was clear that she was in immense pain.

"Please be okay," Aarif whispered as his tears streamed down his face.

The transition finished. But no sooner than Juri had returned to her usual self, she collapsed. Her eyes were still wide open, but she wasn't moving at all.

"Juri!" all three of us cried, Aarif and I dropping down to her side.

While Aarif pulled her into his arms, I checked her pulse and found that she wasn't breathing.

"Juri… please be okay."

CHAPTER 18: YAEL

We'd beaten and escaped the Sunrisers once again, but victory had come with a terrible cost. One we would have to live with for the rest of our lives. Juri had been put through immense pain as she'd saved all of our lives, and now…

Now we had to spoil her even more than we did before, because she'd gone from being the greatest dog in the universe to the greatest dog in the *multiverse*.

"Such a good girl," Aarif said as we brushed her together.

"You want another treat?" P'ken asked in a baby voice. "I'm sure you do."

After freeing us from our cell and cuffs, Juri had fallen unconscious, and was barely clinging to life. Aarif and I had managed to help each other momentarily set aside our panic attacks, P'ken's screaming also keeping us on task, so I could pick her up, and Aarif could take one of the crippled security personnel's com devices so we could see if the transport system was still online. It wasn't, so we had to continue the arduous task of not freaking out as we ran to the engine room. Some more ground troops and security personnel had tried to stop us, but I handed Juri to Aarif so I could make quick work of them.

Once we were in the engine room, Aarif repaired the transport system and we beamed ourselves back over to Ricochet. I got us far away from the Mangalarga, and as soon as I had, I joined Aarif and P'ken in trying to figure out what we needed to do to keep Juri alive. Aarif opened her up and couldn't find anything wrong with her cybernetic parts, which made us all even more worried, since if something was wrong with her brain, heart or any other organ, we were completely helpless.

We all went into full panic attack mode with no task to focus on and no idea what to do, but after an hour, Juri suddenly got back up on her legs and barked a whole bunch of times as her stomach growled, right back to her usual self and demanding food.

We didn't know what had gone on with her and we didn't care. All that mattered was that our doggo was still alive.

Aarif and I mostly recovered once it was clear Juri was okay, and we gave her the large helping of food she deserved, but P'ken was still shaken and remained so for several days. During that time, we finally picked up a cloak, and she barely came out of our room. I was sure getting arrested by the heavily armored and armed troops, stuck in a cell, and nearly having a dog she'd recently gotten to know die on her had all been traumatic, but it definitely didn't help that neither Aarif nor I had thought to cover her eyes as we'd ran through the Mangalarga, meaning the poor kid had born witness to a whole bunch of blood and dismembered Sunrisers. She seemed to be doing better today, but I wasn't sure how much she was hiding.

I'd given both of them a break on their idea pitching duties, and I hadn't managed to think of any usable ideas myself, so we were all taking it easy today and relaxing with Juri. And since there was nothing else on my plate, I decided it was worth trying to further distract P'ken from the intrusive thoughts lingering in her head.

"Hey P'ken, since you've decided to be out and about this morning, do you want to finally know the story of how Juri got to be the way she is?"

"I'd love to!" she exclaimed with a cheerful smile as she fed Juri a treat.

"Great. So, it all started when I went to Toz to attend SlamCon. It wasn't the biggest or best IUWL convention I'd ever been to, but I had fun. I got to meet Ice Pick and Humberto Rodriguez, geek out with some other Autistic fans who had wrestling as their special interest, and I blew way too many gidgits on merch, including a flawless replica of Dragonius' mask, and autographs…"

"I'm liking wrestling, but I don't think I'd like conventions," P'ken said. "They sound so crowded and noisy."

"Oh yeah, they're terrible, but that's part of what makes them fun. Anyway, when I came back to Ricochet to leave, I found that my lightspeed processor had blown out. Burned my thumb trying to fix it, but I had no luck. Previously, I'd had an engineer working for me named Pepe Lavigne, but he was a dick and he quit after calling me, "Impossible to live or work with.""

"Very rude."

"Very, *very* rude," I agreed, pointing at P'ken. "Now, I know my way around a ship, but I'd only studied engineering as much as I needed to to get into the Sunriser academy. Engineers don't tend to become captains after all."

"Bullshit," Aarif coughed. He'd mentioned his hatred for the disrespect Sunriser engineers were paid during many a drunken bitching sessions we'd had about the organization.

"Now, I had places to be and people to rob, and if I was gonna meet my deadlines, I needed to get off Toz soon, and since I couldn't even diagnose what was wrong, I needed to find someone else to fix it. I wasn't looking for a new live-in engineer, but I figured there had to be someone on the planet who'd be willing to do a little freelance work, and who was capable of getting the job done."

"Mother always told me freelancers were people who were too lazy and undisciplined to stay on a proper career path."

"I think she said something like that to me while I was fixing her heaters," Aarif said. "It's nice to have a professional instead of a no-good freelancer," he continued, doing his best uptight feminine voice.

P'ken crossed her arms and pouted. "Please don't mock her."

"So, I put out an ad on subspace network six, saying where I was, what I needed, and how much I'd pay, but I really didn't feel like having to wait for responses," I continued. "I would if I was left with no other choice, but for the time being, I decided to try and go find someone in person. And on decently populated planets like Toz, there are always people who won't ask any questions, looking for work, hanging out in bars. I flew over to the capital city of the planet, Mwot, and went to the bar I had the best feeling about, one called Rhyme Season. The spacious bar/club/restaurant was filled with people of all kinds, rich and poor, reputable and shady, and a band was playing live music. I grew up listening to mostly Cykebian music, so it was always cool to hear tunes from places outside the empire. Oh, P'ken, when the story's done, I'm so sharing some of my favorite bands with you. Hope you like electronica and screamo."

"I... I've never heard any music that wasn't a capella or featuring a string quartet."

"And this is why I mock your mother," Aarif said, scratching Juri's chin.

"Anyway, I asked if anyone there was an engineer, and

offered 20,000 gidgits to anyone who could fix my lightspeed processor. The only responses I got were from a few dirty old men. Thankfully, none of them tried getting near me, so I didn't have to break anyone. There were a few other bars in the area, and if worse came to worse I could always hire a legitimate mechanic, but I wasn't sure if anyone making their living on Toz would be helpful with my specific problem. I still had a good feeling about the bar I was in though, and my feeling was aided by how good the food smelled and how much I was craving some more of the ale I'd had the previous night at the convention's finale party. I decided I'd have a meal and a drink, and if no one who looked like they could help me walked in before I was finished, I'd move on."

"And that's when Aarif came in?" P'ken asked.

"Not before I had a bowl of angel hair noodles in a jasmine and tozberry broth with a dark Geiger ale. Fan-fucking-tastic meal. The soup was warm and citrusy with a hint of spice, and paired perfectly with the ale."

"Is this relevant to the story?"

"My top 100 soups are always relevant. But yes, this is where Aarif comes in. He busted through the door and shouted at the top of his lungs, asking if anyone in the bar was a vet. He was carrying Juri, and both of them looked like they'd been badly beaten up."

"It was bad," Aarif took over. "We'd been sleeping out on the street and we were attacked by some thugs. They took everything I had, and the bastards hurt Juri even worse than they did me. They broke her legs and wounded her internally too."

"Oh my gods," P'ken said, her hands moving over her mouth as her eyes darted over to Juri. "Poor girl."

"I pitied them, but I didn't immediately jump to help," I

said. "I figured there were millions, if not billions of poor people in the universe, many homeless and with injured animals on their hands, and it wasn't my business to help them all. But then, I noticed Aarif's tattoos. Which one was I staring at again?"

"The samurai wielding a flaming balloon sword," Aarif answered. "You wanted to kiss it."

"I did not!"

BARK!

"See, Juri agrees with me!" I shouted.

Aarif glared down at our dog. "Traitor."

Although I definitely had never wanted to kiss it, the samurai tattoo had always been one of my favorites. The thought of Moli seeing it and getting all grumpy about a warrior not being portrayed with their proper weapon was too funny.

"So, I hopped up from my stool and got close to Aarif, observing his arms and all of the other tattoos that covered them."

"Naturally, I was freaked out by her, and hesitantly asked if she could help me. Yael being Yael, she flatly said that, no, she was just looking. I asked what the Hell was wrong with her."

"That's something I'm asked pretty often, so I took it in stride, and took a shot in the dark, asking him if he was an engineer. Turned out he'd studied to be a mechanic, but never gotten any work. I asked how he'd ended up homeless instead of practicing…"

"To which I asked if she'd help my damn dog if I kept answering her questions."

"And I told him, 'Maybe.' One thing Pepe always lacked was imagination, but based on Aarif's tattoos, I figured that wouldn't be a problem here. Didn't know if his mechanic training was good enough to let him fix a lightspeed processor, but I figured we'd both had a stroke of good luck if it was."

"So why weren't you able to get work?" P'ken asked Aarif. "You're so talented."

"That means depressingly little when you have no connections and the job market is bad. I had no choice but to sell bootleg movie files to make ends meet. I got caught, had to spend two years in jail, and, afterward, no one would even interview me, let alone hire me."

P'ken momentarily looked sorry for Aarif, but she quickly broke out into high-pitched giggles, and I couldn't help but laugh with her.

"I'm sorry," P'ken said, covering her mouth. "But with the kinds of things you and Yael do now, it's just funny to imagine you getting caught for something so… *basic.*"

Proud of my apprentice for using one of the words I'd taught her, we broke out into laughter once more, mine intentionally loud and obnoxious. Even Juri seemed to be laughing a little.

"Know what? Forget finding a girlfriend. I need another guy on this ship."

I pounded my chest as I stopped myself. "So, after laughing at Aarif like we did just now, I told him about my ship's problem, offered 500 gidgits for him to just take a look at it, 20,000 if he could fix it, also promising to get Juri help if he was successful."

"I thought carefully about what I was getting myself into, but ultimately decided I had no choice but to try, being sure to tell her I'd never done anything like this before. We properly introduced ourselves, and we walked over to Ricochet."

"Now, after getting on board, from the look on his face, I *thought* Aarif was gonna be another snob who was gonna make fun of my baby. But then, he smiled and said it had character. And it was at that exact moment I decided I loved him."

"It was also the first time I experienced one of your death hugs," Aarif said, shaking his arms. "Still got the fractures."

"Aarif set Juri down, and I took him down to the engine room. I was gonna give my best shot at words of encouragement, but before I could say anything, he'd already gotten to work. Just watching, I was already intrigued and impressed. I could see that he was moving like someone who'd graduated from the academy with a specialty in engineering."

"After a few minutes of tinkering, I told Yael that I was pretty sure I'd fixed the lightspeed processor. She was confused by how I'd finished so quickly, and I told her I just looked at what was going on and did what I thought made sense. I reiterated that I'd never done this before, but insisted we test it out so we could get to a vet."

"Since Aarif wasn't all talk, it was at this point I decided I needed him as my full-time engineer."

"She turned down my idea of going to a vet, saying that they could take a long time to see, and instead suggested using some of Jellz's spare parts to fix Juri up. I thought she was crazy, but she convinced me by saying that if Juri had weapons built into her, no one would ever be able to hurt her again. It was also at this point she let slip that she was a professional thief, which, combined with everything else, made me think I might be making a terrible mistake."

"And it turned out to be the best terrible mistake you ever made," I said with a smirk. "After that, we flew over to one of Jellz's hideouts, spent a few hours making sure we knew what we were doing with all of his junk, and turned Juri into what she is today. And once we were done, Aarif agreed to become my full-time engineer for a price I still regret being talked into today."

P'ken was looking at me with awe again, but there was also confusion mixed in there. "Incredible... but if neither of you are doctors, how did you perform such a complex surgery? Even if you did understand all the technology you were working with, how did you know what to do with it?"

I put my brush down and cracked my fingers. "I do have *some* medical knowledge from all the studying I did to get into the academy, and we pretty much did everything based on that and instinct."

"I was scared out of my mind the entire time," Aarif said, continuing to brush Juri and smiling down at her. "But something about being with Yael gave me the confidence I needed to get it done."

"It would have been too scary for me, even if I did have your mechanical knowledge," P'ken started. "but I do understand what you mean. There really is something about you that inspires people, Yael."

"Oh, please, continue," I said, still not tired of my apprentice singing my praises.

"Well, it's like when we were captured. I know I was scared and screaming at the time and that I've needed to be by myself for the past few days, but if you hadn't been with me, I wouldn't have been able to move at all. Even when you were doubting yourself or keeping me in the dark, I never lost hope that you had an idea."

It would definitely be a good amount of time before I got sick of this. It was as interesting to hear as it was fun. I knew I was cool, but I'd never seen myself as an inspirational figure. When I'd stood up to Morphea or other bullies as a kid, Molina had never fought back alongside me. She'd always stay behind me where she felt safe. But now, things were different.

Wait, I thought. *That's it.*

"Kissing up to the boss is something I never tried, but I

hope it works out for you," Aarif laughed, shaking his head.

"Shut up, dude," I said with a toothy grin. "I think I figured out how to win over Moli."

CHAPTER 19: MOLINA

As I'd predicted, Yael had beaten Captain Asparago. However, while I had great sympathy for the crew of the Mangalarga, many of whom had been horribly maimed, that wasn't what bothered me most. No, what got to me far more was the knowledge that Yael had a strategy she hadn't used against me, seemingly because I was someone she didn't want to hurt.

She'd beaten me while wearing kid's gloves.

Yael's bounty had been increased to 200,000,000 gidgits, and with Asparago having failed, Captain Douglas and the crew of the Lipizzian would likely be assigned to capture this clear and active danger before the trail on her went cold. They were the best of the best, and could possibly succeed where Asparago had failed, but I'd already made up my mind days ago: Regardless of orders, I'd be the one to capture Yael.

But if I was going to take her on, I couldn't leave anything to luck. I needed a plan that had no chance of failure. And in order to come up with one, I needed help.

After re-reading Captain Asparago's report to make sure I hadn't missed anything crucial, I scheduled a meeting for first thing the next day, and mulled over what I would say to my senior staff in order to acquire their assistance.

The next morning, I arrived in the conference room, ten minutes before the meeting was set to start, after enjoying a simple breakfast of blueberry jam on toast and black coffee. While I waited for the others to arrive, I stared at Yael's new wanted poster. While the picture of her they'd used on her previous poster had been adorable and captured her personality perfectly, she'd evidently been so unhappy with it that she'd actually been bold enough to send a new, sauce-free, picture of herself to Zenith Command. She was still gorgeous in this new one, but it seemed like she was trying too hard to seem tough and cool.

Commander Revudan arrived at the meeting on time, but everyone else was tardy. Commodore Pen was three minutes late, Security Chief Michaels was seven minutes late, and Kaybell came in fifteen minutes late.

I sat at the head of the table and tried to focus on what I had to say, rather than the way everyone was glaring at me.

"Thank you all for coming," I began, holding in a "finally." "No one is happy about the current status of this ship, least of all myself. There has been no change in our orders and we still remain without an official mission. However, I believe that for the good of the careers of everyone aboard this ship, as well as the universe at large, it is the duty of the people in this room to take up a mission that we haven't been assigned. Captain Asparago failed in her mission to capture Yael Pavnick, and it appears that she's been permanently paralyzed beneath the waist. I fear that similar results await any other captains who attempt to take her on. However, I believe that with my intimate knowledge of her, and the combined knowledge and experiences of all of us, we can formulate a plan that will allow us to redeem ourselves and bring this thief to justice.

If you do not wish to disobey direct orders and join me in this endeavor, I understand, but I ask you to please speak up now, and order you to not discuss what I've said with anyone else."

Everyone looked around at each other, save for Kaybell, who had turned her attention to her watch while I'd been speaking. Commander Revudan didn't have anything personal against me, so I believed I could count on her support, but I still didn't know Pen and Michaels too well as individuals, and Kay was angry with me for reasons other than my failure as a captain. If worse came to worse, I could make do with only half of the senior staff at my side, but I wanted the support of them all.

"I'm with you, Captain," Commander Revudan unsurprisingly said, speaking up first. I nodded at her in acknowledgement.

"I'm sorry, Captain, but I can't go along with this," Michaels said, sneering at me. "I've already disappointed enough people, and the last thing I need is to also be dishonorably discharged."

"Very well," I said. "You are hereby relieved of duty. Lieutenant Yang-Xi will take over all security matters until further notice. Dismissed."

His sneer not leaving his face, Michaels got up and exited the conference room. As he did so, I turned to Commodore Pen.

"I've been serving aboard Parallax-class ships for the past twenty years," he moaned. "I'm not about to go back to doing vending machine maintenance on a base. Count me in."

I only needed half of my senior officers, but I desperately wanted Kaybell's help. I needed to fix things between us.

"Commander Bythora?"

Kaybell finally looked up from her watch and glared at me. She rose to her feet, standing tall and proud as ever.

"You say that we'll defeat her using our 'combined

knowledge and experiences,'" she began. "Does this mean you've decided to become tolerant to views outside your own, and accept that they may be correct? Because as much as I agree with the sentiment of this mission, I cannot properly serve as your first officer for it if you aren't willing to consider what I have to say and value my input."

I stood up as tall as my small body allowed so I could look Kaybell in the eyes without having to significantly tilt my head.

"I am not a Cykebian noble, the most I can ever hope to be is an honorary noble, and I will never be a princess. As a commoner, I was raised with different values from all of you here. I'll confess, I have long found it difficult to find common ground between the morals of the nobility and the values Sunrisers are meant to have. However, *as* a Sunriser, and as a friend to several of you, it's my duty to find that compromise and work to better understand you all, without thinking that I know best." I clasped my hands behind my back. "Commander, I promise you I will listen to and consider everything you have to say, without passing judgment. And should you ever feel that I am emotionally unequipped to complete the mission, I will step down and allow you to take command."

Kaybell slowly sat back down, crossing her legs. She glanced at her watch, before looking back at me.

"I believe those terms are… *acceptable*."

My senior officers and I had been strategizing for the past several days, all the while searching for any sign of where Yael was. We were unable to gather any leads, her ship most likely having been equipped with a cloak since Captain Asparago had found her with ease, until we received a transmission. Another damn transmission from Yael herself. I couldn't *not* listen to it, but I'd had a complete diagnostic of the ship run after I'd done so to ensure she hadn't infected any of our systems this time.

"Hey Moli!" she began, her voice filled with exuberant joy. "So, I know things didn't go great the last time we saw each other, but I haven't been able to stop thinking about you. And I have a feeling there's been a similar situation over on the Noriker. I know you said we wouldn't have any more date nights… was it a date night? I'm gonna call it a date night. Point is, I can make it worth your while. I can't give you any information on the Banshees, but there are plenty of other bastards I know who I'd be happy to sell out. Just so long as you promise not to try and arrest me. I can't imagine you'd let me choose the location again, so you can pick any planet and any venue you'd like. I'm in the Gwyntama system right now, so just let me know when you're free and what you wanna do."

"What could her true goal be here?" Kaybell asked, standing at my side on the bridge. "We don't have anything else she could want."

Seated in my chair with my hands folded in front of me and my legs crossed, I shook my head. "There's no ulterior motive here. She really does want a date with me."

I'd told Yael to her face that we wouldn't have any more nice nights together, but either she could tell how much I still wanted to spend time with her, or she was thinking that offering up other criminals as bait would be enough to draw me out.

As tempting as her offer was, however, especially since there was no doubt she knew the whereabouts of some truly awful criminals, I wasn't going to allow myself to be distracted.

"All she's done is save us the trouble of having to track her down," I said. "We can set the exact date and time we want to put our plan into action, and give ourselves as much time as we still need to strategize. Her affection for me shall be her downfall." Out of the corner of my eye, I could see Kay smirking. "Suggestions for the date and location we send her?"

"She said she was currently in the Gwyntama system," Commander Revudan said, almost immediately. "That's a little over two days from our current position. I believe we could have everything ready in that time."

"We should arrive at our destination before we tell her where to meet us," Kay said. "We can give ourselves as much time as we need to plant cloaked mines all around the designated planet." Kaybell elevated her head and looked away from me. "Gha'Yun, five days from now. We spend two days flying there before we send her a message saying that you want to meet her on one of the planet's famous beaches in three days. We use the extra time to both set up the mines and other traps around the beach itself, and with her only in a bathing suit, she won't be able to hide any gadgets or weapons."

Their ideas were all sound, but I had to wonder how much I could set things up without tipping off Yael. I was what she was after, but no logical person would knowingly walk into a trap unless they knew exactly what it consisted of and how to get out of it.

But I knew how deep her desire went because my feelings were the same. The difference between us was that she was no longer prioritizing a mission over those feelings, while I was. She overestimated her own abilities and underestimated mine. She would walk into any trap I set because of how much she wanted to be with me, and because she didn't think I was capable of outsmarting her.

"Set a course for Gha'Yun," I said, lowering my hands.

"And bring up a registry of all the planet's beaches. I need to select just the right one."

"Yes, Captain."

I turned my head to Kaybell and saw that her smirk had persisted. When I'd assured her that I would value her input, I'd meant it, and I was happy to have the opportunity to prove that. In an ideal world, I'd be able to hold onto both Kay *and* Yael, and they'd be friends themselves, but Yael had done everything she could to make that impossible. She'd made a decade of bad decisions, and it was finally time for her to pay for them.

Gha'Yun had been part of The Cykebian Empire for centuries. While there were farmers, traders, and even 20,000 employees of Gbeho Metalworks who lived on the planet, the bulk of its economy was based around its highly profitable vacation businesses. Along with its well-renowned beaches, there were exotic locations to explore such as the Lushan Jungles and the Okoro Volcanoes, amusement parks for families, and gargantuan shopping malls. Duke Barrows III had become one of the wealthiest men in the empire through his successful management of the world.

The beach I'd decided to meet Yael on was known as Clownfish Bay. Named after one of the most popular species of fish with their hotel guests, the beach featured turquoise waters, sparkling sand, hourly tours through the bottom of the ocean, and multiple exclusive clubs, entrance to the beach also paying for access to a neighboring spa. It paled in comparison to Kay's private beaches, at least in her opinion but it was still one of the five highest-rated beaches on the planet, and one with some of the best security, to supplement our own.

Fifteen hundred cloaked mines had been planted within the planet's atmosphere and beyond it, each one individually capable of crippling Yael's hunk of junk, all of them having been activated an hour ago, and not only would they serve as a preventative measure in case Yael got back to her ship, but odds were Yael would know we'd be planting them, and would have her engineer try to disable them, thus keeping him busy. In addition, hundreds of troops were on the beach disguised as guests, Kay having paid for all of their admittance, with thousands more in the neighboring town, where Yael's ship would be parked, twenty snipers with blasters set to stun were all in position, the beach's security had been tipped off to keep an eye out for people matching the descriptions of Yael's engineer and Headmistress Amatyn's daughter, just in case they decided to crash the party, and Kay had command of the Noriker, standing as the last line of defense in the event Yael made it past everything else.

Had we been acting under Zenith Command's orders, we could have activated the mine field before Yael even showed up and taken her down that way, but since we were acting independently, we'd had to set up the mine field in secret, and we could only keep it up for an hour. Kay was friends with some of the duke's children and she'd gotten them to cover for us and give us some leeway, but they'd made it clear that even with their help, if we denied passage to paying guests for any more than an hour, the planet's governor would be calling Zenith Command and demanding an explanation. As helmsman, Commander Revudan had the unfortunate duties of sending out frequencies to all ships trying to get in or out of the planet's atmosphere that no one was permitted to enter or leave at the moment, and dealing with their complaints.

No, I would meet with Yael like she wanted. I'd show her

a good time, lower her guard, and take her in the old-fashioned way. Also motivating this strategy was how dangerous we knew her dog to be, how little we actually knew about it, and how essential it was that engagement with it be avoided at all cost, an order that had been given both to my troops as well as the beach's security. I wanted Yael's new friends brought down as well, but not if it meant facing off against the monster that had ravaged the crew of the Mangalarga. However, I was fairly certain that the dog would be nowhere near the beach. She wouldn't use it against *me*.

I walked onto the beach wearing a single-piece, burnt orange bathing suit and sunglasses, my bag containing a towel, sunscreen, a water bottle, and a stun baton. The hot, grainy sand was wonderful against my feet.

The beach was packed with civilians, families on vacation, couples and throuples on romantic getaways, and groups of friends all prevalent. I didn't know how powerful any of them or their families were, but I didn't care. Even if a chase were to occur, this time around, political ramifications were the last thing I cared about.

"Moli! Over here!"

As I turned around, I swallowed and braced myself for what I was about to see. Sure enough, stretched out across a bright yellow towel and wearing a neon blue string bikini, was Yael, her smile brighter than the sun which was bearing down on us, and her exposed body the sexiest thing I'd ever seen.

I had to remember why I was here. I had to remember that, right now, she was the enemy. But her long legs, completely exposed muscles, and cute as a button face all had me enraptured.

"Hello, Yael," I said nervously as I approached her. "You look… wow."

"Right back at you. Great job picking this place."

I tried to recompose myself as I unpacked my bag and laid out my burnt-orange towel, but despite all the mental preparation I'd done, in her presence, I was helpless.

"So, what have you been doing since we last spoke?" I asked as I sat down on my towel, directly next to Yael. "*Ignoring* the incident on the Mangalarga."

Yael sat up straight without pushing down on the ground. "A bunch of stuff. I've been training my new apprentice, while also watching *tons* of wrestling with her, my friends and I have tried out a few new board games, and we've also been stuck debating what to do with all the gidgits we have now, cause we are *loaded*."

I tilted my head back and snapped back to reality just a bit. "I take it that last part means the rumors are true? You're officially a Banshee?"

"I mean, if you *wanna* talk about work… yeah, I'm a Banshee." Yael stretched her arms out above her head. "And it's just as awesome as I thought it would be."

While I was happy to have confirmed that she did have information she could offer us about the Banshees, I instantly regretted bringing them up so early. I needed Yael to feel comfortable and *I* wanted to have some final, happy memories with her.

"You talked my ear off about your passion for wrestling at the steak house," I said as I took my sunscreen out of my bag. "How'd you get into it in the first place? It doesn't exactly scream 'You' in my mind."

"I'll answer that question, but do you want some help putting that on first? I'm already all sunblocked up but, you know, my enhancements let me reach places others can't on their own."

As much as I wanted to say no, and as much as I knew I

should have said no, I couldn't pass up that offer.

"Please," I said, meekly handing her the bottle.

"After I first left Cykeb, I was really bored," she said as she rubbed the lotion into my arms, the warmth of her hands sending a rush through my body. "I was all by myself, flying around in Ricochet, and taking any jobs I could get. To pass the time, I spent a lot of hours on board game forums. And on one of those forums, I ended up chatting with a user named 'Nina Rose.' You see we'd both been obsessed with the same game lately, 'Bat Country.' Only, she'd been getting to play it, and I'd been stuck *watching* people play it. After a few days of getting to know each other though, she invited me over to her house to play. I wasn't about to say no to that, so I set a course for Zazanka. When I got there, I saw the trophies she had, and how jacked she was, and I learned that 'Nina Rose,' along with being her username, was also her wrestling identity, and that she was part of the IUWL. After we played a round of Bat Country, which is an awesome game by the way, she showed me some of her matches and explained to me the intricacies of her storyline, and from that moment on, I was obsessed. I don't know if I would have gotten into it so hard if Gia, Nina's real name, wasn't so hot, but I think I would have. Of course, she's nowhere near as cute as you."

By the time Yael was finished speaking, she'd made her way to covering my back. And the further down she went, the more I wanted her to mount me and do things to my body I'd only ever experienced in my imagination. I wanted to know just how flexible she really was.

"I'm not sure if I could get into it, but I'm glad it makes you happy." I let out a soft moan as Yael pressed down against my spine. "And it's nice that you're still into board games."

"You still play them?" she asked as her hands continued to work their magic.

"No, unfortunately. I tried getting my friends into them while we were all at the academy, but they dismissed any game that didn't require great mental or physical ability as juvenile. And so that was the end of that."

"Wow, that's the worst thing you've told me about them yet. What exactly *do* you have in common with them?"

My shoulders stiffened. This was an easy question, but I hated that she was asking it like this. "We're all Sunrisers. Deep down, we all believe in the same things. The same values. And even if they don't care for any of the things we did when we were growing up, I've come to enjoy nearly every new activity they've introduced me to." I smiled. "If you hadn't been dismissed so unfairly, I think you would have liked them too."

As I turned around, Yael squirted more sunscreen onto her hands and rubbed it into my legs. "Now you're saying I was dismissed unfairly? Last time, you seemed to be defending the psychologists' position."

"That… may have been me projecting," I said, thinking back to that moment. "I defended them and attacked you because… well, I'm not sure, but I think it was because I didn't want to feel like I'd snuck into the Sunrisers. Like if I'd shown a single one of your symptoms that I wouldn't have gotten in."

"And what exactly made you change your tune?" she asked. "Besides what I'm doing right now, I haven't done anything to endear myself to you as of late."

I lowered my head. "No. No, you haven't. But I also haven't been doing the best job in either my social or professional lives. It's entirely possible that even with the things that make you stand out, you would have been a better captain than me. I'm sorry."

Yael smiled back at me and lightly slapped my leg as she finished applying the sunblock, closed up the bottle, and dried off her hands with her towel.

"Don't worry about it. I wasn't mad. And even if I had been, I could never *stay* mad at you." Yael slowly reached a hand forward and lightly tugged on my hair. She was looking directly into my eyes, which was already rare for her, and she was doing so like I was the most precious and sacred thing in the universe. "I know I could never get you to leave the job you love. And I know, from your perspective, what I've been up to lately is pretty horrible. However, I'll remind you that I would *never* do anything like I did to the Mangalarga unless forced to, which I was. My point is, I fucking love you, Moli. Always have. And I want to spend each and every day with you, but I'll compromise with a date every month or two to fit our busy schedules. I just need to know that we're in this together."

Tears formed in my eyes and they quickly streamed down my face. She'd actually said it. She'd actually said she loved me, and not just as a friend. She'd said what I'd always been too scared to say through our teenage years. And even fully aware of the awful things she'd done, I couldn't help how I felt. I still had the same feelings I'd hadten long years ago.

Without thinking about it any further, I closed my eyes, grabbed the sides of Yael's head, and pressed my lips against hers. As soon as our lips made contact, Yael's tongue swirled around my mouth like a tornado of bliss, while her hands tugged on my hair. I definitely wouldn't have felt the same way if my first kiss had been Zanthum, but it was one of the most amazing things I'd ever experienced, and even better than I'd imagined.

Yael took her hands off my hair and, in one swift motion, picked me up by my sides, lay back on her towel, and placed me on top of her. Evidently, she was a bottom too.

Not wasting a second, I wrapped my legs around her chest and resumed kissing her with more passion than I'd ever put into anything else. I didn't want this to end. I wanted to do this forever. I wanted to experience so many more glorious firsts with my best friend, and that meant I only had one option."

"Yael… I love you too." I said as I came up for air. Looking down at her, I could see I was making her just as happy as she was making me. "And that's why I'm placing you under arrest."

CHAPTER 20: YAEL

"Are you being serious?"

"You're completely surrounded. Even with your physical enhancements, you have no chance of making it back to your ship. You *will* be put in a cell. And I promise you, it's for your own good."

I hadn't expected Moli to kiss me today, but the fact that she had made me so ridiculously fucking happy. For a moment decades in the making, it was everything I could have hoped it to be. Raw, unbridled pleasure was all I could feel in those moments, and when I'd picked Molina up and put her on top of me, it had been an act of pure instinct.

I'd completely forgotten that I'd expected her to try and do her job. Her trying to do it while still mounted on me though was less than expected.

"What about the deal we made? I can get you a bunch of nasty criminals who you wouldn't rather smooch."

Moli took my hand. "You'll still tell me about them. And you'll also give me the information I need to capture every single member of The Order of the Banshee. Your bounty is 200,000,000 gidgits. Still one-hundred million lower than Madame N'gwa's, and compared to the combined bounties of every other Banshee, almost insignificant. If you *can* get us all of them like I think you can now, and volunteer all the information we need willingly, that should be enough to get you out on probation after just a few months. I know you love your life as a thief too much to leave it, but if you can stay off the radar like you have for the last decade… then yes, we can be together."

I tightened my hand around Moli's. This was definitely a better offer than her previous one. If nothing else, not having the Sunrisers constantly after us would help put P'ken at ease. And it was clear that she'd enjoyed the kiss just as much as I had and wanted to do much, much more than that. God, especially with the position we were in right now, did *I* want to do so much more.

"No."

I swiftly sat up and banged my head into Molina's, sending her flying off of me and onto her back. With Moli dazed from the headbutt, I hopped up to my feet and sprinted down the beach.

Molina's proposal was solid. But I had a better idea.

Seconds after I started running, muscular people of various genders and levels of attractiveness charged toward me. Just as I'd expected, Molina had planted her troops all throughout the beach. It was almost disappointing how uncreative she was. I knew she'd plant mines around the planet so we'd been able to pick them up pretty quickly, even with their cloaks, and Aarif had guaranteed me he could disable them by the time I returned to Ricochet. If I was right, there would be even more troops in the town I'd parked in, the beach's security would be looking to get me as well, and—

"Shit!" I screamed as I was shot in the head by a laser and given a major headache.

And there would also be snipers. I hated snipers.

While I was still a bit dazed, I was surrounded by Molina's

cronies, all either armed with stun batons or holding laser-cuffs. Before diving head first into them, I tapped on my ear, turning on the new, fancy, micro-communicator I'd bought with Ricochet's cloak.

"Aarif, get the ship running," I said. "I'm running back, and we need to go as soon as I'm on board."

"On it," he said. "Really hoping you were right about being able to fight off an army."

"I was looking forward to maybe meeting Molina today," P'ken said. "You've made her sound so wonderful."

"She's everything I've said and more. But don't worry. You'll meet her soon enough."

The way the Sunrisers on the beach swung their batons at me, they may as well have been moving in slow motion. I quickly broke each of their arms, and, when the remaining members of the group attempted to put me into holds, I grabbed each of them by the wrist and flung them across the beach, all the way into the ocean.

It was at this point that many of the civilian beachgoers either turned all their attention to me, or ran off in a panic.

I cracked my knuckles as I braced myself for the next batch of poor suckers who probably only took this job in the hopes of becoming honorary nobles, but before they even reached me, I was shot in both the side of the head and the back of the head.

I dropped to one knee and pounded a fist into the sand as I tried to shake off the pain.

It seemed Moli hadn't set up all her measures without thinking about them. She was gonna keep me busy with her troops, while her snipers slowly whittled down my stamina. This… could actually be a problem.

"Stay down!" Moli shouted as she struck me from behind with a stun baton. A buzzing sensation went down my spine as my muscles contracted, my mouth dried up, and my heart pounded so hard it hurt.

I reached my arms behind me, grabbed Molina's wrists, and flung her over my head, crashing her against the sand. "How are you still conscious?! That headbutt should have knocked you out!"

"It's because I'm not losing you that easily!" Molina kicked herself up to her feet and came at me once more with the baton, but as quickly I dodged her strike, another sniper shot hit me, this one in my right knee. "How much did it hurt, Yael?! she screamed as I struggled to stand back up. "How much pain did you put yourself through to become this indestructible abomination?!"

"Unimaginable agony!" I screamed back. "Just like imagining the rest of my life without you!"

"What's going on over there?" Aarif asked, worried.

Moli grit her teeth. "Flirting time's over."

I was grabbed from behind by some more troops and put in a Hiidravden hold, but it only kept me still for a second before I broke out of it and, subsequently, broke the legs of the two hairy guys who'd put their hands on me.

"It's always flirting time with us, Moli. That's our problem. If we'd stopped and done what we just did a decade ago, we wouldn't be here right now. We would be in bed, together, having amazing, fucking—"

"Be quiet!"

Molina charged at me once more with her baton, looking to get more and more angry with each step. I really hoped she wasn't taking the moves I was using to defend myself too personally. If she was, then my next one needed to put her to sleep for sure so I didn't have to keep hurting her.

I kicked the baton out of her hand, wrapped my arms

around her waist, and suplexed her over my head and into the sand, right on her back, with more force than I'd used with either the headbutt or throw I'd used on her previously. It didn't matter how much love or adrenaline was fueling her, she wasn't getting up from this for a while.

A simple punch to the head could have caused a concussion and damaged her beautiful mind, and also would have been far too boring. When we were old ladies celebrating our 50th anniversary on a leisure planet, enjoying the best noodles and beer in the universe, I wanted to be able to point to that wacky time we were fighting against each other and say, "Remember how I took you out with a sick wrestling move?"

Yeah. It would definitely be worth it.

"Fuck!"

While I was staring down at Molina, three more sniper shots hit me, one in the head, one in my left knee, and one in the arm. By shooting me all over, they weren't just beating down on me, but weakening each part of my body so the ground troops could stand a chance. It was smart. Painful, but smart.

"You sound like you're in pain," P'ken moaned. "Tell us what we can do to help."

"Just stay put on the ship," I ordered. "So long as you're with Juri, none of the troops will risk breaking in, meaning I can focus on being awesome, and not have to worry about you."

I continued sprinting across the beach, serpentine style, before leaping over the next wave of troops. If I didn't waste time fighting them, the snipers wouldn't have the time to get a clear shot of me, and they wouldn't be able to take advantage of my weakened state.

By continuing this strategy, I made it all the way to the

neighboring town of Totoff without breaking anyone else's bones and without getting shot a single more time. There had been one troop who'd managed to get the drop on me, but I'd quickly dispatched him by stabbing a nearby family's umbrella through his foot.

As soon as I got into the town filled with hotels, casinos, and massive, artificially grown palm trees, things got a little more sticky as the troops coming after me stopped being in bathing suits, and started wearing body armor and their full standard kits, none of them hesitating to shoot at me with their assault blasters. These guys I had no choice *but* to take out.

I made my way through them with a combination of punches, kicks, grabs, and a few wrestling moves, the cross body block and power slam proving particularly effective, taking care to watch their hands carefully so they didn't catch me by surprise with a flash or smoke grenade. The area was too crowded for them to use their Viseph gas cannons, but those others were fair game.

Unlike the losers on the beach, thanks to their armor, these guys took more than one hit each to knock out. A few of them even had the chance to say things to me like, "Drop dead!", "Die, you bitch!", and "Burn in Hell." For whatever reason, they really wanted to kill me.

"Hey, how much more do you think these guys I'm beating up would hate me if they knew I was ten seconds away from having public sex with their boss?"

"*You were?*" Aarif asked in amusement. "*Go, Yael.*"

"Isn't public sex completely inappropriate?" P'ken asked. "And shouldn't you wait for marriage to have any sex?"

"Awwwwww," Aarif and I hummed together.

The troops kept coming, swarming out of the hotels, casinos, restaurants, shops, and apartment buildings. Every time I thought I'd dealt with the last of them, more of them poured out of somewhere. It was like a never-ending stream of enemies in a video game.

Individually, each one of them was nothing to me. But all together, especially once they *did* start utilizing their grenades, they were more troublesome than I'd expected. By the time I was halfway to where Ricochet was parked, I was getting tired, and I'd taken about a dozen more sniper shots all over my body.

Just when I thought that I might not make it back, however, the troops stopped coming. It seemed unlikely that Moli wouldn't have positioned troops all the way between the beach and my ship, so I wasn't too sure what was going on. Adding to my confusion was a single, non-armored and unarmed woman standing in the middle of the street, down the block from where I was. All the civilians had fled inside, so it had just been the troops and I up until this point, and as I got closer, I could see her cracking her neck and knuckles.

As I got closer, I was able to make out who she was. She was wearing a blood red tank top, black tactical pants, and combat boots instead of her uniform, but her long, vermillion hair and sour expression were unmistakable. For a first officer, beaming down to fight me hand-to-hand after getting reports on what I'd done to the last thousand-plus guys was beyond stupid.

"Hey, you're Moli's 'new best friend,' right? Well guess what, we just kissed! And it was amazing! And we were gonna fuck like no one's business, if she wasn't so brainwashed by you asshole, buzzkill—

During my smacktalk, she punched me in the side and knocked me to the ground.

"That hurt!" I shouted, aghast, as I pressed down on where she'd hit me. "How did that *hurt*?"

"What's happening out there?"

"Going on silent, guys," I said. "I think I may need to start paying attention."

Ms. Grumpy Face attempted to stomp down on me, but I rolled away and kicked myself up to my feet. Looking down for a second, I could see that she'd made an indent in the pavement.

"Holy shit," I said as my lips curled and my eyes widened on their own. "A Sunriser commander with enhancements. I have *got* to know your story." I blinked. "Wait, aren't you a princess?!"

Instead of saying anything back to me, the commander unleashed a series of strikes, ones that I was only barely fast enough to block, and which still hurt my arms to do so.

Genetic enhancements had been illegal for as long as they'd existed. One would think the smug and proud Cykebian nobles would love to make themselves physically superior to everyone else, but receiving them was always a gamble. Even with the best surgeons, who tended to be the less reputable ones, there was a one-in-five chance of the procedure completely destroying someone's body.

Moli's friend had taken the gamble though. And it had paid off.

"I've been looking forward to this, you filthy little commoner," she said with a sadistic grin as she kept up her assault.

I spat out blood as a punch from nowhere got me right in the jaw, causing me to stumble back. Not only did the sharp pain hurt worse than her previous punch, but it was infinitely worse than the pain any of the troops or snipers had managed to cause with their blasters and batons.

"You will never harm me or my captain again."

As fascinated as I was by this woman, this was bad. I had

no idea if she was stronger than me and, even if she wasn't, I'd taken a beating, while she was fresh. Not to mention that I was still surrounded by snipers.

I was gonna have to go all out, and hope that Ms. Grumpy Face was strong enough to take it, but not so strong that it wasn't enough.

"Alright, bitch," I said, wiping blood off my mouth. "Let's see who had the better surgeon."

I kicked myself back up once again and charged her, my head tucked down and my arms open wide. The commander tried to get away, but before she could, I wrapped my arms around her, tossed her up into the air, grabbed her by the ankles, and slammed her into the ground, pavement flying everywhere.

If I could have, I'd have gone for an airplane spin to make her dizzy, but I hadn't been in the right position for that. A few months after wrestling had become my special interest, I'd called up Gia and asked her to perform an airplane spin on me so I could know what it felt like and, while she was a bit weirded out by the request, she'd still gone for the idea, and it was—

"Shit!" Seemingly unfazed by the slam, the commander got right back up and kicked me in the neck, cracking *something* in there. "Focus!"

"If you were thinking about your ship coming to save you, you should give up that hope," Ms. Grumpy Face said, bouncing on her feet. "We have it completely surrounded."

"That just means I'll have more goons to deal with when I'm done with you."

She came at me with another flurry of attacks, most of which I was able to block, but a few of them made contact with my face and torso, each one hurting more than the last. Her style seemed to be a mix of the standard Cykebian Mixed Martial Arts everyone learned at the academy, and another form I was unfamiliar with. But odds were she was equally unfamiliar with krav maga.

I waited for an opening in her defense and, when I found it, I swiveled to the side and jabbed two of my fingers into her eyes. With as much force as I'd used, her form and stance completely fell apart, and her hands instinctively moved to cover her face. I used this opportunity to grab her shoulders and repeatedly knee her in the liver, delivering blow after blow, as fast as I could, before switching things up and repeatedly striking the side of her right knee. When I thought she was sufficiently battered, I moved to put her in a blood choke so I could stop her circulation and knock her out, but before I could even get an arm around her, she cracked something in my neck again, this time with her left leg, and headbutted me.

I blinked, and in the space of the time I did so, the commander had started laying into me with a barrage of nothing but body blows. I tried to raise my arms up to respond, but they didn't listen.

Oh no. Did she fuck up my nervous system?

The commander closed out her assault with a single, ungodly painful punch to the head that made my brain feel like it was rattling around, sending me to the ground for the umpteenth time. I wasn't sure I was even capable of throwing a punch that strong. Her surgeon probably *was* better than mine.

But like Moli was earlier, I was fighting for love, and she was just a cog in a machine.

"I don't want to kill you here, but I'd be more than happy to do so," the commander said. "Stay down."

Just as I was about to say something witty, metallic blue

vomit erupted from my mouth and got all over the commander and the ground, prompting my opponent to shriek in disgust.

The side-effects of the querlious energy shot I'd taken couldn't have kicked in at a better time, as, for a moment, the commander was completely distracted.

I forced my body to move in a way it didn't seem to want to, and tackled the commander's right leg, bringing her down to the ground with me. I grabbed the largest chunk of pavement that was within reach and smashed it into her face, before pressing down on her neck with my right arm, putting all my body weight on it. My neck was completely busted and severely burnt, but I could still breathe. If *she* couldn't, it didn't matter if she was a little stronger than me. She tried pushing me off, but I refused to budge, using my free hand to hold on as tightly as I could to her hair.

Eventually, she was down and out.

"I'm a goddamn champion!" I shouted as I slowly stood up. "Moli, I really wish you could have seen that!"

My moment of glory was short lived. As soon as I'd declared victory, I was riddled with sniper fire. I'd pushed my body to its limits and I'd been softened up. I couldn't dodge the sniper fire, and I couldn't continue to stand. And to make matters worse, as I collapsed, Ms. Grumpy Face got back up.

"You may be one of the smartest commoners I've ever met." She pressed down on my face with her bootheel and put what felt like all of her weight down on it. "But no commoner should be so arrogant."

CHAPTER 21: MOLINA

When I woke up in the medical unit, Revudan and Pen were standing over my bed, eager grins on their faces.

"The plan worked," Revudan said. "We got her."

The relief I felt from hearing those words almost managed to distract me from the splitting headache and back pain Yael had left me with. And looking at the troops filling the rest of the beds, I could see that she'd once again gone easy on me, everyone else having had bones broken.

"Bring me up to date," I said. "What's our status?"

Pen replaced the grin on his face with a more professional look. "Yael Pavnick is secured in a cell. After capturing her, we were able to get her engineer and apprentice to surrender, and put them in their own cell far away from Yael's. Her ship is in our tractor beam, and her dog is still aboard it. We'll be beaming food and water for her."

"You've been unconscious for three hours," Revudan took over, her own grin having faded as well. "As you can see, your old friend filled the entire medical unit. Everyone we didn't have room for was sent on shuttles to the nearest Sunriser base. Fortunately, there were no casualties."

"No troops remain on the planet and all the mines have been taken down. Commander Bythora has written her report, but she hasn't sent it out yet. She wanted you to be able to inform the supreme general of our success yourself."

This had gone just as well as I'd hoped. There was a chance that Father would be initially enraged that I'd disobeyed his orders, but once I assured him that she could lead us to the rest of the Banshees, my path to redemption would be cleared.

"Am I fit to return to duty?" I asked.

"Dr. Chihiro already healed the bulk of your injuries. You can return whenever you feel ready."

I pushed myself up and elevated my head. "Good. I'm going to rest, and, while I'm doing so, read through Kay's report before I contact my father. You're dismissed." The two nodded and walked away, when I continued to say, "And… thank you. I couldn't have done this without you both."

"Of course, Captain," Revudan said with a smile.

"I did it so I wouldn't have to spend the rest of my career staring at peanuts and chocolates my allergies won't even let me eat," Pen groaned. "What's so great about them anyway?"

Once they were gone, I went onto my watch and read the reports. It was mostly what I'd expected to see, save for a position in Kay's report where she mentioned fighting Yael hand to hand and significantly injuring her. That shouldn't have been possible, and it was something I'd need to discuss with her.

Fully informed of what had transpired, I got out of bed, changed out of my gown and into my uniform, and left for my office. Walking through the corridors, I could feel a warmth that had been lacking recently. I wasn't fully out of the cold just yet, but I was well on my way there, and the fact that we'd managed to take this first major step had livened up the crew.

I arrived at my office and sent out a video call to my father. Naturally, I couldn't expect him to respond immediately, so I was left waiting. Staring at my swords on the wall, I wondered if I'd have fared better against Yael if I'd tried to use my blade against her, rather than a stun baton. If she was good enough to implement *wrestling* moves into her fighting style, then I should have been just as capable of effectively utilizing a sword.

After a little over half an hour, the supreme general appeared on my monitor and I stood in attention as I faced him.

"Captain, do you have something to report?" he asked.

"Yes, sir," I said. "My crew and I have successfully captured Yael Pavnick."

Father didn't flinch. "Your orders were to stand by and respond to distress calls. Do you understand that you have committed an act of insubordination?"

"I do, General, but after the incident with the Mangalarga, I couldn't stand by and watch a similar fate befall another crew. I knew I was the only one who could capture her without any casualties, and I did just that. I also have her accomplices in custody, as well as her cybernetic beast, and, as she's been made an official member of The Order of the Banshee since our last encounter, I believe I can get her to give us information that will allow us to capture them all."

When I'd first thought of disobeying orders, I'd assumed that, no matter what, I would either be relieved of duty or court martialed. Ironically, Yael doing something as horrid as joining up with the Banshees was what could potentially allow me to maintain command of the Noriker. But it still all depended on how my father saw things, and how angry he was that I'd gone against my given orders.

I couldn't show it on my face, but I was glad that Morphea wasn't present to influence his decision.

"Regardless of your motivations or your results, insubordination is not tolerated by the Sunrisers. You will receive five demerits, and you will send me reports from every member of your senior staff so my advisors and I may decide if they should also receive demerits. You have one week to capture another Banshee and prove that this prisoner can be used as a reliable source of info. Should you fail to do this, you will receive another five demerits and be court martialed. Do you understand?"

I swallowed without showing my fear on my face or body. I'd thought capturing Yael alone would remove any chance of being dishonorably discharged, but clearly, even if he wasn't showing his emotions either, Father was enraged. He must have taken my actions as a personal betrayal, and now only further, fast results could make things up to him.

"Yes, sir. I understand." Father ended the call and, once he was gone, I took a deep breath in and out. "Entropy is chaos. We are extropy."

One week wasn't a lot of time to apprehend a member of one of the universe's most elusive group of criminals, and Yael was my only chance of doing so. For her own good, I needed her to give me the information willingly, but if she continued to refuse, I'd have no choice but to interrogate her. No, I wouldn't be able to do that properly. I'd need to have Kay interrogate her. Before I went to see Yael, however, I had other matters to take off my plate. I needed to talk to her with a clear mind.

"Commander Bythora," I said, pressing down on my com device. "report to my office immediately. Commander Revudan, you're in command."

I sat down at my desk, nervously sheathing and unsheathing my sword repeatedly, until my 1st officer arrived, at which point I allowed her in, and folded my hands in front of me.

Kaybell was clearly mighty proud of herself for having been the one to actually take Yael down, and much as it usually annoyed me, it was actually nice seeing this side of her again. However, she also showed evidence of her fight with Yael. Her face was covered in cuts and scraped, and was badly bruised, and the way she walked displayed exhaustion.

"First off, I'd like to thank you for your crucial role in capturing Yael. As we knew was a possibility, I was taken out of commission, and you picked up my slack."

"Having your back is my primary duty," Kaybell said. I held in a smile.

"Second, I just spoke with the supreme general. We have one week to use Yael to capture another Banshee, or else I will be court martialed, as will possibly you and the rest of the senior staff."

I'd expected some kind of response to that, but her expression didn't change.

"All that means is that we'll have to get the information out of her as soon as possible," Kaybell said. "Even if she's as smart and as talented a thief as the rest of the Banshees, she most certainly isn't made of the same stuff as them, and lacks their experience."

As much as the thought of putting her in *one* of our interrogation chambers hurt, at least *one* of us needed to come out of this with our life intact. I needed her to open her eyes, stop being stubborn, and see that just this once, I'd beaten her, and she needed to listen to me.

"Kay," I said, hardening my voice. "You beaming down to fight Yael, while evidently an effective move, was not part of our plan. Not only that, but you were in good enough condition afterward to write your report. Why did you beam down, what made you think you could take Yael on, and, most importantly, *how* did you fare so well against her?"

Kaybell smirked.

"I beamed down because I felt I could be more useful on the ground than I would be standing on the bridge. As stated in my report, I was able to keep up with her thanks to the injuries she'd already sustained and the early stages of exhaustion she was in. I've maintained a strict diet, workout routine, and training regimen all my life, and I've had personal combat tutors since I was four. It's not my fault if our troops aren't of the same caliber as a princess."

She was clearly hiding something. I could see it in the way her lips had moved. And if she was hiding what was the most obvious explanation for all this, then I had a whole new set of problems. No one, not even a princess, was supposed to have genetic enhancements.

Right now, I couldn't worry about this. I needed to focus on a single task. I would hope I was wrong and just imagining things, and get to the bottom of things once the Banshees were finished off once and for all.

"Very well," I said, unfolding my hands and stroking my hair back.

"Regardless of how this all turns out, it is immensely satisfying knowing that this monstrous woman is locked up in a cell and completely at our mercy," Kaybell said.

"I asked you to not refer to her with any more derogatory terms."

"I'd say after what she did to the Mangalarga, it's warranted."

"And I'd say that I'm *ordering* you to not refer to her that way again."

Kay opened her mouth to speak, but closed it before she said anything. She turned around halfway and walked over to where one of my swords was hanging.

"I'm not going to apologize. For this, or for my recent behavior. A princess never apologizes. However, I will admit that I've allowed my temper to get the best of me. I am not used to failure and I did not handle it well. Any problems I had with you, I should have come to you with in a respectful and dignified manner."

I smiled at my friend. Cykebian royals being taught to never apologize and that everything that went wrong was someone else's fault was yet another thing I didn't agree with, but I wasn't about to say that now.

"Thank you for saying all of that," I said. "I appreciate it. And, since I'm not a princess, I'm more than willing to once again say that I'm sorry for disrespecting you and your beliefs."

Kaybell turned back to me, but her stiff face had softened ever so slightly. She unclenched her hands and allowed her arms to hang at her sides.

"Before I took her down, the thief said that you two kissed. And were going to do a lot more. Is this true?"

Yael was unpredictable, but I hadn't anticipated her blabbing about what we'd done to someone she didn't even seem to care for. Everyone knowing was inevitable, however. Troops had been watching us and, once they were conscious, rumors of what we'd done would spread all throughout the ship. Kay having been told about this only meant I had to deal with the annoyance now and not later.

"Yes, it's true," I said as I stood up. "None of what Yael

has done has made me stop caring about her and, when we were together on that beach, I let my feelings run free. Feelings I should have acted on a long time ago. And, if I can trust you with a secret, once Yael has helped us captured the Banshees and been pardoned, I plan on pursuing a real relation—"

"You stupid commoner!"

Kaybell stomped toward my deck, her teeth gritted and her eyes filled with fire, and I half expected her to slap me for being so unprofessional, but instead she firmly placed her hands on my face and pulled me in for a kiss.

I didn't kiss her back, too stunned to move at all, but her tongue maneuvered all around my mouth. My body didn't weaken from pleasure like it had when I'd kissed Yael, but it still felt nice. If Yael tasted of noodles and beer, then Kay tasted of red meat and berries. No matter how good it felt though, I knew this wasn't right.

I pulled away and started to say something, but before I could even get a full word out, Kay interrupted me again, keeping her hands firmly planted on my head.

"Shut up and listen," she said. "You're mine. Understand? *Mine*. You belong to me, not some trash who you had the misfortune of being stuck with as a child. And yes, I'm calling her trash, because that's what she is, whether you can see it or not." Kay lowered her hands off of my head and gripped my hands. "I understand the appeal she may have as your lost love, but that can't possibly compare to everything you and I have been through together."

"Kay," I said, struggling to find the right words for this situation. "I'm flattered, but… where is this coming from? You've never, *ever* expressed this type of interest in me. Are you jealous?"

"Of course not!" she shouted, tightening her grip on my hands. "And of course I've never mentioned these feelings before.

Imagine how my parents would react if I told them I was in love with a commoner! No, I had to wait for you to at least acquire the title of an honorary noble. But when I heard what your old friend said, I knew I couldn't wait any longer." Kay grinned as her eyes watered. "I knew there was something special about you from the moment I laid eyes on you at the academy orientation. It's why I pushed so hard to become your friend, and why I always stuck by your side. Not because your father was the supreme general, or because I wanted to befriend a charity case, but because I could see that even if you weren't perfect and even if you held views which needed, and still need, to be corrected, that you were the only one worthy of being with Princess Kaybell Kose Bythora, daughter of Stephen and descendant of Leon, first emperor of Cykeb and founder of the Sunrisers, future ruler of The Holy Cykebian Empire."

I had no idea what to say. I'd never even suspected that Kay held these kinds of feelings for me. While I'd always found her to be one of the most gorgeous women in the universe, I'd never thought about her that way. And I definitely didn't feel the same way I felt toward Yael. But how could I possibly say any of that without breaking my best friend's heart?

"Don't throw your life away for this woman," Kay said, choking up. "I'm the one who's been there for you for the past decade, the one who didn't run away, the one who stands on the right side of the law, and the one who loves your adorably silly sword obsession, even if I don't quite understand the appeal. I love you, Molina."

There were those words again. Words that had never been said to me in this way before today, but had now pounded against my heart twice.

I slowly pulled my hands away from her and used one of

my thumbs to wipe the tears from her eyes. I then walked around my desk and wrapped my arms around her.

"I love you too, Kay. And I hope you'll understand that this is a lot for me to take in, and I need time to think about it. All right?"

Maybe if things didn't work out with Yael, I *could* eventually make a happy life with Kay. I'd read articles about how the person you marry should be your best friend, and both Yael and Kaybell fit that description.

Kay wrapped her arms around me. "I understand. But *please* make the right choice."

The right choice. If Yael didn't agree to work with me, I wouldn't have a choice. I'd lose her forever.

I couldn't waste any more time prioritizing other things, or waiting for my mind to be clear. I needed to speak with Yael immediately.

CHAPTER 22: YAEL

Things were not going according to plan. Things were not going according to plan at all.

After telling Molina I loved her, I was supposed to escape back to Ricochet and fly away through a disabled minefield. My declaration of love, proclaimed while in a sexy bathing suit after rubbing sunscreen all over her, would then linger in her mind until she was inspired to leave her life behind for me, just like P'ken. Just like I'd been inspired to leave my life behind by Madame N'gwa.

Now that I was stuck in a cell on her ship though, there was a chance I'd be dropped off at a Sunriser base before she had her change of heart. And if that happened, my only chance would be to either break out, which I wasn't sure I'd be able to do while also rescuing Aarif and P'ken, or to hope that the Banshees weren't so ashamed of me for getting captured right after joining them that they left me out to hang.

Speaking of my friends, I had no idea what Moli had done with Aarif and P'ken. Odds were they were both just being kept in a separate cell, but it was possible they were keeping them more comfortable in an effort to get information out of them that they could then use against me. Telling Moli I'd joined the Banshees, and thus could potentially have lots of information about them, hadn't been one of my best ideas.

The only thing for sure was that Juri and Kidney were no doubt still on Ricochet, and my baby was being towed by a tractor beam. After reading Captain Asparago's report, there's no way they would have let Juri come on board the Noriker.

We were all still together. I hadn't lost yet.

What I was *going* to lose was my mind if someone didn't show up to talk to me soon. I'd been conscious for at least two hours and, far worse than the laser burns all over my body, was the boredom I was experiencing. No tablet, no music, no fidgets, no nothing. I would have killed to go a few more rounds or trade some barbs with Ms. Grumpy Face. No, all they'd left me with was a plian, itchy robe to change into.

I passed the time working out, pushing through the pain, and imagining wrestling matches in my head, but it was difficult to focus on either task while stuck inside a dank, enclosed space.

Oh shit, I thought. If I don't get out of here soon, I'm gonna miss the IUWL Championship Qualifiers.

As I feared missing an event I'd tuned into every year in recent memory, I heard footsteps coming toward me. They were fast and hard, whoever was walking down the corridor definitely in a rush, and moving with purpose.

"Leave us," Molina said as she stepped in front of my cell's forcefield. The security officers who'd been watching me did as they were ordered and walked away.

Moli had changed into her uniform, which was fine by me as she looked just as cute in it as she did in her bathing suit, and she was looking as uptight and flustered as I'd ever seen her, which was beautiful to see.

Seeing her made me relieved and horny all over. I'd flirt my way out of this, and, if I was extra good, we'd have a quickie before she sent me on my way.

"Finally," I said, hopping up and down and lightly flapping my hands "Been waiting for you to show up. Since you've got me as your prisoner, why don't you come in here so we can pick up from the beach."

Molina turned her head in all directions, presumably to make sure no one was listening, before glaring back at me. "We don't have time for games, Yael. This is serious."

"Got it," I said in a gruff voice as I clenched my face. "Super cereal."

Moli shook her head and sighed. "Listen, I have been given one week to capture another Banshee, or else I'm going to be court-martialed. As I said back on the beach, if you help me catch one, and then assist me in catching them all, I could get you a very, very lenient sentence. But if you decide not to help me, you will spend the rest of your life in prison, your friends will both spend plenty of time there as well, and you will be single-handedly responsible for crushing my dreams. Will you really do that to the woman you claim to love?"

I stared down at my feet as I kicked them around. "I swear I wasn't lying when I said that. And I'm sorry I've put your career in jeopardy. But I'm not going along with your plan. I promise, I'm gonna figure out a plan that gets us both a happy ending without sacrificing the Banshees."

"Enough with the plans!" she shrieked. "Your time to plan is over! You've lost! All you can do now is make the best of your situation and help me save us."

"Nah," I said, looking up at her and tilting my head. "So

long as I can think, I can still win."

Molina turned away from me. "You don't care about my career. You think that I'm wasting my life with the Sunrisers. Maybe you *can* think of a way to once again catch us by surprise and save yourself and your crew, but you won't think of anything that helps me get what I want. You've always been incompotent when it comes to the things you don't care about."

That... wasn't inaccurate.

"Sorry, Moli. They're my heroes. I respect them almost as much as I love—"

"Don't say it!" She raised a finger up at me. "If you're not willing to help me, then I'll just have to rely on friends who will."

Molina walked away from me, and I had no idea what to call out to her. I'd really thought I was good enough to fight through all of her troops, and now instead of making her think about how much she cared about me, I was giving her all new reasons to be mad.

I'd once ended up being dangled off a skyscraper by my leg, and yet this was still by far the most I'd ever botched a plan.

What felt like hours later, a sizable team of security personnel and ground troops came to my cell to give me a sedative to weaken me, put laser-cuffs on my wrists, and escort me to an interrogation chamber. As a kid, I'd always found the technology behind them fascinating. Rooms that could be manipulated at will to create the ideal circumstances for getting answers from prisoners, without having to directly harm them, made possible through a combination of hypersonic particles, matter regenerators, and weather and spatial manipulators.

Now that I was walking into one of the square, black rooms, they seemed far less cool, but I had to stay strong. Madame N'gwa and the rest of the captured Banshees had no doubt been put through interrogation while aboard the Noriker, but they hadn't given up any of their fellow members, and I wasn't about to do so either.

Standard procedure would have been to strip me down, but all the guards did was undo my cuffs, and secure my arms, legs, head, and waist to a chair with titanium alloy restraints. Either Moli didn't want anyone else seeing me naked, or whoever was in charge of my interrogation had something special planned.

Sitting in the dark, I lost all sense of time as I waited for my interrogator to show up. My nose got itchy and I wasn't able to scratch it, I felt the urge to bounce up and down, but I wasn't able to move, my feet fell asleep and pins and needles dug into them, and I couldn't think about anything else since I was so entirely focused on all the movement I wished I could be making.

They weren't doing anything special with the room. But they didn't have to to make me supremely uncomfortable.

"Took you long enough!" I shouted at Ms. Grumpy Face as she finally walked into the room. She held a black case with the Cykebian royal seal on it, and closed the door behind her. "Full disclosure, I find you more irritating than my old engineer found *me*, and I don't terribly like talking to people in general, let alone being interrogated by them, but anything, *anything*, is better than having to sit still with nothing to distract me."

Ms. Grumpy Face pointed her smile down at me. "You're still lively. That's good."

She wore an overly pleasant, smug look on her face. It was a look I recognized. Despite the age difference, she was no different than the bratty nobles I'd dealt with at Lulu's school.

"Remind me of your name? You mentioned it when we first talked, but I really wasn't paying too much attention, so I've just been referring to you as Ms. Grumpy Face in my head."

The commander crossed her arms and giggled. "I am Princess Kaybell Kose Bythora, daughter of Stephen and descendant of Leon, first emperor of Cykeb and founder of the Sunrisers, future ruler of The Holy Cykebian Empire. And your little nickname for me isn't too appropriate, as I'm actually in a very, very good mood."

The princess opened the case she was holding. There were six identical devices inside it, but I couldn't tell what they were.

"Aww, is that supposed to be some kind of torture device?" I mocked. "Hate to break it to you but, as you should be aware of by now, I know everything about how you operate. You can't use that thing on me."

"You think so?" Kaybell asked as she took two of the devices out of the case and approached me. "Because while I very much believe in what this great organization stands for, sometimes I don't agree with its gentle touch."

She placed one of the square, chrome blocks in her hands on my right bicep, a sharp pain hitting me and lasting for only a moment. When she walked away from the device, I could see that it had attached itself to me.

"You're a member of The Order of the Banshee. You humiliated us. You maimed hundreds on the Mangalarga, including our former captain and an old friend of ours, and a few crewmen even died as a result of their injuries. And we don't even have an idea of what your full list of crimes consists of."

Kaybell put the other device in her hands on my left bicep,

the pinch as this one attached itself to me hurting a little bit more.

"But even with all of that in mind, no, it wouldn't be enough to make me go against one of our most important protocols. We're the heroes of the universe, and torture isn't very heroic."

She took two more of the devices out of the case.

"But, Ms. Pavnick, more important than anything else you've done, you have deeply hurt and confused my friend. My *best* friend. The woman I love."

My mouth stretched open in amusement. "Is that what this is about? You're jealous?"

Kaybell placed the devices in her hands on each of my hamstrings, the pinching sensation continuing to get a bit worse with each one.

"You know, Molina had the same idea when I told her how I felt. But no, I'm not jealous of anyone. I simply care about her more than anyone else in this pathetic universe, and I cannot simply stand by as you continue to torment her."

"Torment her? Lady, we've both been dealing with some emotional distress since this all started, but that's because of how much *we* care about each other. Like I told you earlier, if she wasn't a Sunriser, we would have gone nuts on that beach. Don't take it out on me because she's just not that into you."

Kaybell took the last two devices out of the case and placed on one my forehead and the other one on my heart. The one over my heart was painful enough to get a grunt out of me.

"The eldest daughter of the Sunrisers' supreme general and the crown princess of The Cykebian Empire entering the academy at the same time? That doesn't happen by chance. That's fate. Molina's life began the day she met me, and everything before is irrelevant. And you made a big mistake stepping out of your irrelevance."

She opened a pocket in the case and pulled out a remote.

"Ms. Pavnick, do you know where we can find Madame N'gwa?"

"Even if I did, I wouldn't tell you," I said. "And listen, I've met more than a few professional torturers. All very good at what they do and all very experienced. To be effective requires a lot of practice. A first-timer won't have much luck extracting information, no matter how fancy her toy."

"Oh… sweetie." The princess walked up right to me and brushed my hair with her hand. "This *is* my first time doing something like this in a professional capacity. But I've been torturing insolent commoners for much, *much* longer than I've been a Sunriser."

"AHHHHHHHHHHHHH!"

I'd been burnt plenty of times, but this was so, so much worse. My entire body, each and every part of it, was on fire, at temperatures that should have instantly fried my nerve endings, but the pain didn't stop, and from the brief moments I was actually able to open my eyes, there wasn't any external damage. Heartburn had been an expression for over a millennium, but the actual sensation of a beating heart being set ablaze was unlike anything a doctor could describe. The only other thing I could hear besides my screams was the snickering of the princess.

I didn't know how long she let me burn for, but with a press of the button on her remote, the princess eventually stopped the pain entirely.

"That was your first taste of my newest creation," she said, while I gasped for air. "I haven't given it a name yet, but it works on the same principles as the very room we're in right now. It utilizes a combination of hypersonic particles, matter regenerators, and weather and spatial manipulators, but with the effects entirely localized within a person's bloodstream."

"Moli," I said, barely audible. "Moli would never allow this."

"Sorry to disappoint you, but she *ordered* me to do this."

"That's a lie."

"I'm delighted to say it's not." The princess tightly gripped my chin, and the smug smile she'd been wearing this whole time was replaced by a sneer. "She can't bring herself to hurt you personally, but she *does* want you to suffer. Let's try again: Where is Madame N'gwa?"

I really didn't know the answer to that question, but no matter what response I gave that wasn't what she wanted to hear, she was going to turn the damn machine back on.

"You need... to get laid."

My screams filled the room again, this time because my insides were contorting. She'd just mentioned that spatial manipulators were used in this Hellish contraption, and now my chest was bursting like a Gigagian crab was popping in and out of it in an infinite loop, my organs pressed up against one another, and my bones felt like they were seconds away from being ripped out of me, tearing through my flesh and skin, and flying across the room.

"Fuck. Fuck. Fuck. Fuck. Fuck. Fuck."

It was the only word I could say as the princess, now smiling down at me with unbridled glee, turned the pain off. Everything hurt, and something was happening to my vision. Everything had a white tint over it.

"Let's try something easier: When and where will The Order be meeting next?"

That, I *did* know. But N'gwa had made me feel like I was responsible for everyone being captured before. I wasn't actually going to be responsible for that now. No matter what she did to me.

"The deserts of Vhampampa," I forced myself to say. "Three weeks from now. From what Moli said, you only have a week."

The princess turned half way around. "Do you know when a criminal is lying? She turned back to me and hovered her thumb over the remote, her grin widening. "When she opens her mouth."

"I'm telling the truth you condescending — AHHHHHH!"

My organs were put through a shredder, cut up into a billion pieces, while my bones were peeled with a sword and my finger and toenails were torn off one by one. I couldn't see anything anymore, everything blocked out by a bright light. I wanted to keep screaming for as long as the pain lasted, but my mouth clenched shut on its own, and I couldn't re-open it.

I couldn't see, I couldn't speak, and because of the restraints, I couldn't even move. I could still smell and hear, barely, but all I smelled was overly strong perfume, and all I heard was more laughter from my captor.

"Oh, look at your eyes," Kaybell said with amusement and fascination. "I think you've gone blind. I may have taken things a little too quickly."

There were some beeps and bloops from some other device she must have brought, before Kaybell said, "Everything from your heart rate to your oxygen saturation is through the roof. Another hit like the ones you've been giving will probably kill you." She guffawed.

"Well, we can't have that, can we? How are you feeling, Ms. Pavnick?"

I wanted to tell her that I was feeling peachy keen and to fuck off, but I couldn't even open my mouth. No matter how much I told it to, it wouldn't listen.

"Ah, I see, that bad," she said. "Good. The effects should wear off by tomorrow, and then, we'll take things slower. Although, I can't help but wonder. As much as I personally want to hurt you, you're quite tough, and there's no getting around that."

No. No, gods, please no.

"For the sake of our mission, perhaps my time would be better spent extracting information from your friends."

No, no, no, no, no.

"Yes, I think that's a lovely idea!" Kaybell cheered. "That smelly engineer will produce some most harmonious screams."

Please stop. Please.

"But I don't know, maybe the girl should take priority. This might just be what she needs to realize the error of her ways."

Shut up. Shut up. Shut up.

"What's that ancient expression? Spare the rod, spoil the—"

"SHE'S JUST A KID!"

I somehow forced a single scream out, and an eruption of blood from my mouth immediately followed, the sticky liquid getting all over me.

"She'sjustakid. Andneitherofthemknowsanything."

She had to believe me. This woman was a monster, but she *had* to believe me. I couldn't let this happen to P'ken and Aarif. I couldn't be responsible for that.

"You're independent. You don't strike me as the type to share crucial information with others that they don't *need* to know. But, if our next few days together don't procure any fruits, then we'll have no choice *but* to give it a try."

This couldn't be happening. This wasn't how any of this was supposed to be going. Moli couldn't have been behind this. That had to have been a lie to mess with me. It had to have been.

It had to have been.

Each of the devices was pulled off of me, the pinches that came with their detachment now completely insignificant.

"Get a good night's sleep, Yael. You'll need it for tomorrow."

The door to the room slid open and the bitch walked away from me. A few seconds later, the door closed. I was all alone now, unable to see or move, covered in blood, in the worst agony of my life, and filled with the knowledge that my suffering, and the suffering of two of the only people in the universe I gave a damn about, was only just beginning.

Moli... please save me.

CHAPTER 23: YAEL

Deep down, at the very bottom of my food rankings, was the most disgusting thing which had ever been put in my mouth. My parents had both been terrible cooks, and one night, they'd concocted something that could only generously be described as meatloaf. It left me in the bathroom for six hours, puking my guts out on and off.

After three days of not being given any food or water, I would have *killed* for that meatloaf.

They had to at least give me water today. I'd die if they didn't. The princess would probably have me drink toilet water through a funnel, but I'd live.

I rolled over in my bed. Between how uncomfortable it was and how much pain I'd been put through, I hadn't slept in days. Just because the blindness and the inability to speak went away after a few hours didn't mean I wasn't still in constant agony.

Moli couldn't have been behind this. The princess had to have taken command of the ship. Sure, I hadn't treated Moli the best through all of this, but there's no way she'd have ever approved of what was happening to me. No, she was probably confined to her quarters. Soon, she'd break free and get us all out of here.

I'd tried so many times to come up with my own plan of escape, but between the pain and the hunger, I couldn't focus. Every time I'd start to get somewhere, I'd be overwhelmed by a craving or a part of my body would flare up.

The only things I could focus on for any extended period of time were Moli, Aarif, and P'ken. Even if they weren't being put through the same torture I was, anything could have been happening to my friends, and if I didn't talk today, they could make good on their word and *start* torturing them.

They were both so weak. So skilled in their own ways, but in a situation like this, so completely helpless. I should have been saving them, but instead I was stuck waiting to be saved myself. Aarif had been through plenty of crap, so maybe he'd managed to stay strong, but P'ken was probably a nervous wreck. I shouldn't have put off training her for so long. I should have prepared her for this.

As my arm flared up, I rolled over onto my belly. I had to give credit to the princess. The device she'd built was one of the most advanced torture devices I'd ever seen. Dr. Sanban and Dr. Reese would pay any price asked to take a look at it. When Moli came in, slicing through the guards with her sword, I hoped we'd have time to steal it.

I knew nobles could be snobby and cruel, but I hadn't realized there were still such sadistic bitches among them. In the old days, nobles used to torture commoners for fun all the time, but that practice had been outlawed nearly a millennium ago. If Moli really wanted to be a hero here, she'd kill the princess, regardless of how close they were. This woman could not be allowed to become emperor. I may have worked for some evil people in the past, but if she got control of the entire universe, everyone would be fucked, normal people and us hard-working criminals alike.

My stomach growled, yearning for some disgusting, vomit-inducing meatloaf, getting me to roll over onto my back. I closed my eyes and tried to think about anything which could distract me from the Hell I'd gotten us into. Wrestling. Board games. My noodle rankings. None of it worked. All I could focus on was pain.

"Leave us."

Noooooooo. No, no, no, no, no.

I opened my eyes and saw the guards posted at my cell walk away, while Moli approached it. There were bags under her eyes, her posture was sloppier than usual, and her sword was absent, but the guards had listened to her, she still walked like she owned the place, she showed no signs of injury, and her uniform was perfectly neat and tidy. She was still in command.

"Hello, Yael. I'm not entirely sure what I'm doing here, but—"

"You bitch!" I hopped up from my bed and ran straight toward her, resulting in my being tazed and bounced down to the floor by the forcefield. "You fucking bitch!"

Moli stared down at me, pity on her face. I could see many other feelings on it, but all I cared about was the pity. The part of her look that screamed, "You're beneath me."

She stepped closer toward the forcefield. "I know you're angry at me. And you have every right to be."

"Don't talk to me like you shared a secret I trusted you with!" I screamed. "You've been torturing me!"

Moli tugged at her hair. "I've been mad. Mad at you for everything you've done to me. And if you weren't going to help us, then I felt you needed to pay. And so I gave Kay free rein to do whatever she had to to get you to talk. I had a feeling that she'd use torture, but I didn't want to believe it." She shook her back and forth. "I haven't been eating. I haven't been sleeping. And I've been disgracing the Sunrisers." She sighed. "Tell me exactly what she's been doing."

Gripping my chest, I pushed myself up to my feet. Standing took too much energy at this point though, so I sat back down on my bed.

"She's been using a machine she designed," I started. "One that can do virtually anything to a person's bloodstream. One which can induce virtually any type of pain, at any level of severity. All without leaving any lasting effects, save for agony. She's managed to chop off my limbs, stuff my face in a shredder, hammered a rusty nail through my heart, and blown up my brain. She's put me through death over and over again. And she laughed and smiled through every second of it."

Still tugging on her hair with one hand, she covered her face with her other hand. "I'm sorry."

"Save your sorry! I've fucked you, I admit that, but I didn't do anything like this! And you stand there looking like you're still above me, when you've betrayed everything you claim to believe in." My stomach roared. "Are you also the one who gave the order to not feed me at all?"

Squeezing her forehead, she nodded. "I'm so sorry." Moli lowered her hands and allowed tears to stream down her face and smear her makeup, mucus dripping from her nose. "Like, I said, I don't really know why I'm here, but, now that I am, I think you should know what's going to happen. Kaybell wants to take over interrogating your crew. But with what you've told me, I can't let that happen. Not to an innocent teenager. So I'm dropping you and your friends at the nearest Sunriser base, and then I'm going home to be court martialed." She tilted her head up and chuckled. "We're both gonna lose after all."

I wanted to smack her in the face and tear her uniform into pieces. If that forcefield wasn't in my way, and I was in any condition to take her, I'd have already been at her throat.

"Good to know you're not completely heartless."

"I'm not heartless. I steeled my heart so I didn't let my emotions influence me, but I—"

"Emotions should *always* influence us," I cut her off. "They're what keep us from being mindless drones."

"They're what keep us from being effective! They're why you're in a cell right now! I would have captured you right from the start if I hadn't been so distracted by your... everything."

I smiled up at the ceiling. "Please. You never had a chance."

Molina laughed as she rolled her tongue around her mouth. "You're right. You are completely right. How could I, poor, simple, Molina, ever compare to the unrivaled genius of Yael Pavnick? How could I compare to someone who's both smarter than I'll ever be and, thanks to genetic enhancements, stronger and faster than I could ever *hope* to be? Someone so confident in her abilities and herself that she galivants across the universe in search of profit, not caring about who she hurts along the way." With a mocking grin spread across her face, she shook her head. "It's my own fault. I have a type! Selfish bitches with no moral compass who think they're better than everyone else! I don't know what that says about me. Maybe I should see a therapist. I'll have the time once I'm out of a job."

The comparison to the princess stung. I'd never tortured anyone, but I'd still done some pretty awful things. I was definitely selfish. And no one had more of a right to say this to me than Moli.

"I'm not apologizing for anything. Not after what you've

done to me. Maybe I'm a piece of shit, but you're no better. Unlike you though, I'm just fine with that. I'm happy with the life I've got, and the only thing I needed to make it better was you. That's the only reason we're here right now. If I hadn't contacted you to arrange a date, you'd have never seen me again."

"That's what I thought back then!"

Moli lowered her head as new streams of tears went down her face. She walked up to the panel next to my cell, pressed a few buttons, and disabled the forcefield.

"What the Hell are you doing? Is this a trick?"

"You left, Yael!" She picked her head up as she roared at me, her breathing intense. "You left me! You were my only friend, the only one who made the days worth getting through, and you left me without so much as a goodbye!"

"I... I already apologized for that at the steakhouse."

"And that wasn't good enough!" Moli grabbed me by my shoulders and threw me down to the floor. "Yes, I've been having you tortured. Maybe that makes me a terrible person. But you tortured me too! Every day after you left was filled with nothing but pain and suffering! My first day at the academy should have been one of the happiest of my life, but I was left only able to think about you. Even four years later, the day I graduated, I was just thinking about how much more excited I'd be if you were there with me."

I struggled to push myself up, my arms both killing me, but Moli pressed her boot down on my chest.

"I wouldn't have been there with you no matter what I did."

"Maybe not as a student, but you could have been there on the sidelines, cheering me on and supporting me. All the while making a real life for yourself, whether that meant taking over your parents' pickle business or doing literally anything you set your mind to. But no, the Banshees made you think that flying off and becoming a thief would be more fulfilling than standing by me." She pressed down harder with her boot. "If our situations were reversed, I would *never* have left you."

There was no comparing what we'd done to each other. But she'd acted out of anger, ignorance, and desperation. I'd just been a selfish bitch. I really hadn't thought leaving would hurt her so much. I knew she'd miss me, but I thought she'd move on with all the new friends she'd make at the academy. No, I'd abandoned her. I'd let her suffer. And here I'd been, acting like nothing but her job was standing between us getting together.

"I'm still pissed," I said. "And I know it's not enough, but I'm truly, truly sorry." Her face didn't soften, but the pressure from her boot did. "Tell me what I have to do to make things right."

Molina tilted her head. "You could give me information that would let me catch the Banshees."

"Done," I said without hesitation. "And then, after you've captured them, if *you* want to make things right, after you've captured them all, you'll have at least monthly dates with me."

"Really?" she spat. "Just like that, you expect me to believe that, after everything, you're willing to give them up. And you *still* want us to be together? Even after what I've done to you?"

I smirked up at her. "We've both put our jobs and our personal beliefs ahead of each other. The Banshees saved me when I was in the darkness and I owed them everything, but don't think for a second I thought they were more important than you. I thought I could make things work and have it all, and that you'd be willing to leave your career behind at the first sight of me, but I didn't realize how much *that* meant to you. Another thing I'm sorry about. If you really want to stay a Sunriser that much, then I won't take it away from you. And I'll just have to make things up to the Banshees by saving them, again, this time without having to screw you over."

Moli's face crumpled as the tears and mucus continued to flow. Her leg shook until she fell right on top of me, which would have hurt like Hell if her skin didn't feel so nice. As she continued to cry, she wrapped her arms around me tightly.

"I love you."

I hugged Moli tightly. Tears would have been forming if I'd had any water in the past few days. "I still kinda hate you for what you've been letting the princess do to me. But I love you too."

We put our hands on each other's heads, tugged at each other's hair, and kissed.

It hurt. Doing anything at this point hurt. But the pleasure so completely overwhelmed the pain. Just like on the beach, she tasted of sashimi and beer, and everything that was wonderful about this terrible, dark universe we lived in. I hadn't wanted to settle for the deal she'd made and I'd thought I could make a plan that could get me everything I wanted. But I was wrong. She put her essence into her beliefs, and I couldn't take that from her.

But I could live with doing this every month. Yes, that would definitely make life much, much better.

"A genius, unstoppable in a fight, and completely gorgeous," Moli said as she came up for air. "I really got the total package."

"And I've got a girl who's just as smart and capable as I am, who's as fit as any normal person can be, and who's as adorable as they come. I'd say we both win."

I'd loved the feeling of her on top of me at the beach, and I loved it now. In all my fantasies, she'd always been on top. And in my more recent ones, she'd always been in her uniform, giving me orders that I'd have to follow, *or else.*

"I don't believe I've seen anything so grotesque in my entire life."

Hearing Kaybell's voice caused all the pain I'd been put through over the past three days to hit me all at once. It was paralyzing.

Moli got off of me and stood up, allowing me to see the princess standing outside my cell. Her arms were crossed and she looked at us with contempt.

"Kay, I—"

"I didn't find you in your office, so we figured you'd be here," the princess cut her off. "However, I didn't expect you to be degrading yourself in such a horrid fashion."

The forcefield was still disabled. If I was capable of moving at all, I'd have already started bashing her skull in

"You should be *honored* to have my love," she continued. "How could you possibly do this to me?"

"Can't help it... that I'm smexy," I snarked, feeling like I was biting down on nails with each word.

The princess glared down at me with a look of death, before looking back up at Moli. "Molina, explain yourself. Please tell me I'm missing something."

Moli stepped closer to the monster. "All you need to be concerned with is that Ms. Paynick just agreed to give us all the information she has on The Order. We can capture them all." She twisted her hip and smiled down at me. "But we're not going to."

I'd just agreed to give Moli the information I'd been fucking tortured for, and now she was saying she didn't want it?! What was she thinking?

"That's *not* an explanation."

"No, I suppose it isn't," Moli said, turning back to them. "The fact is, as much as being one means to me, none of us deserve to be Sunrisers. We've been insubordinate, cruel, and ineffective, *you've* broken additional laws by getting genetic enhancements, and we both need to be court martialed."

The princess stepped closer to Moli. "Regarding the work I've had done on myself, it's been in the best interest of the universe. In the name of making myself the most effective Sunriser possible. The crown princess of the Cykebian Empire *must* be strong, and is above any and all laws." She clasped her hands in front of her. "And regarding more recent events, *I* have only been following your orders, and if she's agreed to give us the information, then my methods have not only been effective, but worth it. And you still haven't told me what I just walked in on. You were enjoying yourself far too much for that to simply be a deception."

Oh yeah, there was *no* way she'd faked that.

Moli closed the distance between herself and the princess entirely, taking her hands. "Kay, you're my best friend. But I love Yael. And from what she's told me, you've taken absolute delight in the nightmarish pain you've been causing her. Was she lying?"

The princess raised both of their hands up and smiled. It was strange to see her look at someone lovingly rather than with malicious glee.

"Not at all. And there's nothing wrong with that. Torturing commoners has been a pastime for nobles for as long as the empire has existed."

"What are you talking about?" Moli asked, fear in her voice. "I'm aware that it used to be commonplace, but it was outlawed centuries ago."

The princess snickered. "Officially, yes. But again, for

people like me, the law is meaningless. Nearly all noble families have continued the tradition, with the crown aiding them from the shadows as we have peasants kidnapped off the streets. Just because we needed to look better in the eyes of the rest of the ignorant universe didn't mean everyone needed to be denied their fun." She raised one of her hands and stroked Moli's hair, Moli looking to be frozen in place. "Whenever you're not with me on Cykeb, I indulge myself with my brother and sisters. But once you became an honorary noble, I was going to bring you in, and introduce you to the joys of inflicting pain on…" She paused and sneered down at me, "lesser forms of life."

Moli pulled away from the princess and nervously took a few steps back. "You've always had sides to you I didn't like, but everything else about you let me accept it. Right now, I don't even know who I'm talking to."

"The same woman I've always been," the princess said as she followed Moli into the cell. "The woman you belong with."

Moli shook her head. "No, no, no." She paced around in a circle, tugging on her hair. "Why did you join the Sunrisers? I'd assumed that even if you saw yourself as better than everyone else that you still cared about protecting others and making the universe a better place. But if you just see everyone who isn't a noble as a toy to play with, then what are you doing here?!"

The princess appeared to be caught off guard by that question.

"No, I don't care about the lesser life forms on an individual level. But I do still care about the universe as a whole, the same as you. We *all* want to make it a better, safer place. For Cykebian nobles to rule over." The princess grabbed Moli's arms and got her to stop pacing. "I've always loved you in spite of *your* faults. Your being born a commoner, your inability to see some of the basic facts of the universe, and smaller things like your fashion sense from when we first met. You admitted before that it was wrong to be intolerant of my views, so why can't you accept me in spite of what you see as *my* faults?"

"Because it's not equal!" Moli shouted as she pulled away. "Because it's not the same at all!"

"So loving a criminal who hurts people and spreads chaos wherever she goes is okay, but loving the princess of the greatest empire the universe has ever known is unacceptable because I follow in the footsteps of my ancestors?!"

Moli stayed silent and froze. As the silence lingered, she bent down, sat next to me, and took my hand.

"Yes."

My heart tingled. Between Moli's proclamation, her taking my hand, and the way the princess's face was twitching, I momentarily didn't feel any pain.

"This is all her fault," the princess growled. "Well I'm not about to lose you that easily." She raised her hand to her com device. "Commander Bythora to all personnel, Yael Pavnick has escaped her cell. I will be attempting to subdue her, but should I fail, lethal force is authorized to take her—"

Molina roared as she cut the princess off and tackled her to the floor, which was super hot to witness. "You crazy bitch!"

"I'm just doing what I have to to save you!"

It was thrilling to see Moli fight for me like this. It was *so* thrilling, I momentarily forgot the princess was even stronger than I was. She had no issue grabbing Molina by her collar and tossing her across the corridor.

"You're dead, you wretched little commoner," she said,

standing back up and drawing a gamma knife from its sheath. One of those blades was capable of inflicting severe radiation poisoning with a single cut.

There were such terrible things I wanted to do to the princess, but right now I had to focus on being practical and surviving, as I could barely move. Whatever I did, I needed to be quick about it.

She roared as she stabbed her knife down at me, but I rolled out of the way so that it missed me by an inch. She continued to try and put a hole in me, while I rolled around the floor, trying and failing to kick myself up. Out of the corner of my eye, I could see that Moli had gotten back on her feet and tears were streaming down her face, ruining her makeup.

"All right, that's enough of that." Kaybell bent down, grabbed me, and stood us both up, putting me in a lock. "I'm gonna carve you up real good."

It would have been so cool to raise my legs up and steal the gamma knife from the princess, but that wasn't happening. My body wouldn't listen to me, and she slashed me across the stomach.

"Gaaaaaaaaaaah!" I screamed, the poison instantly taking effect as blood spilled down my legs.

Under normal circumstances, the radiation inflicted from a single gamma knife cut would kill a person in twelve hours. My enhancements could potentially buy me more time, but with each cut I took, I'd have much less.

"Yael!" Moli called out as I screamed. She charged at Kaybell, but was easily dispatched once more by a kick to the jaw.

As weak as I already felt, the poison made me feel even more pathetic, with nausea and numbness being added into the shitty mix that was my current condition.

"Just last a little longer, Moli," I said, breathing heavily. "I can get us out of this."

Kaybell slashed me again, right across my chest. The slicing itself was nothing compared to what her machine had been doing to me, but my head was spinning and I was seeing double. Everything was blurry and I was going to vomit again, but nothing was coming up.

"I could keep at this for hours without killing you," she whispered in my ear. "But I really should just cut your throat."

The princess tightened her grip on me as she raised her knife up. Moli was on the floor, barely moving at all. She wasn't going to get me out of this with a quick assist.

I wasn't ready to die. If I did die, P'ken and Aarif and Juri and Kidney were goners as well. They'd turn Ricochet into scrap metal. And if Kaybell was angry and crazy enough to kill her friend, if she killed Moli, the universe would become completely worthless.

"No," Kaybell hummed. "One more thing before you die like the vermin you are."

She released me from her lock, but before I could make a move, she elbowed my jaw, my head banging against the wall on my way back to the floor.

Kaybell bent down, gripped the sides of Moli's head, and planted a kiss on her lips, Molina making loud but weak noises as she was forced into it.

My whole body shook. I'd caused Moli so much pain over the past ten years. As recently as a few days ago, I'd suplexed her and knocked her unconscious. I'd always thought I was doing what was best and that I could make things right in the end. But looking at the pain on her face as she was assaulted, I could see how stupid

I'd been. For someone I loved as much as her, I couldn't let her feel any amount of pain, not even for a second.

"Get away... from... my... Moli!"

Leaping back up with energy pumping straight from my heart, I charged toward the princess. She spun around and was quick enough to draw her knife, driving it forward as I came right at her. My legs were moving on their own and I couldn't stop them. But I also wasn't going to let a damn knife be what stopped me now.

The knife plunged through my torso as I gripped the princess's head and smashed it through the wall, over and over again, until her face was as beaten as she'd left Moli's, not stopping until she was unconscious.

She'd had the better surgeon. But she did *not* love Moli more than I did.

Moli, still shaken, opened her tear-filled eyes. I couldn't imagine what she was feeling right now. Being hurt like that by her best friend. Again. And like usual, I had no idea what I was supposed to say.

"Yael... your stomach."

I stared down at the knife in me, which I'd barely felt until she'd pointed it out. Now? Now, it hurt like Hell.

"Yeah, probably need to do something about that. But I've been stabbed before. I can fix myself up once I'm back on my ship."

Molina softly pressed one of her hands against my cheek. "Your ship?"

"What? Were you still planning on putting me in a cell, forever?"

"No... no, I guess not."

Even with her injuries and her tears, I could still see how beautiful she was. How she was everything wonderful wrapped up in a small package. She'd shown a capacity for vengeance and cruelty, but that just showed she was a human with flaws, who'd been pushed to her limit. I was far from perfect, and so was everyone else. We were all fucked up in our own ways, and pain and hardship only served to bring our worst traits out to the surface.

"Yael, look out!"

Moli shoved me aside as once again, Kaybell once again getting back up after I'd assumed victory. Kaybell charged at us and kept herself from stabbing Moli, but that just gave Moli the chance to kick the knife out of Kaybell's hands, grab her arm, and throw her over her shoulder, slamming her into the floor.

"Thanks for the save," I said, that maneuver having been stupid hot.

"We saved each other."

With one more punch, I took Kaybell down for real.

Moli gave me a quick peck, and while I would have preferred a full-on makeout session, there was a knife in me, I was slowly dying of radiation poisoning, and this bitch wouldn't be unconscious forever. I still really wanted to kill her, but I had a feeling Moli wouldn't like that. So it'd have to wait for another day.

"Come on, let's go get your friends."

Holding hands, we quickly walked to the elevator and went down to the next deck, where there were more cells. The guards raised their blasters when they saw me, but Moli ordered them to stand down and walk away. They were confused, but they weren't about to question their captain.

"Yael!" Aarif shouted as we found the cell he and P'ken were in.

"Oh my gods, there's a knife in you," P'ken panicked.

"Yeah, we should really get moving."

Neither of them seemed injured or malnourished. They'd actually been treated like Sunrisers were meant to treat prisoners. The two got up off their beds as Moli entered a code and disabled the forcefield.

"Hold on," Aarif said. "You two are together. Are you *together* now? I swear, Yael, if this was all some crazy, secret plan of yours…"

"No, no, none of this was to plan," I laughed. "But we are together. Finally." I looked my friends up and down. "You two… seem all right. P'ken, have you not been scared?"

P'ken raised her head, brimming with confidence. "I wasn't going to be the one to save us. But the least I could do as your apprentice was stay strong in the face of danger and trust that my teacher would get us out of trouble once again."

Aarif gently nudged his elbow against mine. "Honestly, I thought we were totally screwed this time. But I had to stay strong for the kid."

It hurt, but I giggled. I'd recruited these two because I saw parts of myself in them. But I saw more in them than just my past struggles and adversity. I'd seen that they were the best.

"Come on, everyone! We have a rat, a dog, and a ship to get back to!"

I pulled on Moli's hand and walked forward, Aarif and P'ken moving as well, but Moli didn't walk with me.

"Yael… I can't come with you."

I turned around, confused. "Why? What are you talking about? You still want to be here when that psycho wakes up?"

She shook her head. "I don't deserve to be a Sunriser, but I still believe in what it means to be one. And that means I have to report to Zenith Command and face the consequences for my actions."

"No, no you don't. Consequences are for losers."

Moli smiled. "I love that you think that way. But I need to do this. And we don't have time to argue. You need to go and treat your wounds immediately."

"No! I don't want to lose you again!"

"You won't. This is just something I need to take care of then… then I'll come and find you."

My legs were shaking. I wanted to grab her and run to my ship and not give her a chance to leave me. I hated the awkwardness of Aarif and P'ken watching this conversation, and I fucking hated the knife and radiation that were killing me.

I wanted to argue. I wanted to argue so bad. But she was right that I didn't have time to.

"Fine," I grunted. "But you better come back to me soon. I'll be planning out our dates, adventures, and crazy and wild sex."

Moli leaned forward, being careful not to press up against the knife, and softly pressed her lips against mine and gently kissed me.

"I promise I'll see you soon. I love you, Yael."

This wasn't a total victory. I wasn't walking out of here with my best girl on my arm. But at least getting to this point, this point right here, made everything I'd been through worth it.

"I love you too."

I leaned forward and gave her a kiss this time, and in the brief seconds it lasted, I fantasized about the full lifetime of happiness that awaited us.

CHAPTER 24: MOLINA

"Captain Molina Langstone, you stand charged with insubordination and unethical treatment of a prisoner. How do you plead?"

The Council sat around me in a circle, all of them in tall chairs. It consisted of my father, three of his top generals, and, worst of all, Morphea. The chambers we were in were only ever used for advisory meetings and court martials. They were candle-lit, and the Sunriser emblem was emblazoned on every wall.

I recognized the three generals my father had chosen for today. They'd all been present when I'd been promoted to captain. They were all heroes. And disappointment was written all over their faces.

"Guilty."

In contrast with the disappointment of the faces of the generals, sadness showed through my father's stoicism, and Morphea was barely trying to hide her satisfaction. Even if she didn't hate me, her chances of one day becoming supreme general had never been stronger.

I wasn't sure if I regretted my insubordination. It had gone against what I believed in, but I'd done it to make up for my own mistakes. I'd succeeded and I might have prevented other ships from ending up like the Mangalarga. But even if my father had been more appreciative of what I'd done, I still may have approved of what I'd let Kay do to Yael. And there was no defending that.

"And what is your stance on the council's position that you have failed in your duties, both as a captain and as a Sunriser as a whole?"

At the start of all of this, I'd captured the eleven members of The Order and then fought off an attempt to rescue them despite how much firepower and how many back-up plans they'd had, capturing another member in the process. But even then, I'd frozen up in the face of danger. When I wasn't in complete control, I lost it. And every single interaction I'd had with Yael further proved that I was not emotionally prepared for the job.

And when given my final assignment, "get information out of Yael," even with the cruel and inhumane methods I'd used, in the end, she'd only been willing to talk as a way of saying sorry to me. Victory through pity. She loved me, but that's what it was.

"I agree."

During the flight back to Zenith Command, Kaybell and I had once again gone without speaking, this time without even bridge interactions as I'd had her confined to quarters. Without her and without my career, Yael was all I had. When I got back together with her, I could try being friends with her team. The engineer from the middle of nowhere and the normal girl seduced by adventure. I didn't imagine we'd ever have high tea, ride horses, or play light-squash. I'd miss all those experiences.

Without them, I'd been left with a lot of time to think about what I was going to do next. All I'd ever dreamed of was becoming a Sunriser. I definitely didn't want to be a thief, but I did need a job I could continue to perform once I was living with Yael. The best idea I'd had was to focus on my swordplay and participate in the competitions I'd always wanted to partake in, but as fun as that sounded, it didn't sound like a career. And as of late, I hadn't even felt a desire to practice.

"Before the council votes on whether or not you should be stripped of your rank and dishonorably discharged, do you have anything more to say for yourself?"

I lowered my head and tugged on my hair. Along with my future, I'd also thought about what I was going to say here.

"I was raised to be a Sunriser. I believed I fully understood what it meant to be one. However, somewhere along the line, I forgot my own beliefs. And I made mistakes which I can never take back. I have no doubt that your vote to condemn me will be unanimous, and I hope that you'll vote similarly regarding Commander Kaybell Bythora. I also hope that you take a serious examination of the influence of Cykebian nobles on this organization. From what she told me, Commander Bythora seems more like a rule than an exception."

"Thank you, Captain."

General Augustus proposed the first vote and, within ten seconds, five hands were raised and I was no longer a captain. Morphea proposed the next vote, clearly getting a rush from it, and while this one took over 30 seconds to complete, all five hands were once again raised.

For the first time in over seven years, I was no longer a Sunriser.

My father shed a single tear and quickly wiped it away, before ordering me to hand in my earrings and leave the premises. I'd gotten all my tears out a few days ago when I'd decided to give everything up and my best friend had assaulted me, so I had none to spare now.

I gave my father, each of the generals, and even Morphea a respectful nod, before handing my earrings to the former, and exiting the chambers.

While I had no more tears to spare and I'd braced myself for this moment, it had still been exhausting. I was drained, out of breath. And I became even more tired as I stepped out into the hall, and was greeted by Kaybell, Revudan, and Pen's glares.

Revudan and Pen had been just as disgusted by Kaybell's actions as I'd been, but they'd been outraged that I'd turned down the chance to get information from Yael and save their careers.

"Commodore Pen, Commander Revudan, the council is ready for you," an officer said.

Pen and Revudan got out of their seats, not taking their eyes off of me and bumping into me on their way into the council's chambers, leaving me with just the ex-friend I still held a small amount of love toward. Once the doors to the chambers were closed, she rose from her seat and walked up to me, their arms all crossed in front of them.

"Princess," I said. "Is there something you'd like to say to me? I'm no longer your commanding officer, so I can't stop you."

"*Princess?*" Kaybell laughed. "You haven't called me that in a decade." She elevated her head. "I haven't apologized for anything since I was four, when my father struck me for doing so. But he's not here right now. So please, *please* believe me when I say I'm so, so sorry for how I acted a few days ago. I can't believe I forced a kiss on you against your will. And, as much as I may loathe her, it was also wrong of me to try and kill our prisoner. I've screwed up completely both professionally and socially. I have no doubt I'll be dishonorably discharged just as quickly as you were, and it will be well deserved. But that won't hurt nearly as much as if you can't forgive me and give me another chance.

I could hear it in her voice. As privileged and smug as she was, in this instance, she really was in pain, and feeling deep regret over what she'd done. My friendship was the most important thing to her.

"I'll be returning to my parents," Kay said. "They'll no doubt be furious with me, but I don't have anywhere else to go." She swallowed, looking to be in physical pain as she did so. "But please don't make me go back alone. I'm not so stupid that I think you'd want to be my girlfriend after what I did to you, but we can still be *friends*, and I'll do whatever I have to to prove that."

I'd cried for hours over what I knew would happen today. I'd cried for hours over my own actions. And I'd cried for hours over what these two had done. But this was something I hadn't cried about yet, or even anticipated happening at all. They were being sincere here.

Looking at her now, I didn't see the woman who'd violated me and tried to kill Yael, or the woman who had gleefully tortured her on my order. No, I saw the woman who'd passionately forced herself into my life. The woman I'd gone rafting with down Jyaria Falls on our most recent shore leave. The woman I'd celebrated every birthday and holiday with for ten years. The woman who gave me the motivation to get out of bed and live my life.

But none of that mattered.

"I appreciate what you're saying," I said. "I really do. But no amount of apologies or sincere regret is going to change the fact that you take joy in torturing people, and have done so for years. If you can admit that you're monsters and that you need to change, and you promise me that you'll work to change and be better, then maybe we can still be friends. I get it. I'm not perfect either, and I have flaws I need to work on. But I need to hear you say it and be as sincere as you were just being. And if there are any other secrets you've been keeping from me, now would be a good time to share those too. If you can't do this, then get out of my way. Because I'll never want to speak to you ever again."

She opened her mouth, but no words came out. Her face contorted into various expressions, before it settled on barely concealed frustration.

"Molina, I'm trying here, and I know that to you, as a commoner, the idea of what we do must be frightening. But even if you're too scared to ever give it a try yourself, you could talk to my father about it at dinner one night. Hearing from the emperor himself why this tradition persists should ease any fears you have."

She was trying. She was trying her damndest. She cared about me more than anyone else this side of Yael. I was sure that she would do virtually anything I asked of her right now in order to keep me in her life. And if there was anyone in the universe who could convince me that torturing innocent people could be morally right, it was the emperor.

I softly smiled at the two, and she smiled back at me, hope in her eyes. I raised a hand up and gently placed it on Kaybell's face.

"Goodbye."

I walked through the two as heartbreak and pain overtook them. I would treasure the memories I had forever, and I'd always be grateful, but there was no saving them. Not right now.

"Molina, get back here!"

"Molina, please!"

"Just give it a chance!"

If I was lucky, one day they'd have a change of heart. But somehow I doubted that day would ever come. Odds were, Kaybell would only become more maniacal upon one day assuming the position of emperor.

I shouldn't have felt any sympathy or love toward her after what they'd done, but I did, and I couldn't help that. I was going to miss her dearly.

My own heart broke as I walked. In a perfect world, I could have Yael, and I could have Kay too, and we'd all be a family. But the two lives I'd lived weren't meant to mix. And I was heading toward a brand new one.

Whatever new job I found, I never wanted to be in a position where I could hurt anyone ever again. Being a Sunriser meant protecting the universe, but it was also a level of responsibility that I just hadn't been ready for. I needed to find another way to help people, one that I was more equipped for.

I'd dedicated my life to extropy. To fighting against the chaos of the universe. And I'd failed. Now, I wondered if there was a way I could make a difference as a part of the chaos instead.

CHAPTER 25: YAEL

It felt like it had been forever since I'd been chased down the side of a mountain by an angry mob.

"Yael, don't these people seem a little overly angry about us taking a portrait?" P'ken asked, her voice squeaky with fear.

I glanced down at the framed portrait of the third baroness of Vakaxta held under my arm. "Uh, not really, considering the people of this world worship it as a god. Did I forget to mention that?"

"Yes, you did 'forget' to mention it!" P'ken shouted. "You always 'forget' to mention something! I'm beginning to think you do it intentionally!"

"You're learning!"

There were only a handful of small settlements on Praceus. Fewer than 300 people in total inhabited the world. About half of that population lived atop the planet's highest mountain, and it was all of those people who were currently chasing P'ken and I down the snow-covered, rocky hill, pitchforks and torches in hand. I got why they were mad, but the current baron of Vakaxta wanted the portrait of his ancestor, and he was paying what used to be my annual income for me to get it.

"Ahh!" P'ken shouted as she ducked under a projectile pitchfork.

"You know, if you take the portrait, I can carry you, and I won't have to slow myself down," I told her.

"No, no," she panted. "I need the cardio."

The member of the mob who'd tossed his pitchfork charged ahead of the rest of the crowd and grabbed P'ken from behind. I was about to step in and get him off of her, but she proved perfectly capable of doing that herself, flipping her assailant and flinging him back at the rest of the mob, forcing them to momentarily slow down and stumble.

"Looks like you're good on combat training, though," I said.

"Not at all. My form was sloppy. You couldn't see that?"

"Sorry. A bit too focused on trying not to die."

We continued running, dodging more pitchforks, torches, and a few glass bottles as we did so, but clearly I'd made a wrong turn. I'd thought we were going down the same way we'd gone up, but instead, we found ourselves standing on a sharp cliff. On one side, we were surrounded by the mob, and on the other side, a 300-foot drop.

"Return our god, and you will be allowed to go free!" an old man shouted over the rest of the mob's swears and murmurs.

"Look, if you had the gidgits to match what I'm being paid to take it, I'd happily give it back," I said. "But since I doubt that's the case, I can't help you. Sorry."

"Then you will die!" a woman around my age screamed.

"See, I would, but I've got plans. So dying would be pretty rude, and everyone on my ship has been trying to make me more polite."

"This is no time for jokes!" the old man declared. "Hand

over our god. Last warning."

"Yael, what's the plan?" P'ken whispered. "If we try and fight them all, we could end up slipping and falling off the cliff."

I licked my frozen lips as I examined the mob. I turned my eyes momentarily to P'ken, before glancing down at the mist-covered forest surrounding the base of the mountain. If we were pushed off, we'd most likely be dead before we even touched the ground.

Smirking, I took P'ken's head and gripped it as tightly as I could. She softly grunted, and looked absolutely terrified, having become accustomed to the kinds of things this look on my face could mean.

"Yael…"

"If we tried to fight them all, yeah, we'd probably end up slipping and falling, resulting in our untimely deaths."

"Kill them!" the old man screamed as the mob charged towards us once more.

"So we're gonna skip straight to the falling!"

Right before we could have pitchforks plunged through us, I flung P'ken and I off the cliff, sending us into freefall.

"Yaeeeeeeeeeel!" P'ken screamed in horror, alongside general high-pitched screaming.

I'd never fallen like this before, and it was one Hell of an experience. My heart beat like a machine gun, pounding hard against my chest, the freezing winds all around me pressing down on my body with even more force. My hair blew all over the place in the wind, and with each moment that passed, it became more difficult to breathe.

I never would have been able to try this stunt a few weeks ago. I would have just fallen to my death. But now I had someone's arms to fall into. A comforting heat engulfed my hand and passed through the rest of my body as I did just that.

"Tell me this isn't something you do on the regular," Molina said with a concerned smile, reaching out of Ricochet.

In one hand, she held the portrait she'd taken from me. Her other hand was clasped around mine, my free hand still holding onto P'ken.

"No, no it isn't," I said, unable to keep myself from smiling back at her. "And while I kinda enjoyed it, I don't think P'ken wants to ever do that again."

"Please pull us up!"

As Molina did just that, we shared a giggle. She'd been very clear when she'd returned from Cykeb: She wouldn't directly help in my stealing, but she'd always be there when I needed her. So far, this arrangement had been working perfectly. But there was one change I needed to make.

―――――

"There's my superstar!" Jellz said, his multi-colored, distorted skin the result of some poor choices in experimental skin cream.

"Nice to see you too, Jellz," I said, seated in my cockpit with a beer in one hand and a bag of gummies in my lap.

I'd finally gotten back to my manager shortly after the stab wound and radiation poisoning I'd received aboard the Noriker had been treated. He'd been bewildered and pissed by the story I'd told him about what happened, but he was willing to let it all slide, and focus on the fact that I was now loaded. I made it clear to him that he was still my guy, but for not believing in me, he wasn't seeing any of the initial sum the Banshees had given me.

"You got the baron's portrait?"

"Yup," I said, popping some gummies in my mouth. "You

think those villagers will get over it?"

"Who cares? It was never theirs to begin with and my cut for this job is enough gidgits to upgrade all my safehouses. Gods, I love you getting Banshee clients!"

Jellz was startled as a thunderous banging sound echoed from his end, enough so that he coughed up a stuffed narwhal I'd seen him swallow two years prior.

"Jellicimo Horzinski, we know you're in there!" a masculine voice shouted. "Come out with your hands up!"

I giggled uncontrollably. For whatever reason, I found Jellz's birth name hilarious.

"Send me those gidgits as soon as you get them," he said, picking up his shotgun. "Clearly, I need them."

The call ended, and I poured all of my remaining gummies into my mouth. As mad as I'd been with Jellz, I was happy to be talking to him again, and the thought of what he was probably doing to some Sunrisers right now was pretty funny.

Once I'd finished chewing and swallowing all of my gummies, which ranked 8th on my candy ranking, I stepped out of the cockpit, where Molina was waiting to wrap her arms around my waist and kiss my neck.

No longer wearing her uniform all the time, and not wanting to dress as preppy as she had when we were teenagers, her new wardrobe consisted primarily of lots and lots of leather. She insisted it was what she liked and that she wasn't wearing it to turn me on, but I didn't really care. She'd look amazing in anything.

"I hope his cut isn't too big," she purred. "There are some *very* fancy swords I'd like you to get me."

"Your wish is my command."

I would have been perfectly happy to have Molina as my kept

woman, but she'd insisted that even though she didn't want to be a thief, she still wanted to work. Right now, that meant participating in sword-fighting tournaments, but we were workshopping other ideas for what her future could hold.

"Yael, look!" P'ken shouted from below, choking out Aarif. "I think I got the technique you showed me right!"

"Very good!" I cheered as I walked down the stairs. "And what did I tell you about the sleeper?"

"It's not a crowd pleaser, but it's very effective!"

Grinning at the sight of a new wrestler being born, I jumped down to the main area and separated P'ken and Aarif so the latter didn't get knocked out or die.

"Remind me why she can't ever practice on Molina," Aarif panted.

"Aarif, just keep at it a little longer, and I'll get you those abs you want."

P'ken giggled into her hand while the annoyed Aarif rubbed his neck. Once P'ken's training was complete, she'd be a demon in combat, packing a unique blend of Cykebian Mixed Martial Arts, wrestling moves, and top-level gymnastics. Traditionally trained opponents would be entirely unprepared to face her.

"Anything we should know about your chat with Jellz?" Aarif asked as Juri and Kidney appeared, the former chasing the latter around.

"Not really," I said, chugging back the rest of my beer and tossing the bottle aside. "But I do suddenly want a stuffed narwhal."

DEWDEWDEWDEW. DEWDEWDEWDEW.

"Now who's calling?" P'ken asked.

I smiled at my new watch. With all the excitement from the job, and the awesomeness of making out with Moli, it was easy to lose track of time.

"Just someone I arranged to rendezvous with." I pointed a finger at each member of my crew. "Stay right here!"

Molina hadn't spent too much time alone with Aarif and P'ken yet, but they'd all been getting along. Aarif and Moli enjoyed sharing embarrassing stories at my expense, while P'ken was more fascinated and engaged by Moli's sword talk than I'd ever been.

I ran up the staircase, went into the cockpit, and adjusted the ship's defense systems so that inorganic matter could be transported aboard. Once I'd confirmed that the transport had been completed, I set our defenses back to their normal state, and sent over payment to the delivery ship. When I got back down to the common area, three massive boxes were present, and Juri and Kidney were sniffing all around them.

"You order something?" Aarif asked.

"I ordered a *lot* of somethings!" I cheered, skipping over to the boxes. "From box #1…" I drummed on the top of it before unlocking the seals and grabbing for whatever was at the top.

"That's a Benkinian dress," P'ken said, looking at it with awe. "A really expensive looking one."

Specifically, the dress was primarily metallic blue, it had the standard length and poofy shoulders of this style of dress, a large, fancy bow was right below the collar, and the black parts of the dress resembled living shadows, encroaching on the rest of it.

"And this whole box is filled with ones just like it, as well as more shoes and accessories than one person could ever need."

"It's… all for me?" She sounded like she was about to faint.

"Heh, no. It's, uh, it's for both of us."

P'ken's face lit up, while Aarif stepped toward me, suspicion on his face.

"Explain."

"No need to look at me like I'm possessed," I said, putting the dress back into the box. "I've just been looking at the dress in my closet and it's been growing on me. Plus, as far as a signature look goes, dressing like this will stand out more than a hat with a tragic backstory that most people will never know. And, I figured if it's gonna be *my* signature look, my apprentice should have outfits of the same quality. Plus, you know, you helped save us all back on the Noriker."

While P'ken came over to me to look at the contents of the box, Aarif crossed his arms and glared at Molina.

"You said something about how she looked in the dress, didn't you?"

Molina clicked her tongue. "Maybe."

While P'ken pulled out other dresses, heels, hats, and more, putting them back in the box after she was done looking so as to avoid putting them on our filthy floor, I made my way to box #2. "Aarif, this next box is for you and Juri."

Aarif came up right next to me as I unlocked the seals and opened it up.

"Holy shit."

Inside the box was a year's supply of dog food, the good stuff that Cykebian nobles fed *their* dogs, as well as some brand new toys for Juri, both high-tech and low-tech. And right on top of it all was a card. Typically I found cards pointless, but seeing as his gift was digital, it felt more natural than just telling him what I'd done.

"Dear Aarif," he read. "Thanks for having my back for the past six years. The way you saved my ass on the Noriker is only the latest in a long line of reasons why you're responsible for my still being alive. Along with a raise to your salary, I've deposited 30 million gidgits in your account. You're the brother I never had, Yael."

Aarif turned to me, his eyes wide, as I opened my arms up for a hug. He wrapped his arms around me and whispered, "You think of me as a brother?"

"Duh, dumbass," I laughed. "And come on, be more excited about the gidgits."

"Oh, I am. I *am*." He pulled away, grinning. "Not a half bad net worth for the street rat who just happened to be able to fix your lightspeed processor."

I slapped him on the back, knocking him into the box. "So you see me as a sister, right?"

"I mean, I've never really thought about it," he said, straightening himself out. "But I guess so, yeah."

While we'd been hugging, Juri had jumped into the box and Kidney had started crawling around it.

I turned to P'ken, who was still enraptured by the fineries I'd purchased. "And this goes for you too, kid. I know you've still got your mom, but as far as I'm concerned, you're as much a part of this family as that one."

P'ken put down the shoes she was holding, looking like she was about to cry. "Really?"

"For sure. All of us here? The six of us? We're a big, happy, weird-ass family."

P'ken's tears ran down her face as she charged at and hugged me. At least until the time came when Lulu tried to have me killed, the job that had brought my apprentice to me would occupy the top of my rankings.

Moli gently held my hand. "Sounds good to me."

P'ken slowly pulled away, wiping her tears off her face. "So, what's in box #3?"

"That," I said, banging against the top of the box. "is all for me. Mostly wrestling merch, and some neat-looking beers and snacks, but there are some other nicknacks as well. There is, uh, one other thing in there, though. And I need to take it out immediately."

Moli, Aarif, and P'ken exchanged curious glances while I opened up the box, andI seemed to even have Juri and Kidney's attention. Maybe their animal instincts tipped them off to what was coming.

"Is... is that...?"

Inside the large shipping crate, sitting at the very top, above my snacks and merch, was a tiny box with a velvet exterior. As I pulled it out and dropped to one knee, Moli's hands covered her mouth, P'ken furiously fanned her face, her tears continuing to come down in force, and Aarif uttered a barely audible, "I'll be damned."

"From the day we became friends, we were always meant to spend our lives together. We were apart for so long, and we went through so much so we could be together again. We're all a family here, 100%, but I want to be able to call you, you, my perfect, adorable Moli, my god damn wife." I opened up the box, revealing the most expensive diamond engagement band I'd been able to find. "Molina Langstone, will you marry me?"

"Say yes! Say yes!" P'ken, smiling and blubbering, shouted.

BARK! BARK!

Molina's face was completely free of tears. Instead, from ear to ear, there was the biggest smile on her face. Plain and simple ecstasy, love, and joy.

"Of course I will."

I squealed with glee as I took the ring out of the box and slipped it on her finger, Aarif and P'ken applauding. I jumped to my feet and we placed our hands on each other's heads, pressing our lips together.

Life hadn't gone the way I'd planned. I was a criminal, and that wasn't always easy. Sometimes it meant being horrifically tortured and throwing myself off of cliffs. And the same traits of mine that had gotten me rejected from the Sunrisers still found ways to make things hard for me.

But I didn't care. Despite my social struggles, I had friends, pets, and an absolutely flawless fiance, all of whom I loved and adored.

With them by my side, I wasn't just the happiest woman in the universe. I was the happiest woman in the multiverse.

CPSIA information can be obtained
at www.ICGtesting.com
Printed in the USA
BVHW071005211122
652422BV00005B/185